Abide With Me

The Barn Church Series

Book Three

by

SHELLIE ARNOLD

Kaleidoscope Publishing
Reflecting God's Truth

ABIDE WITH ME BY SHELLIE ARNOLD
Published by Kaleidoscope Publishing
1738 Oak Trail St. NE, Massillon, OH 44646

ISBN: 979-8-9865367-8-1
Copyright © 2017 by Shellie Arnold
Cover design by Eva Marie Everson and Elaina
Lee, edited by Stephanie Arnold
Interior design by Karthick Srinivasan

Available in print from your local bookstore, online, or from the publisher at:
www.kaleidoscopebooks.net

For more information on this book and the author
visit: http://www.shelliearnold.com/

Library of Congress Cataloging-in-Publication
Data Arnold, Shellie.
Abide With Me / Shellie Arnold 2nd ed.

Printed in the United States of America

PRAISE FOR *ABIDE WITH ME*

As a licensed counselor, I've worked with heartbroken couples enduring crucibles of strife. Shellie Arnold's writing breathes fresh realism and hope for hurting readers. Authentic characters rise from her novel to demonstrate the immensity and gravity of true marital love. More than a syrupy pit of infatuation into which we fall, true love involves sacrifice, sustaining effort, and a Savior's grace.

~Tina Yeager
LMHC

Prepare to be completely captivated and swept up into the midst of a tremendously powerful story. Marriage, mayhem, and the majesty of God all rolled into one fabulous book. Cover to cover, author Shellie Arnold delivers yet another poignant page-turner in the Barn Church Series.

~Clint and Penny A. Bragg
Authors and co-founders of Inverse Ministries, Inc.

Abide with Me is a story of love, divided loyalties, and greed. It's also a story of grace and forgiveness. This is one powerful novel.

~Ane Mulligan
Author of *Chapel Springs Revival*

Shellie Arnold has done it again! The stories Shellie creates demonstrate how life can get in the way of our best plans, in devastating ways. But God can bring healing. As a pastor, I am always looking for creative tools to assist me as I counsel people. *Abide With Me* has become one of those tools! The day I finished reading this wonderful story, a couple came into my office desperate for help to save their marriage. They had forgotten how to talk to each other, so they didn't. (I won't give away the good stuff, but the chime method Nicholas uses to speak back into Angelina's life—they should teach this stuff in counseling courses.) I told them about the couple in this story. They loved the idea and it started them back down the road to healing their marriage. When a story can do that it's magical, in the best and most God-like way!

~Tina M. Hunt
Pastor
Ashland First Church of the Brethren

Acknowledgments

In my opinion, this story is the story of every marriage. It's the novel I wanted to write for the longest time, the story I wanted to tell first. But God had other plans, and rather than this manuscript being book one in The Barn Church series, it became book three.

The plotline changed too many times to count. Every time I thought I had the story nailed down, a new set of problems awaited me. So I made revision after revision and changed layer after layer. Much like God does with us as He redeems, restores, refines, and heals. As I sat to write this acknowledgements page, I realized even the process of creating the story mirrored my spiritual life and my marriage. Both are always a work in progress.

So once again, my first thank you is to God. Who is faithful to convict and teach and lead me, even when we have to go over a lesson one more time. God, You know how much time and effort You spent convincing me to marry. Thank You for pushing me and pushing me, then pushing me again. Thank You for teaching me as I live.

To those who have read my previous novels and shared with me how their lives were touched. Thanks for letting me see some of the fruit of my labor.

To my agent, Tamela Hancock Murray, thank you for supporting me writing what I feel called to write.

To Eva Marie Everson and Jennifer Slattery, thank you for helping me birth this book during a season when I couldn't push alone.

To Dory Stewart and the Medina County Writers Club. Several revisions back I knew the story wasn't working, but couldn't figure out why. Thanks for telling me why and how to begin to fix it.

To Officer Jim Conley of the Akron Police Department, thanks for the tour and the abundance of information you shared. All was invaluable to me.

To my new Sisters in Crime friends. Thanks for the quick responses about legal procedures. I admit I panicked before I thought of consulting you, then sighed with relief that you were in my life.

To my speedy betas: Tina, Tina, and Terry. Grouped together like this you sound like a girl band. You're not, but you still rock.

To my number one fan, thanks for all the cheers. I hear them, even from this distance.

To my family, it always has been and always will be for you, first.

To Stephen, thank you for listening and brainstorming with me, for listening again when I said "that won't work because...", and for letting me plot aloud. In moments when I struggle to find God and His love, I find both in you.

Dedication

To my husband, Stephen
You know how scared I was to marry. You didn't have to accept the love God put in your heart for me. Even with all we've been through, it's better than we thought it could be, isn't it?

PROLOGUE

Present day, Las Vegas, Nevada

Wearing her newest Oscar de la Renta cocktail dress, Angelina Rousseau stopped in the ballroom's open double doorway. She clenched her jeweled evening bag and resisted the urge to pat the French twist rooted at her hairline. Attending the wedding of internationally-renowned interior designer Rita Dade demanded certain fashion and etiquette. Rita—who considered her clients her friends, and had won awards for work in Angelina's home.

She scanned the chandelier-lit room from columned wall to columned wall. To her right and left, twin harps worthy of a cathedral filled the space with the classic "Unforgettable." At the far end where the groom stood on stage, garnet roses overflowed urns the size of small cars and scented the room like an English garden.

Rita hadn't been kidding. No expense was spared—not for Angelina's plane ticket and opulent suite upstairs, or this, Rita's fourth Las Vegas wedding. Over three hundred guests had been invited. Had Rita flown all of them here?

A tuxedo-clad usher caught her eye. "Bride's side?"

"Yes," she whispered. "Near the back, preferably an aisle seat."

He settled her hand into the crook of his arm. They stepped forward.

"Are you alone?" he asked.

When *wasn't* she alone?

Then, she almost stumbled. Had he actually tapped her wedding rings? The platinum band set with its three-carat diamond tilted on her finger as if losing its balance.

They stopped, and he turned. "May I have a dance at the reception?"

She lifted her chin and caught him eyeing the gold wrap grazing her collarbone. He winked at her and left.

Angelina sat. A blush sprouted from her chest. If only she had the nerve to shed the organza wrap and expose her bare shoulders, simply to get another reaction from the handsome usher.

How long had it been since her husband's dark eyes rested on her, sparkling with appreciation? Since his soft, women-would-kill-for-those lashes fluttered against her cheek or traced her jaw? And if she let her parched heart drink from another man's desire this weekend, when she returned home and saw Nicholas again, would he know what she had done?

Would he even care?

She folded a hand over her custom wedding rings, Nicholas' gift on their third anniversary. Did the rings he'd proudly given her then mean anything to him now?

Angelina stared at the minister holding his black book and standing beside Donatello, the groom. Then, the flirtatious usher passed by and winked again.

Dare she respond?

The entire weekend stretched before her. Later in her suite, she could open her balcony doors. Let moonlight stream in; let the soft night breeze stir the sheer curtains. If she gave in to the forbidden, the filigreed bed—the kind romance novels vividly describe—would keep her secret. She could touch and be touched. Smile at whispers of her beauty. Pretend the physical pleasure reached all the way to her heart.

And like a scarlet letter, the sin would surely shine on her face, especially when she and Nicholas next attended The Barn Church. And on that exact Sunday, the sermon topic would probably be adultery.

Or worse, hell.

She glanced at her sapphire-studded watch. 3:23 P.M. Nevada time meant 5:23 P.M. back home in Rowe City. Nick's plane would have landed in Alabama about the time hers had landed in Vegas. He would spend the evening working in his office downstairs. Tonight, he probably wouldn't realize he was alone in their house, not even when he slid between the satin sheets on their enormous bed.

Six thousand square feet of Venetian plaster, custom furniture, imported marble. And emptiness.

Was there any worse hell than living lonely in a marriage? At what point should a woman admit her marriage was dead?

The lights dimmed. Fiona Price, fresh from her world tour with Andrea Bocelli, emerged from the flowered hedge behind the stage singing "Con te Partiro." The ushers lit ivory candles on brass stands lining the red satin aisle-runner. *He* reached her row and winked yet again.

To her embarrassment, her heart jumped like a jubilant child. She'd not experienced this kind of sizzling spark since she fell in love with Nicholas, with one exception: Over a year ago, she'd felt an intense attraction to Rick Matthews. The sight of the married stable owner in faded blue jeans and boots had made her toes curl. What woman wouldn't be drawn to a quiet, cowboy type who showed almost maternal care for his horses? But Rick was also kind and committed to his wife.

Fiona's solo ended. The wedding march began. The audience stood.

Although Rita had described her gown, Angelina was still taken aback. Her friend's dress was stunning. Handmade in Italy, hundreds of glass beads—each its own prism—dangled from the long sleeves, swirled across the bodice, and danced down the twelve-foot train. A wide diamond choker graced her neck.

Rita's steps were sure. And the expression on her face—Rita's heart was wide open. Her glistening eyes said, *finally, I found you.*

"Please be seated," the minister said. "A wedding is a great way to start the new year, right, everyone? Dearly beloved, we are gathered together to witness the union of this man to this woman."

Angelina's heart squeezed as if making a fist. Weight, like heavy hands, pressed down on her as the minister charged the bride and groom.

She squared her shoulders. For heaven's sake, this was Rita's *fourth* marriage, and Angelina had attended the last wedding. Sentimental rhetoric was an expected part of the program.

The fortyish pair in front of her shared a lingering kiss. The gentleman whispered in his companion's ear, provoking a gentle elbow to the ribs. He draped his arm around the woman—make that wife, his wedding band was now clearly visible—and brushed reverent fingertips down her neck.

And it hit Angelina. The reception would be fraught with couples dancing and sharing unspoken memories via long looks.

Rita and her groom turned to each other and clasped hands, their every expression shown on two large video screens flanking the stage.

"I promise all of myself to you." Donatello's voice shook, but his hold on Rita was solid. He raised her hands to his lips, a common enough European gesture, but the way he looked at her, like she was the only woman in the world …

Rita laughed and cupped his cheek, her face aglow. "Donatello, you showed me what real love is. You shared God's love with me. I promise to be your wife from this day forward."

Angelina shifted in her seat. How did a couple go from such loving anticipation on their wedding day, to tolerating, then despising each other as had happened to her own parents before her mother's death? She'd hoped she and Nicholas would be fortunate. She'd hoped they would find themselves blessed with a deep relationship.

Rather, after almost a decade together, she'd learned familiarity didn't breed contempt, but indifference.

She blinked, surprised at rapidly pooling tears. *Lock 'em up, girl. Lock 'em up.*

What was wrong with her? She never cried, especially in front of others.

Although she had to admit, she'd almost cried in front of Rick. Over Nicholas, and her marriage, and the incessant loneliness she faced.

The soloist sang again, another love song. The longing, the bliss of the piece, did something inside her, forcing aside a rusty latch that secured her deepest yearnings. She could almost feel the cellar doors of her heart fly open.

A frightening wind roared in her ears.

Was it too much to ask to feel connected to *someone* in this world? To a husband after ten years of marriage? To God, after years of attending church?

Anguish burned its way up her throat and tears gushed forth. She couldn't stem the flow.

She clutched her evening bag and rose. She was seconds away from total meltdown and unable to stop it.

Watching her steps through the sea swimming in her eyes, she fled. She pushed the back doors open as the first drops left her chin, crossed the smoke-hazed lobby, and turned the corner behind the lounge.

A hand touched her shoulder.

She turned to see the handsome usher.

"Please," he said, "may I help?"

PART I

CHAPTER ONE

*T*en years ago, St. Augustine, Florida

"I'm so happy, Nicholas. We're going to be so happy."

And she'd never be lonely again.

At the edge of the McDonald's parking lot, Angelina snuggled against him on the wide front seat of his car.

He raised a large Coke with two straws to her lips. "Here you go, Mrs. Rousseau."

Coke dribbled down her chin, and she laughed. "I am Mrs. Rousseau, aren't I?"

"For the past half hour."

She dipped a McNugget into honey mustard. "Not bad for a free meal. Sweet of the courthouse clerk to give us a gift card."

He looked through the windshield at afternoon rain. "I wanted better for you, Angie."

"This is better." She squeezed ketchup onto folded napkins. "Way better than the mac and cheese I usually split with Phoebe."

"Don't think I don't know if you'd married someone wealthy—a doctor, a lawyer—your dad would have continued paying your tuition and shelled out for a big church wedding."

"Who needs a boring church wedding with all that God stuff? You didn't really want that, did you?"

"No, but I'm just saying. You gave up everything for me. I want to give it all back to you, and more."

"That's not true. Daddy disowned me when I told him I wanted to change my major to study art. He's always belittled my interest in art.

And he wouldn't have paid for any wedding, especially one in a church. The minute I moved in with Phoebe—black sheep number one—I became black sheep number two. Taking back my car and cell phone were just formalities."

"We won't live with your sister long."

"She works days. And besides, my room is at the other end of the house."

"We'll get our own place soon," he said.

"She's gone so much; it's like we do have our own place."

He gave her the last fry, then kissed her. If every married kiss turned out to be as passionate as these first ones …

He pulled away, his breath hot on her face. "Wow. The motel's not far. You want anything else? From the drive-thru?"

Angelina laid her head on his shoulder. "A vanilla shake?"

He drove his land-yacht Buick around the building, ordered, and sped down A1A to Vern and Verna's Motor Lodge near St. Augustine Beach. Sixty-three dollars bought a room with two double beds, a sputtering window air-conditioner, and a rear view of Vern's rusty work shed—a sight so distinct if this weren't her wedding night, she'd be tempted to sketch the image onto paper.

Nicholas closed the threadbare curtains over the dingy window.

"This place is a dump," he said. "Almost as bad as some of the places I lived in as a kid. I should've pawned my computer."

"No, you shouldn't have."

"I could buy it back later—"

"Shh." She pressed a finger to his lips. "It's Valentine's Day, and we're married. The day's already perfect. Tonight's just icing."

"Icing, huh?" He kissed her again. "Angie, I love you so much. I wish we didn't have to go to work tomorrow night."

"I love you, too. Going to work's not so bad. At least we're there together."

"Right," Nick said. "Denny's is a great place for a honeymoon."

She knew he hated working as a nightshift short-order cook, so she smiled up at him. "We can have a honeymoon every day if we want."

"Someday, Angie, I'll give you everything you want. Anything money can buy."

"But all I want is a life with you. I love you."

He shook his head. "Love isn't enough. It doesn't buy houses or pay bills. One day, I'm going to make enough money so you won't have to work." He took her face in his hands and gazed deep into her eyes. "I'll work, and you won't, okay?"

Her eyes widened. "You mean when we have children?"

"Yeah. I guess."

"I want children. Remember?"

"When we have enough money."

She knew about his parents, that his father left his mother before Nicholas' birth. Collette Rousseau—a French immigrant—had worked two and three jobs at a time to provide for her son until he reached adulthood, then returned to her hometown in Lyon, France. Nicholas would never have been able to go to college if he hadn't done well in school and gotten full scholarships.

"I can work even after we have children. I've told you before; I'm not a princess you need to pamper."

"I want you to be able to pursue your art. You want to finish your degree and paint, don't you?"

"Yes. More than anything."

"You're so beautiful. I still can't believe you married me."

She glanced in the mirror above the dresser and told herself not to resent what she saw there. All her life, she'd been praised for her looks as if she were the mastermind behind her own DNA. She'd gladly relinquish her waterfall of dark hair, her camera-ready face, or modelesque figure to be less shy and more comfortable in her own skin.

She looked into his warm brown eyes. "Tell me again why you asked me to marry you."

"Because the first time we met, I knew my heart was tethered to yours." He grinned that grin she loved, flashing his dimple. "I love the way you wring your hands or fiddle with your many bracelets when you're nervous."

She looked down and saw she'd been caught doing exactly that.

"I love when the artist in you forgets she's shy and points out details and colors I don't notice."

She felt herself blush.

He lifted her chin. "I even love your sometimes annoying optimism."

"Annoying optimism?"

He kissed her. "Only sometimes. I guess we might need it if we hit tough times. But one day we'll have money. I'll buy you expensive jewelry. A dozen new necklaces to wear all at once, like you like to."

"I'd rather travel with you. Go to Paris and visit the Louvre."

"I'll take you. I promise."

He once again took her face in his hands. Hunger leapt from him. "I can't wait to be with you."

He kissed her like every fantasy she'd ever envisioned about her wedding night. So many times they'd come close to having sex, but he'd always stopped, refusing to take advantage of her before marriage as had happened to his mother. He released her only to pull his shirt over his head, then reached for her blouse buttons.

"I don't want to hurt you." His breath came fast. "You have to tell me if I hurt you."

"Okay." She slid her bracelets off both wrists and lay them on the dresser.

"Promise?" he asked.

"Yes," she breathed. "Now, stop talking!"

***

Nicholas woke in a sweat. He'd dreamed his credit card payment for the hotel room had been denied, and the manager was banging on the door, yelling they had to get out. He sat up, reminding himself he'd paid with cash, but couldn't quite get back his breath.

Leaving Angelina to sleep, he slipped into the bathroom. He braced his hands on the tiny counter and tried to ignore the scent of mildew from the shower tiles, the rust ring at the bottom of the sink, the way his bare feet stuck to the laminated floor. He wished he was wearing socks.

He raised his gaze to the chipped and cracked mirror.

"You're an industrial engineer," he whispered. "You can figure out a better way to do almost anything in the workplace."

Sure, his grades had slipped before graduation from working nights to save for Angelina's ring. So professional recruiters had picked others of his classmates. He simply needed to be patient. Finding a great job was only a matter of time, right?

He ran a hand through the back of his hair, down his neck. He should have waited to marry her. Impatient to make her his wife, desperate to finally give in to how badly they wanted each other, he'd focused on the short-term goal of getting married.

Now, he was so embarrassed over where they'd spent their first night together, over sharing McDonald's Chicken McNuggets as their first married meal, he wished he hadn't done it. He could have given her more, given her better, if he'd just been willing to wait a little longer.

He rubbed his neck again and caught the distinct whiff of body odor. Hoping the tub wasn't as dirty as it looked, he stepped in to shower.

A spray of sludge hit him in the face. He leaned away, gritted his teeth as the pipes cleared. He watched the brown-gray water disappear down the drain and immediately knew how to fix a problem in the kitchen where he worked. The backup wasn't caused by the drain's position, or—as his boss had voiced—by the way Nicholas stacked the dishes. Rather, he'd bet the drain line itself had not been cleaned in years.

He scrubbed his body, washed his hair, all the while creating in his mind a mechanism that would protect the drain and prevent back-up in the sink. With the absence of an exhaust fan, the bathroom steamed quickly. He emerged from the shower knowing he had no paper on which to draw the design, so he drew on the fogged-up mirror. If he could sell his idea to Denny's, or better yet, a national plumbing fixture company, he might make royalties for the rest of his life.

The door opened.

"Nicholas?"

Her long hair was tousled, her face slightly flushed. She'd wrapped herself in the faded bedspread. He hoped the stains on its surface weren't fresh, left from previous guests. Never again would he take her to a low-class place like this one.

"I promise I'll provide for you," he said. "And I want another wedding. I want to buy you a beautiful dress and have a big reception and a two-week honeymoon at a fancy resort. The kind of place you stayed at when you were younger for all your beauty competitions."

She shrugged and grinned. "This place has its own unique character. What are you drawing?"

"Remember how I'm good at figuring things out? I have an idea."

"Only married a few hours, and you're already bored with me?"

"What? No."

"Come back to bed."

"Just a sec. I think I know a way to, um, if we do it this way, hmm …"

"Your brain doesn't turn off even when you sleep," she said.

"Nope."

"Are you a morning person who needs to always be working on something?"

"Yep." He glanced back at his diagram.

"I'd rather sleep in, then spend the day wandering through a museum."

"What? I like museums okay."

"I guess it'll be up to me to get your attention back if I feel neglected."

She blew on the back of his neck just below his errant curls. She kissed the same spot and he turned, catching the edge of the bedspread so her body was revealed.

"Oh, you've got my attention." His gaze traveled down, then up to lock with hers. "I've never craved anything or anyone like I crave you, Angie."

"Isn't that a good thing?"

"If you always want me as much as I want you."

She pulled him from the bathroom. She'd turned on the bedside lamp, illuminating their pitiful surroundings, so he focused on her instead.

He wrapped her in his arms. "Tell me again why you said yes to marrying me."

"Every time you say you love me, it feels true. I've never felt safe with anyone the way I do with you. I'll be happy if I wake every morning next to you."

"I love you, Angelina. More than I thought I could ever love anyone."

"Show me." She drew him back to bed. "Show me every day for the rest of our lives."

"You can count on that. I promise."

Chapter Two

Six months married, Troy, Alabama

Angelina would never have guessed August in Troy, Alabama, could be as humid and hot as Florida's east coast.

She drank the last few drops of the bottled water and looked around at the empty cars in the parking lot. She felt safe enough here with the windows down, but the heavy heat was getting to her. She knew she couldn't have gone in with Nicholas to the job interview at Warren Engineering, but he could have at least found her a seat in a waiting area or lobby with air conditioning. The AC in their car had given out near Tallahassee when they'd refilled the tank. How much gas would be used if she cranked the car and turned on the fan for a few minutes?

She doodled in the notepad she'd brought along. She sketched the cars in their neat rows. The front of the building with its imposing gray doors.

Finally, Nicholas emerged from the office building. A man in a business suit followed, called to him and handed him something, then went back inside. For several moments, Nick stood in place.

He returned to their car. Started the engine, and with a squeal of tires, raced onto the highway. He threw a crumpled envelope onto the seat between them.

"Nicholas, you're scaring me."

His knuckles whitened as he tightened his hands on the wheel.

"Where are we going?"

He checked the rearview mirror. Checked the traffic to their right and sped across two lanes to the exit ramp.

She grabbed the armrest on her door. "Nicholas, please."

Lately, he'd been moody. More than once, he'd lost his temper at work. Frankie, their manager, had written up the incidents and placed Nicholas on probation. She'd told herself it was because Nick had trouble sleeping during the day. Because they had little to no privacy while staying with her sister.

When he'd told her about this job opportunity, they'd both been filled with hope. The idea of traveling for the interview had sounded perfect. Not only a chance for them to get away from her nosey sister and the parade of random guys who frequently visited her, but maybe, just maybe, a chance at a real job for Nicholas. He simply wouldn't be happy until he made a lot more money.

He turned in at an abandoned Shoney's, swerved to miss a pothole, and stopped, facing a billboard advertisement for a local strip club. He slammed his hand against the steering wheel and turned away from her. She thought she heard him curse.

She waited. Sweat poured down her back as the car baked on the pitted asphalt.

She was getting hungry, and the cereal box they'd brought to snack on was almost empty.

"I guess they didn't offer you a job." She paused. "That's okay. We'll be okay. It's only three-thirty. We can be back home in seven hours. We'll change clothes fast, go straight to Denny's like nothing ever happened, and you can keep looking for other work. We'll just tell Frankie he's confused about us asking for the night off. No one has to know we came here."

"I'll know."

She looked at the envelope. "Did they give you anything for your time and travel expenses?"

"A hundred-dollar check."

Which they couldn't easily cash. Their credit union was back in Florida.

His head hung so low, she thought he might cry. She'd never seen him cry.

"We should get something to eat," she said. "I know you're exhausted from working last night then driving straight here. We'll talk while we eat, then I can drive home, and you can sleep."

He finally looked at her, tears bubbling in his eyes. "We can't afford to eat out and get a hotel room."

"We could look for one of those check cashing places. Or we can just go home—"

"I don't want to go home!" He wiped his eyes. "Look. I screwed up. I thought this was a done deal. I thought I'd be surprising you right now with a new job and a new life. We could move here and, I don't know, finally start our life together?"

He banged the steering wheel again.

"Between when they called me last week and now, they lost a big contract, and now the company is being bought out. They can't hire me. They can't hire anyone. Probably half the people there are going to lose their jobs. And I might as well tell you … it won't do us any good to drive back in time for our shift. I'm sorry, but the last few nights, with Frankie flirting with you and giving me grimy grunt work, I can't take it anymore."

"He doesn't flirt with me. He's married. And he's old enough to be my father."

"Which doesn't stop him from putting his arm around you when you come in the kitchen, or licking his lips as he watches you leave it. He makes sure I see him."

"He hasn't said anything bad to me."

"Yeah, well, he's said it to me."

She could almost read in his eyes the type of lewd comments to which he was referring. And she'd thought older men, married men, were above that.

A coldness ran through her. She'd thought after all these years she'd developed good enough radar to sense when a man was just looking at her for her body. But she'd been married to Nick for six months now. She'd let down her guard, thinking she didn't need to worry about that any longer.

Now she felt sick inside. Knowing Frankie was ogling her and making sure Nicholas knew about it explained a lot about Nick's behavior and that of the other night shift girls. No wonder the other waitresses rarely spoke to her.

She crossed her arms. "You quit, didn't you? Even though Frankie said he was going to help you meet someone in upper management about your ideas to streamline the kitchen?"

"Yeah, because he'll never do it. He'll never introduce me to anyone."

"Did you quit for both of us?"

"Yeah."

"Not giving notice will really help us find new jobs." She reached for the cereal box. "We can split what's left of the drive so you can sleep."

"Angie." He placed a hand over hers. "I can't stand to watch you eating cereal. We'll get a burger. Just let me get hold of myself. Are you mad?"

"I don't know what I am. You're not like you used to be."

"Because I'm worried about money."

"Then why did you spend what little we had saved on that sham real estate investing course? You didn't tell me you'd done that, either. Now, we don't even have jobs."

"Don't you see how awful this has been for me? Knowing every night instead of us going to bed together in our own place, we schlepped off to jobs we hate? Watching you get hit on at work, and you didn't even know it? All because I don't make enough money to support us. That's why I'm angry and frustrated. That's why I bought the stupid course."

Somehow, they both looked up at the barely-clothed, air-brushed model gazing at them from the billboard.

"Great idea," he said. "You'd probably make boatloads of money."

He couldn't have hurt her more if he'd slapped her.

Six months married. He knew all her insecurities about her appearance. That he'd so carelessly joke about her selling herself that way …

She got out of the car and ran, across the cratered lot, past a rusty dumpster to a narrow band of trees. She sagged against a pine and let herself cry.

She heard his footsteps and closed her eyes. Felt his hand on her arm, and before she thought, swung out and barely missed slapping him.

He caught her in his arms, pressed his cheek to hers. "Shh. I know you're scared. I'm scared, too. Don't stop loving me. I'll die if you stop loving me. Don't leave me, Angie."

"When you're so angry, it feels like you leave me."

He kissed her. Hunger and passion erupted as in their first few weeks of marriage. His hands were in her hair; she couldn't hold him tightly enough. The kiss went so deep she thought he sucked the breath out of her.

A short siren sounded, then, a piercing *blip-blip*. At the edge of the parking lot, a policeman exited his car holding a megaphone.

"Sir, please step away from the lady. Both of you, hands up where I can see them."

"Do what he says," Nick said.

"Nothing's wrong here," Angelina said. "He's my husband."

The officer laid his hand on his weapon and approached.

He motioned with his head. "That your car?"

"Yes, sir," Nick said.

"You broke down?"

"No, sir, not exactly."

"Got some ID on you?"

"In my wallet."

"Turn around," the officer said as he reached them. "I have to frisk you. You got any weapons?"

"No," they answered.

"Let's see that wallet, and you can tell me why you're out here skirting the woods."

They walked back to the cruiser.

"You got any ID, ma'am?"

"In my purse. In the car."

"Let's go get it."

He verified their IDs, then took off his shades. "So, what's your story?"

Angie stared at the ground as Nick answered the officer. She grabbed Nick's hand.

"I'm at the end of my shift," the policeman said. "You two look like you could use a bite to eat. How about you follow me up to the new Shoney's. I'll get you some food and help you figure out where you go next."

She waited to speak until they got back in Nick's car. "Do we have to go with him?"

"You mean legally?"

"Yes."

"I guess not. But why shouldn't we? Might as well get a free meal. We've got nothing better to do."

"Except go home." Her stomach growled; she glanced at Nick. "Don't laugh!"

***

Nick followed the detour signs off the two-lane highway and finally had to admit the truth. They were lost. On the outskirts of a place called Rowe City.

But there was no city. There were mostly peanut fields and corn fields and deer crossing signs, which in the coming darkness would not be visible at a distance. Rowe City didn't waste money on street lights.

"We should have driven home the way we came," he said.

"But the officer said we'd save time and gas if we went this way."

"He obviously didn't know about the detours."

Nick rolled to a stop at a four-way. Frame houses dotted the landscape. Across the street, one sat with its front porch light shining brightly. A large yard lay to the left, then beyond and behind that, thick woods. One day he'd love to own property like that.

"Let's go back, see if we can find the highway." Angelina raised her head from his shoulder. "It's getting dark, and don't we need gas?"

"I think we're heading east. If we keep going, we should eventually reach Dothan, the next big town."

"Big like this one?" She half giggled.

"You haven't smiled like that in a while." He checked the road in all directions—not a vehicle in sight.

He put the car in PARK. "Being married hasn't been easy like we thought it would be."

"No, it hasn't."

"Now do you see why having money is so important? Why I want to make lots of money for us?"

She blinked against tears and nodded.

He held her tight. "Don't cry. My mother cried all the time over my father leaving her, over not having enough money, out of constant fear she'd lose one of her jobs and not be able to pay the rent. It's like I've already failed you."

"You haven't failed me."

"Angie, I can't even get us home." Headlights approached from behind. He put his twenty-six-year-old Buick in gear. "Next country store or gas station we see, we stop and ask for new directions."

"Good idea."

He pulled forward, passing the wooden house on the left corner. Was the speed limit really thirty-five here? His headlights flashed across headstones, then a large wooden sign which said *Rowe City Gospel Church "The Barn Church."* No cars sat in the grass parking lot, but the lights burned inside the huge barn-like structure.

He slowed. "My mom asked for help from a church once. They gave us food from their food bank and helped her find another job."

"My dad always made fun of Christians and churches. Especially those with signs that read 'Turn or Burn' or 'Try Jesus—If You Don't Like Him the Devil Will Take You Back.' Do we have to stop at a church?"

"There's nothing else around here. No stupid sign out front. Maybe this one's just a bunch of do-gooders."

He turned in.

"If you're going in there, I'm going with you," she said. "I'm not staying out here by myself."

As they got out of the car, he scanned the area by the faint light of a crescent moon. The night pulsed with the chorus of cicadas. The sky looked like the bottom of a dark blue bowl.

"Nick, it's so peaceful here. Is this just how Alabama feels?"

"I don't know."

He led her to the large double doors. He knocked, listened, but no one came. From inside, he heard a belt of laughter.

He pushed open the door with a creak.

"Shush, you." A slender woman, probably in her mid-fifties, dusted padded pews on one side of the center aisle. A man did the same on the other side, his shoulders shaking as he laughed.

"I'm thinking about telling that one this Sunday. Pierce will never know."

"Don't you dare. Even if he is grown and has his own life, our son wouldn't want you telling that story to the whole congregation."

Nick stepped inside and felt a quiet he'd never felt before.

"Excuse me. Ma'am? Sir? We're lost. I wonder if you might give us some directions."

A look passed between the two of them.

"I'll keep going." The woman continued dusting the pews. "You go find out what they need."

The man approached and extended his hand. "Daniel Crane. My wife is Kay."

"Nick and Angelina Rousseau. We're driving back to Florida from Troy, got lost after the detours. Can you direct us back to the highway?"

"Are you in a hurry?"

"No, sir, not particularly, but it's getting late, and we've got a long way to drive."

"You looking for a hotel, son?"

Kay finished cleaning a pew and walked over. "Daniel, don't pry."

"I'm a preacher. Prying's what we do."

"No, sir, we're going to drive on home."

Kay elbowed Daniel. "We'd be happy to have you stay with us. Our guest room hardly gets used. It's the house on the corner. Come on, Daniel, lock up. We're going home."

"You're willing to leave with only half the pews dusted?"

"They'll keep. Priorities," Kay said.

Nick turned to Angie. "Let's do it," he whispered.

"I don't know. Shouldn't we just go home?"

"If it gets weird, we can still leave."

She sighed. "Okay."

"Thank you, Mr. and Mrs. Crane. We'll meet you there."

***

Nicholas opened his eyes to the glaring sunlight. A rooster crowed. Was that what had woken him? How cool was that?

He reached for his watch on the small bedside table. Just after seven. He'd slept straight through the night, even though he was in a strange bed, in a strange house, in a little town that seemed to be stuck in an earlier, slower time. No wonder his brain was firing, anxious to get up and get moving.

He sniffed deep at Angelina's hair where it fell across his face. She was snuggled tight against his side, her hand fisted on his chest. Part of him wanted to turn to her and make love in the quiet of the morning. But another part wanted to go talk to the people who'd opened their home. Something about the couple made him feel welcomed.

Pipes rattled in the walls. He remembered the sound from one old house he and his mother had lived in.

"You think too loudly." Eyes still closed, Angelina pulled the quilt up to her chin.

"I didn't say anything."

"I didn't say you did; I said you're a loud thinker. Why won't you sleep late when you have the chance?"

He stroked her hair. "Can't."

"Last night, Kay said they'll be gone all day, but they don't mind us staying here. We could lie in bed all day. Go for a walk through those woods you admire so much."

"We could." He smelled bacon and grinned. "Or, we could go see what smells so good."

"Oh, Nicholas. Really?" She buried her head under a pillow. "I don't want food. You know I'm not a morning person."

"You can sleep later. Let's go see what they're doing today. I bet this place looks even better in full daylight."

While Angie brushed her hair, he dressed quickly, left, and eased the door shut behind him. He took several steps and stopped to listen.

"Be quiet, you." Kay's voice came from the kitchen. "And don't flip those pancakes too early."

"You're a hard woman, making a man wait on his pancakes."

"Ooooh. Like you might wither away."

"I like your apron."

She giggled. "Quit, you. We have company."

"They're still sleeping."

"Nope. I heard a floorboard. Flip the pancakes."

Sure enough, the floors creaked as he walked down the hall through the center of the home, turned right into the dining room and kitchen.

"Good morning, Daniel. Kay. Thank you again for letting us stay the night."

"It's no trouble at all," Kay said. "Daniel's finishing your first batch of pancakes."

"I thought these were mine." Daniel reached for bacon drying on a paper towel; Kay swatted his hand.

"Go on to the table, you two," she said. "I'll start another batch and bring your plates."

The men sat.

Daniel leaned forward. "See, if you irritate them enough, they won't want your help anymore."

Nicholas laughed. "Is that your best marriage advice?"

"Not my best, son, but it's good stuff. Would you mind giving me a moment to bless our meal?"

"Okay."

Daniel bowed his head. "Dear God, thank You for this food …"

Nicholas glanced over.

Daniel placed a hand on his shoulder. "Thank You for our new friends, Nicholas and Angelina …"

His throat tightened, and he lowered his gaze to the table. Sure, over the years he'd heard a prayer or two, but he'd never heard anyone pray for him. Daniel's doing so seemed to spotlight a deficit he hadn't known was there.

His mother had worked to support him, loved him, and cheered for him. But self-confidence, a feeling of security had always eluded him. He couldn't remember a time a man had touched him, let alone with genuine kindness and care. More than a financial provider. Was this what he'd missed not having a dad?

"Please bless this food, Heavenly Father," Daniel said. "Amen."

Heavenly Father.

What else was Nick missing?

Chapter Three

Angelina looked out the back seat window as Daniel drove them all down the long dirt road. When the wind blew, the fields moved in waves much as the Atlantic did back in St. Augustine. But there were no strip malls here. She'd not seen a McDonald's or video rental store on the corners they'd passed.

In the front seat, Kay turned around. "If you two don't really want to stay, don't really want to do this, say the word, and I'll take you back to the house."

"We're fine," Nick answered for them both.

If Angelina had had her way, she and Nick would still be in bed, talking about what they were going to do next. Or maybe already driving, almost halfway home to St. Augustine.

"Don't you love it here?" Nick whispered in her ear.

"I don't know."

"Everything smells so fresh. It's quiet and peaceful, and I don't know, homey."

"You mean white picket fence homey? Having babies homey?"

Their eyes met, and she felt the jolt, that lovely jolt from knowing he wanted her, only her.

He grinned. "Yeah. All I need is a good job."

Which he wasn't going to find here in the land of fields and fences and dirt roads.

He kissed her cheek. "Let's just take the day, Angie. Forget about everything and see what happens. We can have Kay drive us back later if you really want to leave."

"All right."

They turned down a single-car width lane and rolled to a stop. Four old frame houses, one of them two-story, sat apart on the sloped ground. In the distance, a large tractor drove across a field, clearing a path through what looked like hay.

"Tell me again why they're doing this," she whispered to Nick.

"Daniel and Kay are schoolteachers. So, they're off in the summer."

"But they run the church all year."

"Right. Last spring a tornado whipped through, damaging several farms and homes. Daniel said someone from The Barn Church knows the Skinner family, so the congregation decided to help them. Cool, huh?"

"Doesn't school start in a week or so?"

"That's why they've got to finish now. Various people from the church have been out here all summer. They're like a big family."

The excitement in his voice made her smile. "You're really enjoying this, aren't you?"

"Yeah. I've never done construction work before. They'll be hanging the last of the siding on the main house. Today I'll learn how." He kissed her quickly. "I'm going with Daniel. Find me if you need me."

"Well—" She was about to say *I'd rather stay with you*. But he was already gone.

Probably a dozen cars and trucks were parked in the yard. Children ran in circles playing tag. Women of various ages stood on the porch or went in and out of the house.

Kay opened Angie's door. "Overwhelmed?"

"A little."

Kay studied her. "Nick makes friends easily. Not so easy for you?"

Angie got out. "You could say that."

"Angelina, you might be the most beautiful person I've ever seen."

Kay cocked her head. "That's the problem, isn't it? To men, you're an opportunity, to women you're a threat. How terribly lonely for you."

She looked out into the fields. How could this woman, a near stranger, know so much about her? Since meeting last evening, they'd barely spoken.

"Most people think my looks make me confident."

"Instead, you've had to be leery of everyone, haven't you? Oh, you beautiful girl. You're safe here. Come meet the other ladies. Let them welcome you."

"Why would they?"

"Because that's what people who love God do. And like I said before … if you really want to leave, I'll take you home."

They walked toward the main house.

"I've never known anyone like you, Kay. Especially from a church."

"That's too bad." Kay glanced at her as they walked up the stairs. "Thanks for not judging me based on my faith or my appearance."

"What?"

"I'm a pastor's wife, and I'm not as young and attractive as you." She gestured to a short, round woman who stepped forward with a grin. "Angie, this is my best friend, Millie Newman. Millie, Angelina Rousseau."

Millie caught her hand and patted it. "Look what God made. Youngin', you are lovely."

She didn't know what surprised her more—being called youngin' or being told she was lovely, then looked upon without jealousy, speculation, or judgment.

She remembered her father mocking people of faith. *Christianity is just a lot of people claiming to have the same imaginary friend. They're as mean and greedy and thoughtless as the rest of us. They'll stab you in the back like everyone else.*

Hadn't he done exactly that when she hadn't complied with his directive to pursue a business degree?

How she'd always wanted friends. Dare she take a chance Kay's kindness was real? That the other women would be as hospitable?

She turned to Kay. A slow, loving smile spread on the woman's face, and she opened her arms.

Angie sagged into the embrace. She couldn't remember the last time anyone other than Nicholas had held her.

"I'd like to stay," she said. "Would you introduce me to the others?"

***

He couldn't believe how at home he felt in this little town, in this old frame house, with people he'd met last night.

Nicholas knew it wasn't only the quiet of the country or the smell of peanut fields across the road or even the fact he was sitting in an old rocking chair on a house-length porch. He'd found something in Rowe City. He'd found freely-offered friendship and a sense of home, and if he let himself think it, he figured he was also finding a curiosity about faith.

In the nearby rocker, Daniel reached in his shirt pocket. "We worked hard today. You did, anyway. I prefer supervising. Want some Juicy-Fruit?"

Nick laughed. Daniel had indeed been quite the supervisor. "Do you always chew that awful gum?"

"None as good as Juicy-Fruit. I love the stuff."

"Yes." Kay rose from the swing at the end of the porch. "He always chews it. Spends a fortune. We should buy stock in the company."

Daniel popped his gum. "That's a good idea. Married a smart woman—smart enough to pick me."

"Smart enough to know when she's about to burn dinner." She patted Daniel as she walked by.

Nick waited to speak until she'd shut the door behind her.

"Did Kay leave us here on purpose?"

Daniel rocked. "Probably. Your engine's been running since we got back from the Skinner farm."

"My engine's running?"

"Yep. If these rocking chairs had wheels, you'd be twenty miles ahead of me down the road."

"I guess you're right." Nick slowed his pace. "How come you're not beating me over the head with a Bible and screaming at me about hell like some street-preacher with a megaphone?"

"Would that help you?"

"No."

"That's why."

They rocked in silence.

"When you prayed over breakfast this morning, you said *Heavenly Father*. It got me thinking. I never knew my father." Nick shifted in his seat. "He got my mother pregnant, left her right before I was born."

"Tough row to hoe."

"She worked two, sometimes three jobs at a time." He'd lost count of the times they'd moved, the number of one-room apartments they'd lived in. Thankfully, he'd stuck with the same schools. He'd been smart, made friends easily, and his mother had made him study like crazy. "I hardly ever saw her, but I knew she loved me. My dad never looked back."

"I grew up without a father," Daniel said. "Leaves a boy feeling like he's got no safety net under him."

"Exactly. I don't know how to relate to God as the kind of father you prayed to this morning. When I picture God, I think of someone distant and aloof. Not someone you have a conversation with."

"If you've never had that point of connection, it's tough to get a grip on the idea. You get close to Him, you'll want Him to tell you what to do, especially when you don't know what to do. That's asking for wisdom. The judge part, that'll come one day, too, but not like how most people think. God would always rather show mercy than extend judgment."

"The contrasts confuse me. Do you have, like, a chart I can study?"

Daniel laughed. "That's the first time anyone's asked me for a chart about God. I'll give you a Bible. Read the book of John. Chapter fifteen talks about Jesus being a vine and those who believe in Him are the branches. A branch connected to the vine will grow. A disconnected branch just plumb dies."

"So I can get to know God by reading the Bible."

"Partly. How'd you get to know Angelina?"

Nick smiled. "My junior year at college was her first. I saw her in the cafe, almost dropped my tray. Couldn't think two words, you know? But I knew I had to meet her."

She'd been sitting alone at a two-seater booth. The whole time he'd stood in line he watched her, curious to see what guy would join her. No one did.

"I'll never forget it. I walked over, kind of sat at her table without asking. Our eyes met, and I knew everything had just changed. I said, 'My mother says I'd be a great catch.' Then I just looked at her until she laughed. I kept talking. Every time I saw her, every time we went out, I just kept talking, figuring I'd grow on her. If I didn't know what to say, I'd laugh and smile and say, 'Hey.' We'd sit there staring at each other because neither of us could fight what was going on inside us. I fell quick; I fell hard. She did, too, but I didn't know that at first."

"So, you spent time with her."

"Yeah."

"You talked about yourself and let her get to know you. You asked questions so she could tell you about herself."

"Well, yeah. I wanted her in my life. I wanted to know everything about her."

Daniel rocked and nodded. "That usually works."

***

Angelina opened the oven to check the peach cobbler. "How will I know when it's done?"

"When the top is firm." Kay handed her a knife. "If this comes out clean, it's done."

She tested the cobbler, closed the oven. "Not quite."

Until now, she and Nicholas ate cereal or mac-n-cheese at home, then a real meal at Denny's during their shift. No more Denny's meant she'd have to learn to cook.

"Could I maybe have the recipe?"

Kay grabbed bowls from a top cabinet. "My grandmother taught me how to make cobbler. I've never seen the instructions written out. I'll have to make it again soon, pay attention, and write everything down."

"I can set the table."

Angelina arranged the bowls, silverware, and napkins. She sat. "What you said today about making friends being difficult for me? You were spot on. How did you know?"

Kay stirred stew on the stove. She poured two glasses of tea, brought one to Angie, then sat as well.

"I had trouble making friends for the opposite reason." Kay sipped. "I was a skinny child, cross-eyed. Wore coke-bottle glasses before having corrective surgery. I was a terrible klutz, always running into things. Back then, everyone thought any condition like that was practically contagious. No one wanted to be my friend; maybe that helps me recognize those who are friendless now. I know the look of lonely."

This woman, she could cut right to Angelina's heart.

"I was so spatially-challenged my mother enrolled me in modeling classes in hopes I'd learn how to walk straight," Angie said.

"You know, I wondered if you'd ever done professional modeling. Your posture and the way you carry yourself make you appear confident. You're not, are you?"

"No. I learned to walk a certain way, stand and sit a certain way. I guess now it's second nature, but it's not natural. The modeling classes plus my looks gave her the idea of entering me in beauty pageants, which I hated. I was always so nervous I threw up before walking across the stage. I've never liked having all eyes on me."

"Me, neither, not after growing up with people staring at me," Kay said. "I wanted friends, but I didn't like being a spectacle."

Angelina turned her glass on the table, drawing lines through the condensation with her finger. "I can't remember a time I wasn't lonely. Until I met Nicholas, who's never been lonely."

Kay lowered her glass and set it aside. "Daniel was the same. My, that man—he could swoop into a room and make friends with anybody. He connected with people without even trying, while I sat there wringing my hands, scared spit-less I'd do or say the wrong thing."

"That's how I've always been, too."

"When Daniel set his sights on me, well, at first I didn't believe him. Why would he pick me? I figured it was some flight of fancy, a phase that would end with me having a broken heart." She laughed. "But he kind of latched on and never went away."

Angie laughed, too. "That's what Nick did to me. I couldn't *not* think about him because he was always there.

"One night, I had a late lab, and he knew it. He waited for me outside the classroom. But he was so tired from working nights, napping before classes, then going to school all day, he fell asleep on a couch in the hallway. I walked right past him. Didn't even realize he was there. While waiting for the elevator, I dropped a book. He shot up, calling my name, having no clue where he was or that he'd fallen asleep. I told him he'd lost his mind. He said, 'No, just my heart, to you.'"

"That's a good one," Kay said. "Men like Daniel and Nick … they can knot up a girl's feelings, can't they?"

"I feel like I can't breathe when there's conflict between us."

"Of course you do."

"How can that be a good thing?" Angie asked.

"Why wouldn't it be? If you feel like you can't breathe, you know you've got to fix something."

"I know Daniel and Nick are out there talking about God and the Bible. Should I be scared of that?"

The older woman reached for her hand. "Oh, sweetie, how you must have been hurt by those who should have loved you. You have no idea how much God loves you, do you?"

"My dad always made fun of churches."

People don't change, he'd say. Faith's a crutch.

"He liked bringing up the Jim and Tammy Faye Bakker scandal, Catholic priests molesting kids, and scary-looking guys who shoot up abortion clinics."

"Poor representatives, I'm sad to say. And I think you're confusing church people with God, although church folks should be imitators of Him. No wonder you're skeptical and worried your husband might be learning about God." Kay rose, returned to the stove. "Want to check the cobbler again?"

"Okay." She followed. "I was never allowed to question him. It only took me disagreeing with him a couple of times for him to cut off all contact." She realized now, her father was nothing if not a tyrant.

"I'm so sorry," Kay said.

Angelina removed the cobbler, sat it on the stove.

Kay carried the pot from the stove to the table and sat it on a trivet. "All done. I'll call the men."

"Kay." Angelina's heart pounded. She wanted to talk more about God. To learn. But she didn't know where to start. "Does God allow questions?"

"Oh, yes." Kay stopped with her hand on the front doorknob. "You can ask God anything." She walked out to the porch.

Angelina took a deep breath. *Dear God, are You real?*

Chapter Four

Nick groaned as he lay on the bed. His back and arms were sunburned, his shoulders ached from overuse, and he'd cut his finger. One of his most fun days ever.

Angelina entered and closed the door. "Kay gave me this lotion for your neck and arms. It'll take out the sting."

He took off his clean shirt, turned onto his stomach. As he had moments ago when taking a shower, he hissed as she spread the cold onto his skin.

She rubbed in the lotion. "You'll be paying for this the next few days."

"It was too hot to wear a shirt."

"You're from Florida. You should know better."

"There were five of us out there today," Nick said. "Daniel and a wiry guy named Clyde. A big guy they call Deacon Floyd; he's a deacon in the church. And a guy who works at the hardware store. Angus. He's thick, you know? Really strong for his height. Angus was bossing Clyde at the table saw. The deacon and I kept plodding along hanging the siding. Daniel pitched in here and there, but he never stopped talking and telling jokes. Some of them were doozies. Still, I laughed most of the day. I think my face hurts almost as much as my back."

She set aside the lotion.

"Angie. I've never been around men like them. Kind, but still men." They made him want to be a good man, a good husband.

"The women were nice. I didn't feel like they were talking about me or staring at me," she said. "Before long, Kay had maneuvered me through the group until I was hugged by all of them."

Nick grinned. "Kay maneuvered you?"

"Don't think for one second she doesn't run Daniel."

"Yeah, but in a good way. Have you noticed how they talk to each other?"

"You mean teasing like we do?"

"They flirt like they're still in love," he said.

"Kay says Daniel's always been that way. They're such a team. My parents? The only thing they ever agreed on was disagreeing." She paused. "I wonder how they learned to work together so well."

He rolled over and pinned her to the mattress. "I know a good way to practice working together."

She laughed. "Oh, do you?"

"Yeah." He kissed her. "Any chance you want to stay here? Live here?"

He kissed her again. She pulled away and sat up.

"What?" she asked.

"What if we start over here? Have your sister mail our important stuff, or we could drive down later and pick it up. I really like it here. There's nothing for us back in Florida."

She wrapped her arms around her bent knees. "You do seem happy here even though you didn't get a new job yesterday. Was that yesterday? It seems like weeks ago."

He sat up, too. "I like it here, Angie. Let's stay."

"Where? How?"

"Daniel said we could stay with them until we get on our feet."

"You asked him without telling me?"

"I didn't want to say anything to you if there wasn't a way. You've done without a lot of things because of me."

"I haven't."

"Yes, you have. We could get on our feet here if I work two jobs. You'd be safe here with Kay even if I have to work nights. Even if we help pay for food, we could save money faster."

"Money won't make us happy, Nick. My parents had more than enough money, and they weren't happy."

"Why can't I make you understand? We can't live without money. I know what it's like to be evicted, to see your belongings thrown out by the curb, to sleep on the city bus. I ate state-funded breakfast and lunch at school. I spent my childhood living hand-to-mouth. We can't eat only cereal for the rest of our lives."

"I like cereal."

"Angie. I want to give you a home. I want to provide for you."

Like his father had never provided for him and his mother.

She twirled the curls at his brow. "This city's mostly farms. How are you going to find one job, let alone two?"

"Angus and Daniel both say Benson's is always hiring."

"You want to work at a hardware store. I guess it's more secure than flipping real estate."

"It's not perfect. I'll still look for another job. But I have to wait until Monday to apply. The manager's off on Sundays. Although he will be at church tomorrow. Want to go?"

"I don't know."

"A new start's a new start, right? Maybe we give Daniel's church a try."

She looked deep into his eyes. "This is about Daniel, isn't it? And the dad you never had."

"I know it doesn't make sense, but it's like I'm hungry for something he can give me."

"What time does church start?"

"I don't know. We'll get up when we smell breakfast cooking."

"You mean you'll get up when you smell breakfast." She looked at him. "Everything's changing so fast. Where I thought we'd work, where we live. Wondering about God. Will you love me now? Be with me? When you love me, I believe we'll be okay."

"We'll be okay. I promise." He lowered his mouth to hers.

***

Angelina held Nick's hand as they approached the church's grassy lot. Other than Friday night when they'd arrived and stopped to ask directions, she'd never been in a barn. Had seldom been in a church except for a funeral or a wedding, the last being over a decade ago. The weathered, brown-gray exterior of The Barn Church looked old and welcoming and cared for. Kay's doing, Angelina was sure.

Nicholas pointed up. "Check out the window."

"Is that a horse silhouette? In a church?"

"Lots of barns around here have them."

"How do you know that?"

"I paid attention when Daniel drove us out to that farm yesterday. What do you think? You want a house with a barn?"

"I've always wanted horses."

"One day, Angie. I promise."

They passed a small, fenced cemetery. A cemetery. Right beside where people talked about God. It was kind of creepy.

She squeezed his hand and stopped. "Can we go inside after everyone else?"

"I guess. Are you worried about a weird meet-and-greet like in those Hallmark movies?"

"Sort of."

"But you said the ladies were nice."

"They were. I just … I'd rather slip in when everyone's distracted."

He veered her away from the main path to the entrance. "We'll wait here until they've started. But not too long. It's going to be hot again today."

"Thank you. At least I'm not the only one wearing jeans."

"This is a farming community. I don't think you have to worry too much about a dress code."

The large black man Nicholas had said everyone called Deacon and the shorter man named Clyde closed the double doors. Within moments, piano and choir music flowed from the church and seemed to wrap her heart in a loving embrace, much as Kay and Millie and the other women had done yesterday.

Nick led her in. They walked to the far end of the back row. The church was about half full, the congregation and choir stood singing.

The song ended, but the pianist continued playing softly. Deacon walked to the platform, the music stopped. Everyone sat.

He produced a small stack of cards from his pocket. "We have a lot to be thankful for this morning, and we also have a lot of needs.

"The Bartons received an offer on their farm. We'll be sad to see them go but rejoice with them about God providing them new jobs in Tennessee.

"Naomi and I are thankful we heard from our son, Julius, so we know he's alive. We believe he's finally hit bottom, so to speak. He's going back into the drug rehab program in Troy. He wanted us to apologize publicly on his behalf to everyone he stole from—especially you, Pastor. He said he didn't get much for the church speakers." Deacon shook his head. "You all know how we've grieved our boy's choices. We're grateful God always kept reaching for him, as He does for all of us. Let's pray."

Angie scanned the crowd, finally locating Naomi. The short

woman was half the deacon's size and wore a crocheted shawl as she had yesterday, although this one was baby blue. When everyone prepared to leave, she'd given Angie a bowl of corn casserole to take with her. "I heard you say you liked it," she'd said.

Kay and Daniel sat on the front row, their heads bowed with others in the congregation.

But Deacon Floyd looked to heaven and raised a hand. "Father, thank You again for loving us all. For loving my son even more than me and Naomi do. Our church's needs are many—wisdom, help facing grief, strength to endure difficult times. We all need a better understanding of Your love and Your character. At least one marriage here is near breaking. God, help us all submit to Your love; let it work in us and through us."

Never before had she heard anyone talk to God like that. The large man pulled a handkerchief from his other pocket and wiped his eyes.

Nick bumped her shoulder with his. "Isn't this cool? I told you, they're like a big family."

They weren't like the family she'd grown up with, or ever seen before.

Daniel walked to the platform. "I'd planned to continue teaching from Genesis, but this morning God gave me new instructions. You might recognize today's passage as the parable about the prodigal son."

Her ears perked. A vague memory surfaced of sitting beside her sister in a small Sunday school class as someone told this same story. Hadn't her parents fought bitterly the night before? Obviously about one of her father's many affairs, although she hadn't understood that at the time.

The next morning, her mother had taken her daughters to a nearby church, only to return home and pour herself a glass of vodka.

"Maybe faith works for other people. It doesn't work for me," she'd said. "But, after a bottle of this? Nothing bothers me. Not your father's anger or his extramarital activities."

"Deacon, Naomi," Daniel said. "I'll visit your boy this week. I've forgiven him for stealing from the church, but he won't know if I don't tell him. He'll hear it from me, I promise you. We fail miserably when we don't run to meet those taking the tiniest step toward God. God loves your boy, and I'm going to tell him that, too. Too many times the church portrays God as a tyrant. Nothing could be farther from the truth."

Angelina's breath caught as she remembered her prayer from yesterday. *Dear God, are You real?*

Was this God answering? Directing Daniel to speak from the only Bible passage she knew, and use the word *tyrant*, what she'd yesterday thought of her own father?

Now Daniel flipped pages. "Turn your Bibles to Luke 15:11-32 …"

She listened as Daniel explained God's grace and forgiveness, and what he called the "typical salvation message."

"The redemption part of this story is important," Daniel continued. "God forgives the rebel who returns and repents. Most of us here are more like the older son. He stayed and worked with his father every day, but wasn't close enough to realize everything the father possessed was his, too. The older son already owned the land. He could have killed a calf and feasted with his friends at any time. The older son was there all along, but his life was much like the prodigal's—even though his father's love was always there, he didn't enjoy it. Basically, folks, you can lead a horse to water, but you can't make it drink.

"We're all thirsty for love. Some of that thirst can be met by loved ones, a spouse, or a friend. But the biggest part can only be quenched by a close and growing relationship with God—the kind neither of these boys had. Have you walked away from God? Have you never known God? Have you been standing at the trough but remain unsatisfied? God stands before you with open arms."

Angelina looked out a nearby wavy-glassed window. She couldn't believe this picture of God. She'd always imagined Him as being a tougher judge than her own father. The God Daniel now described had pity on those who didn't know Him. He shared all He possessed and welcomed a prodigal like Kay and the women had yesterday—with hugs and kisses and a feast. This God practically threw a party when someone ran to Him.

Laughter erupted in the crowd. Deacon Floyd gave a loud *Ha-ha!*

"What did Daniel say?" she asked Nick.

"The worst joke about three angels walking into a bar."

"When you're done laughing, turn your hymnal to page nine," Daniel said.

People took books from the backs of the pews. Nicholas quickly did the same, slipping the Bible in the shallow rack. Around her, voices rose.

"O Lord my God,
When I in awesome wonder,
Consider all the worlds Thy Hands have made."

She'd heard the words before, although she wasn't sure where or when. For some reason, she thought of Elvis.

"And when I think, that God, His Son not sparing;
Sent Him to die, I scarce can take it in;
That on the Cross, my burden gladly bearing,
He bled and died to take away my sin."

Son. They were singing about Jesus, God's Son whom Daniel said died for her.

The song ended.

"You're dismissed," Daniel said. "I'll wait here in case anyone wants to pray and run into God's arms."

As had happened last night when she'd felt an urgency to continue talking with Kay about God, her heart pounded. She reached for Nick's hand and noticed his knees bobbing.

"Are you all right?" she asked.

"I don't know. Your hand is sweating."

"I know. What are we supposed to do?"

They stared at each other, then she looked toward Daniel. "I think I want to go up there."

"Me, too. I've never felt like this," Nicholas said.

Much of the congregation had left.

"I want to go pray with Daniel," Nick said.

"Me, too."

They walked down the aisle.

"Daniel," she whispered. "This is us running into God's arms."

He led them in prayer.

I think You're real. I even think You love me.

Joy sprang up, the likes of which she'd never experienced, and filled her heart. She felt clean and fresh as a breeze after a hard rain. And held. Held by an unexpected presence.

She was no longer alone.

The prayer ended. Nicholas hugged her and spun her around.

"Angie. It's the best feeling I've ever had."

"Me, too."

***

Nick tossed the thrift store duffle into the back seat. "Is that the last of it?"

"I think," Angie said. "We should probably check one more time."

They walked back into the house they'd shared with Angie's sister, and he knew coming now to get their belongings had been the right decision. Once he started his new job at Benson's on Monday, traveling back anytime soon wouldn't be a possibility. They might have to put their meager possessions in storage, but having his old computer on hand was better than no computer. Who knew? Maybe his resume and letters of recommendation from professors would soon be put to good use.

Angelina took his hand. "Feels like we've been gone longer than a week."

"I know."

Seven days since they'd met Daniel and Kay. Five days since committing their lives and marriage to God. For the first time, Nicholas felt he had a roadmap for his life, and a Father leading the way. Not just the Bible. No, Daniel had given Nick and Angelina his best marriage advice: Everything you need to know about marriage you can learn from your relationship with God. That's your example of how to love each other.

"I can't believe you're moving to podunk Alabama." Phoebe leaned against the kitchen doorway. "I'll have to find another roommate to help pay rent."

Nick was determined not to lose his temper with his sister-in-law. But he did have to unclench his fists.

"Phoebe, we appreciate you letting us share the place." Nick ignored her attitude-filled eye roll. "This is a fresh start for me and your sister. Maybe you could try being happy for her?"

She didn't look at him. "Angie!" she called down the hall. "What am I supposed to tell Dad when he asks where you are?"

Angelina stuck her head out of the bedroom. "Right. Like he cares about where I am or what I do."

Phoebe smiled like a true predator. "He's getting up there. When he dies, there will be money for us."

"You think I want his money?"

"I know you two don't have any."

"We will," Nick said. "I've got a job waiting on me when we get back to Alabama. I start next Monday."

Benson's wasn't perfect, but it was better than nothing, and he'd simply scour the internet for more potential job opportunities.

"Then I guess you got the message," Phoebe said.

"What message?" Nick asked.

"From some place in Birmingham. Jansens? Jamesons?"

"Do you mean Jenkinsons?" Nick asked.

"That's it." Phoebe yawned.

"Phoebe!" Angelina hurried from the bedroom. "Why didn't you tell us when we got here?"

"You woke me up, okay? Today's my day off, so I had a late and somewhat intoxicating night. I'm not your husband's message service."

Nick's chest filled with hope. Jenkinsons was the Birmingham company buying Warren Engineering down in Troy. That buyout was why Warren hadn't hired him. But he'd never spoken with anyone from Jenkinsons. He had no contacts there.

"Did you write down the number?" he asked.

His sister-in-law looked at him like he'd spoken in a foreign language.

"Phoebe, do you have the number or the name of the person who called for me?"

"Probably." His sister-in-law turned to the counter covered with mail and dirty dishes. "Well, don't just stand there. Help me look for it. I think I wrote it on something."

"Angie, let's handle the table," Nick said. "One piece of paper at a time."

"Good idea."

His heart pounded so hard his hands shook. Finding one particular slip of paper in this pile of trash could be next to impossible.

Focus. Think!

"What day did they call?" Nick asked.

"I don't know. Maybe Tuesday or Wednesday. Not yesterday."

An entire week. Would they hire someone else since he hadn't called back immediately?

"Have you taken out the garbage since then?" he asked.

"Does it look like I've worried about taking out the garbage?"

"Well, that's something in our favor."

"Nicholas." Angie touched his arm. "I think I found it."

One end of the envelope was stained and sticky and smelled like Chinese food. Scrawled on the other end was an out of state number, the words "James and sons," and the name Gerald Barker. Barker had interviewed Nick last Friday and given him the check they'd cashed earlier this afternoon before closing their local bank account.

He looked at his wife. Throughout their entire journey from Rowe City to St. Augustine, she'd read to him from the Bible Daniel and Kay had given them, starting in the book of John as Daniel had suggested. The experience had forged a new bond between them.

He wanted to keep that synchronicity.

"Angie, I don't think it's a good idea to wait until Monday to call. Do you?"

"No, and I really like that you're asking me. Thanks for that."

"Everything inside me is new. I won't step all over your feelings again. I promise."

"You two are a little too sweet for my taste." Phoebe hugged

Angelina and offered a half-wave to Nick. "Let me know where you are, sis. I'm going back to bed."

He checked his watch, then waited until he heard Phoebe's bedroom door close.

"Birmingham's an hour behind us," Nick said. "If he didn't leave work early—you know, because it's Friday—he might still be there."

"Or maybe a secretary," Angie said.

He picked up the phone. "My hands are shaking. Can you believe it? God's directing our steps, Angie, just like Daniel and Kay said. I think our whole lives are about to change."

CHAPTER FIVE

First anniversary, Birmingham, Alabama

Across the Birmingham skyline, streetlights and building lights blinked on, cutting through the purple and orange haze of sunset. Angelina knew in a few minutes, from up here the entire city would appear to be covered in glistening jewels—perfect for Nick's homecoming from his first trip abroad for Jenkinsons to Barcelona, Spain.

Spain.

She would've gone with him if she wasn't deep into a school term. Spain had fabulous architecture. Wonderful museums. And was less than seven hundred miles from Paris. She and Nick could have stayed a few extra days and actually gone to France.

"Next time, I'll take you with me," Nicholas had promised.

So far tonight, she'd stained two shirts. Almost every dish in their fourteenth-floor apartment lay strewn across the kitchen counter, dirty. Except for the one Angelina had broken, which she'd swept up and dumped into the garbage.

She'd showered before she created the lasagna—clearly a mistake. She was sweaty and greasy and had sauce caked under and around her newly manicured nails, one of which she'd chipped.

How did a woman cook without making a terrible mess? Without sweating like a weightlifter at the gym?

She slid the glass dish of lasagna into the oven.

Which she'd forgotten to preheat. But was that really important?

Cooking time was a ballpark suggestion, right? If the oven wasn't hot enough when you put the food in, you could simply turn up the temperature a bit, leave the pan in a little longer, and you'd be back on schedule.

So she set the timer, adding thirty minutes to offset the temperature difference.

She loaded the dishwasher. Washed by hand the last dishes she couldn't fit in. She surveyed the table with its linen cloth, crystal goblets, and silver cutlery. The china Nicholas had bought her for Christmas—she'd rather have gone to visit Daniel and Kay, but the dishes were exquisite. All was in place, and if she hurried, she had just enough time to change and freshen her makeup before Nicholas arrived.

She entered their large bedroom. Placed candles on the nightstands, the dresser, the floating shelves on the wall opposite the bed. She lit all twenty, knowing their scent would permeate the air and create a romantic, ethereal atmosphere for their first night together in weeks.

Turning her attention to the embossed lingerie box on the bed, she opened the tissue paper and carefully removed the black lace corset, matching garter, and thigh-high hose. She donned them, snipped the tags on a new siren-red dress, and slipped it on. Added heels, so she and Nicholas would be eye to eye. She could hardly wait to see his expression tonight when he peeled this dress off her.

She checked her foundation, blush, and lipstick in the mirror over the bathroom sink. No matter what he picked to do tomorrow—visit the zoo, the botanical gardens, or even the science center—tonight, she'd rock his world and make him thankful to be home.

Angelina walked back to the living room. She sat on their new plush sofa and flipped channels.

The ear-ripping scream of the smoke alarm startled her.

"The lasagna!"

She rushed to open the oven and thought she'd seared her eyebrows.

Coughing, she lifted out the baking dish, sat it on the stove top. The cheese was charred, the noodles still hard.

Why hadn't the digital timer dinged? She looked closely at it and realized she'd set it for A.M. rather than P.M.

What else had she done wrong? She checked the directions on the side of the noodle box. *Cooking instructions: Boil noodles for …*

She should have boiled the noodles before layering? When making lasagna, you cooked the noodles twice?

On the stove, smoke still rose from the dish. She laid it in the sink, turned on the water, and heard a loud crack as the glass broke. From the abrupt temperature change, of course.

None of it mattered. She wouldn't let it.

She dialed Nick's cell, checking the time. His plane would have landed about ten minutes ago, so he was probably near baggage claim.

She went to voice mail.

"Hey. I kind of ruined dinner. Big surprise, huh?" She laughed. "Could you pick up some burgers on your way? Can't wait to see you. I love you so much, Nick. Hurry home."

After cleaning the kitchen again and carefully bagging the catastrophic lasagna, Angelina re-settled in front of the television. She slipped off her shoes.

At 1 A.M. she woke in the near dark, disoriented.

"Nicholas?"

Surely he would have woken her after he arrived home. Although this wouldn't be the first time he'd let her sleep where she lay.

She rose and walked to their bedroom. Checked the bathroom and walked back through the apartment. She saw no sign of his luggage, no evidence he'd come home at all. Had his flight been delayed?

She checked the airline website. His flight had landed on time. He should have been home hours ago. She should drive to the airport. If he were stranded on the side of the road, she'd see him.

But if that were the case, he'd call for roadside assistance. From his phone. Which he wasn't answering.

Gut-deep fear knotted up in her stomach. What if he'd been robbed in the parking garage? Or car-jacked there? What if he'd been in an accident and was now lying in a hospital unable to reach her? Unconscious and injured?

"Calm down," she told herself. "There's a perfectly reasonable explanation. Don't overreact, just find out what happened."

She changed clothes, folded the lingerie, placing it and its box in the closet. She called airport security. No robbery, assault, or stranded vehicle had been reported.

She called the area hospitals. No patient named Nicholas Rousseau could be found in the Emergency Room. No one with that name had been admitted.

Where could he be? If he were able, he'd call, right?

He'd know she'd be worried and wondering where he was.

She called the police and sheriff's offices, on the chance he'd been speeding and been arrested. Out of character, she knew, but she was desperate for ideas.

The fear stretched and twisted, reaching up her spine.

She scrolled through the contacts in her phone. Daniel and Kay would be asleep this time of the night, but she had to talk to someone, and her classmates at the institute were all single. They wouldn't understand.

She dialed. One ring. Two, three, four.

"Hello," Kay said. "This is the Crane residence."

Angelina fidgeted with the chains at her neck. "I'm so sorry to wake you. It's Angelina."

"Angie? Are you all right? Are you here?"

"I'm fine. And, no, I'm not there. I'm at home in Birmingham."

She felt silly and stupid and embarrassed.

"I shouldn't have called," Angie said. "This was inconsiderate. I'm sorry."

"What's wrong? I know you wouldn't call for no reason. Do I need to wake Daniel?"

"No, I … tomorrow's our anniversary. Nick's flying back tonight from Spain, a big, important trip for his job. But he didn't come home. His plane landed hours ago, apparently without him on it. He hasn't called."

"And you're scared. Of course, you're scared. You've double-checked with the airline?"

"Yes."

"Hospitals?"

Maybe her ideas hadn't been so paranoid after all. "Yes."

"If you don't want to be alone, do you have any friends who could stay with you in the meantime? Maybe from church?"

"We don't know very many people there yet. Although we are learning a lot. My friends from the art institute are all single—I actually got in last fall right after we moved here. What would you do if you were me?" Angie asked.

"I can come if I can find a substitute to take my class. Although I will have to be back here by tomorrow night."

"No, I don't want you to do that. I'm a grown woman, right? A grown, married woman who should have a better handle on her emotions."

"I think you're a wife who's worried about her husband. I've been there a time or two. Since you know his plane didn't crash, do you know if he was actually on it?"

Angelina sank into one of her new dining room chairs and almost dropped the phone on her spotless china. Relief surged through her.

She pushed her hair back from her face. "I bet he had to stay longer than he expected. With the time change, he didn't want to wake me. He'll do that sometimes. If he stays at the office, comes home late, he lets me sleep."

"There ya go. Call his boss or maybe a secretary later this morning to see if they know why he's delayed. You'll feel better if you do."

"Yes. I'll do that. Thank you for talking me back from the ledge."

"Worked yourself up, did you?"

"Terribly."

And suddenly she was exhausted.

"Kay, I'm so sorry I woke you. Will you be able to go back to sleep?"

"I'm over fifty years old; I'm a schoolteacher, and spring break is weeks away. Of course I can go back to sleep."

"I've really missed talking with you. I wish we'd made it down for Christmas, but I had projects to work on over the holiday break."

"I'm so happy for you about your art school. You know I'm only a phone call away."

Angelina rattled off her cell number. "I'm sorry I haven't kept in touch."

"Angie, even if another person isn't nearby, you're not alone. Remember?"

Kay was talking about God.

"He's right there, sweetie," Kay continued. "Always. You can talk to Him anytime."

"Outside of Nicholas, I think you might be the best friend I've ever had."

"Then just hug yourself from me. Goodnight."

"Goodnight."

Angie hung up.

The hint of smoke still lingered. She sprayed air freshener in the kitchen and dining area, opened the windows to the cool night breeze.

In the bedroom, the candles she'd lit earlier had burned out—at least they hadn't started a fire. That would be much worse than carbonizing dinner.

She took off her thin, simple gold band and laid it on the nightstand.

Nicholas must feel so pulled between getting here and proving himself at his job, she thought.

His six-month probationary period wasn't quite over. He was alone on the other side of the world, probably working long hours in an effort to get home.

"I love you, Nick." She hugged his pillow.

"Dear God. Please protect my husband, wherever he is. Bring him home safely. If there's a new problem where he's working, help him figure out how to fix it quickly and efficiently ..."

***

Angelina checked the setting on the toaster and popped down the lever. She didn't want to burn toast this morning, which was often the case.

She yawned. Even having slept in until almost 10 A.M., the sleep interruption last night had clearly impacted her energy level.

She scrolled through the contact list on her cell for her husband's employer and dialed.

"Jenkinsons International."

"I'm trying to reach Gerald Barker."

"I'll put you through to his administrative assistant."

The phone rang once.

"Mr. Barker's office, this is Edie. How may I help you?"

"Hi, Edie. This is Angelina Rousseau. My husband Nicholas works under Mr. Barker. Nick is in Spain. Would Mr. Barker know how to reach him?"

"Your husband is out of the country on business, and you want his boss to call him for you?" The woman's voice turned snide with a heavy dose of *aren't you the clingy one?*

"I'm sorry. I know how that sounds. See, Nick was supposed to fly home last night. Only he didn't. I figure he's had to stay longer than he intended."

She'd left two more messages this morning and was now convinced he probably didn't have phone service wherever he was.

"Please. Would you ask Mr. Barker to call me?"

"He's in a meeting. Give me your number."

"Thank you." She did so and ended the call.

Angelina ate her toast and put away the clean dishes. She debated clearing the table, then decided she'd leave it as it was. Who knew? Nicholas might call her at any minute saying he was on his way. Maybe even walk right through the door.

Her phone rang. "Hello?"

"Angelina Rousseau?"

"Speaking."

"This is Gerald Barker. Ma'am, Nick handles his own travel itinerary with his business account. I don't have any information about his schedule, other than he's expected back in the office on Monday."

"Oh. I guess I thought you'd know if he changed his airline reservation."

"I can tell you he hasn't reported any problems on the Spain project. I have no knowledge of any reason he wouldn't fly home as planned."

She didn't know what to say. Mr. Barker seemed evasive, but she couldn't pinpoint what he might be insinuating.

Still …

"Look," he said. "It's possible his cell doesn't have service. Or the battery's dead. Or he simply missed his flight."

"You're right, I'm sure. I appreciate you taking the time to call me. If you hear from him—"

"I'll let you know. Goodbye, Mrs. Rousseau."

She called Nick's cell again, left another message. She hung up and turned, catching sight of their only wedding photo. A five-by-seven taken exactly one year ago by the paid witness at the courthouse, as Nick's mother couldn't fly over on such short notice.

Nick's mother. Would he have called her?

The third bedroom in their apartment held several still-packed boxes. She grabbed scissors from a kitchen drawer. Somewhere in there was a card from Nick's mother, complete with her overseas phone number.

She started by the door. Found her high school yearbooks wrapped in sweatshirts. Discovered several years' worth of fashion magazines. After hours of searching, she found a box that held assorted papers. Nick's high school and college transcripts. Her grades from her first semester of college in Florida. Check stubs from when they'd worked at Denny's in St. Augustine.

And the card from Nick's mother.

The time difference put Paris well into the evening. However, at this point, Angelina didn't care if she woke the woman.

She dialed.

"*Bonjour.*"

"Collette?"

"Hello. Yes?"

"This is Angelina. Nick's wife."

"*Bonjour!* I have heard so much about you. You make my son very happy."

"You heard from him?"

"Why, yes. I just returned from driving him to the airport, so he can fly home to you."

"Oh, really? He's flying home tonight?"

"*Bien sur.* I wish he could have stayed more than two days, but he must get back to work on Monday, *oui*?"

Nick had been in France for two days?

"Yes, he does have to go back to work on Monday," Angie said. "I'm sorry, I have to go."

"I would love for you to visit me with Nicholas. Lyon is a wonderful place and only two hours to Paris by train."

"I'm sure it is. Thank you again. I really have to go."

She checked her messages. Nick hadn't called.

She dialed his number, waited for the beep initiating voicemail.

"Your mother enjoyed seeing you. Wish I could say the same."

Chapter Six

At Jenkinsons' employee locker room, Nick dialed Angelina. Once again, she didn't answer.

She was mad. He knew that. By missing Valentine's Day, he'd also missed their anniversary. Hopefully, she'd cool off once he explained what had happened. But he couldn't think about that right now. He was almost late for a meeting with Mr. Barker, and he wasn't going to leave a lame message that might anger her further.

Nick showered and shaved. Weather delays meant flying home had taken two days. The last leg to Birmingham had been over-booked. So, he'd rented a car in Atlanta and drove all night, straight to the office. He towel-dried his wayward curls and realized he badly needed a haircut.

He dressed, repacked his suitcase, and wheeled it to the elevator. He stowed it by his desk and carried his computer bag to Mr. Barker's office. He knocked.

"Enter."

"Good morning, Mr. Barker. Should I set up in a conference room to update you on the progress in Barcelona?"

"Didn't you send me photos and spec sheets?"

"Yes, sir."

"Then we'll do it here. You can talk me through it."

Nicholas quickly powered up his laptop and located the Barcelona files. For the next hour and a half, they reviewed the procedural revisions and structural changes he recommended.

"I believe we can increase productivity by at least twenty-two percent, while significantly reducing injuries. A particular repetitive movement is causing the problems." Nick demonstrated the act of lifting an object with both hands and turning it over onto a conveyor-belt.

"Initially, new employees do well at this position," he continued. "However, after a few weeks, the tendons become irritated. Carpal tunnel syndrome is very common. They begin losing dexterity and feeling in their fingers. That's why they start dropping the product—hence the loss in productivity. Not only are they slower, but less product passes quality control inspection.

"We end up having to move these employees to a different position," Nick said. "The cost of training current employees for new positions and replacing them with new employees, who, of course, we have to train, increases our costs. My proposed changes will have a high upfront expense, as we must modify the machinery in zone seven, but I believe we'll recoup that investment within twelve to fifteen months. Thereafter, profits will continue to rise."

"And why is that?"

"Because demand is high. Right now, we can't meet it. Those who inquire are told the product is back-ordered."

"We've been turning away new distributors?"

"Yes, sir. I wasn't aware until after I visited the Barcelona site. That's why I started analyzing this particular manufacturing division. Every other division except one is showing steady growth."

"What other one?"

"I figured you'd ask that, sir." He opened a secondary file and emailed it. "I've just sent you my report. Later today, I'll be speaking with the zone four division director—he was out of town for his son's wedding. Once I speak with him, I'm confident I can ascertain the needed improvements in this area, as well."

Mr. Barker nodded. "Nick, when I first met you six months ago down in Troy at Warren, I had no idea I was looking at one of the most brilliant and thorough industrial engineers and efficiency experts I'd ever meet."

Nick felt his chest relax and realized that until now, he'd been worried about this first project, this first opportunity to prove himself at Jenkinsons.

"Thank you. I really appreciate you saying that."

Mr. Barker leaned forward. "You know, son, a few more jobs with profit increases like this, you can start your own company. Your own worldwide consulting firm."

Nick couldn't hide his grin. "I actually got a side job like that over the weekend. While in Spain, I met a French business owner. After I finished my work—and reviewed my contract to be sure I didn't have a conflict of interest—I went to France. Can't wait to put that check in the bank. Even got to visit my mom for a few hours."

"Maybe you should consider it sooner rather than later."

"Is something wrong, sir? Did I misread my contract? Is my position here in jeopardy?"

"Absolutely not. I'm just saying you could name your price, live your life your way, maybe take that pretty wife of yours with you." He frowned. "Have you spoken with her since you left Spain?"

"With Angelina? No."

"A word of advice from someone who's been married, divorced, married again, and is now working on year eleven of said second marriage. If you're going to be late, call your wife. Especially if you're going to be days late. She didn't sound too irritated when I talked to her, but do you know you missed Valentine's Day? I understand it's not celebrated the same way in Barcelona, so it's understandable you'd forget."

"You talked to Angie."

"She called me wanting to know if I knew where you were. Now, if you were somewhere you shouldn't be, that's not my business, as long as it doesn't reflect badly on the company. I know how it can be when you're traveling and you figure you can get away with stuff. Second marriage, remember? But that kind of thing takes its toll on a relationship."

"No, sir. I wasn't—"

Barker waved away any further explanation. "Either way, forgetting Valentine's Day or forgetting you are married? Not calling on Valentine's Day means you should probably stop for her favorite flowers on the way home."

Nick lowered his gaze. "I'll keep that in mind."

"Great work in Barcelona. I mean that. You look tired. You ready for the Florence meeting this afternoon?"

"I slept some on the plane but drove all night to get here. I'll be ready."

"What about leaving again Thursday to go to Italy? The Florence project is vital to this company. I need your best, even if your wife isn't pleased about back-to-back trips."

"She'll be fine. The trip is a great opportunity for me."

"Then I'll see you at the meeting. And if we run late?"

"I'll call my wife."

***

He wasn't late. At least he wasn't late.

Nicholas rode his apartment elevator up, so tired he was seeing spots before his eyes and was uncertain he could walk more than ten steps after unlocking his door.

Just make it to the couch, he told himself. As opposed to collapsing there in the hallway.

A dozen roses were tucked under his arm. He nearly stumbled out of the elevator, bumping hips with an oncoming teenager carrying a skateboard. The doors closed behind him, catching the longest roses and barely missing his arm.

He jerked away as the doors reopened. Green tissue paper and Baby's Breath fluttered to the travertine floor.

"Hey, mister. This your luggage?"

He'd left it behind. "Thanks."

Nick made his way down the hall, one hand holding his briefcase and pulling his suitcase, the other carrying flowers for his wife.

He'd make it up to her. Tomorrow. He'd do anything she wanted tomorrow evening, but right now he needed food and sleep. Lots and lots of sleep.

He unlocked the door. Opened it to his living room and a group of people he didn't know.

"Hey!" They cheered. "You made it home."

"Angie!" blonde, identical twin girls yelled. "He's back, and he brought flowers."

A skinny Asian guy passed by, slapping him on the shoulder. "Roses. Good choice, bro."

"Pizza delivery."

Behind him in the open doorway stood a delivery boy, his face hidden by a stack of pizzas.

"You buying?" the kid asked.

Nicholas moved to the side. "Um. Just a minute."

Angelina emerged from the bedroom carrying her wallet. Her long, dark hair was pulled back in a ponytail. Her face, flawless. Barefoot, she wore a clingy half-shirt and shorts. She made him think of walking in the surf, then carrying her back to a private hotel room.

She looked past him. Walked right by him and flicked out a stack of twenties.

"Keep the change," she said, as the blonde twins took the pizzas, a bag of two-liters he hadn't noticed the guy held, and carried everything to the dining room table.

"Don't shake the drinks, Josh," one blonde said to the red-headed guy. "Most of us have already showered today."

"I didn't."

"We know."

Everyone laughed, including Angie, who'd set the table with the china he'd bought her for Christmas.

The blondes sat on one side opposite Josh and the other guy. Angelina served everyone soda in their crystal stemware, then sat at one end with her back to him.

"Dig in, you guys," she said. "Juro, pass the supreme box."

"Will do, Angie."

"Are you joining our celebration?" One twin spoke, but both looked at him. "We all got A's on our last projects."

"We're pretty loud," the other said. "You want to eat in the other room?"

He nodded, accepting an unopened pizza and half a bottle of Coke. Still, his wife didn't look at him.

Nick went down the hall to their bedroom. He kicked off his shoes, sat on the bed, and ate straight from the box. Sauce dripped onto his dress shirt. He swiped at it with his hand and succeeded in smearing it across the tip of his collar.

He drank straight from the plastic bottle, set it aside on the nightstand. Angie's humble wedding ring lay beside the lamp.

Oh, he'd screwed up. So, so badly.

"Here! Hold my glass!" The masculine yell came from the living room. "Gimme that controller. I'll show you how it's done."

Electronic battle sounds rocked the bedroom wall. Had Angie bought a video game player?

He laid the pizza box on the floor, grabbed his pillow, and pulled the comforter off the bed. He trudged to their walk-in closet, the quietest place he could think of, removed his shirt, laid on the floor, and closed his eyes.

The sound of the shower running pulled him from sleep. Where was he? What day was it?

He opened his eyes to darkness, but he smelled Angelina. He smelled home.

Reality came rushing back. Yes. He was indeed home, and he'd slept in the closet because of the noise from the living room. Now the apartment was quiet except for the sound of the shower.

Woozy, he fumbled for the light switch near the door, knocked a box off the shelf, but didn't look back.

Nicholas entered their bedroom, put his pillow and the comforter back in place. The clock showed 12:39 A.M. He'd slept on the closet floor for six hours. Still, his brain was mush.

He walked to the bathroom door and found it locked.

He knocked. "Angie?"

No answer.

He knocked harder. "Angelina? I need to talk to you."

The water shut off. "I'll be out in a minute."

Nick waited. Not sure if he was angry or impressed she'd locked him out of the bathroom.

The door opened. His wife stood in her robe, her beautiful face freshly scrubbed. He'd never seen her expression so cold, so distant.

"Shower before you come to bed," she said. "I just washed the sheets.”

“I hope you didn’t speak to my boss that way. Although if you did, it might explain something he said. Did you have to call him?”

“That’s what you want to say to me?”

“I should have called,” he said. “But I got this amazing opportunity. I met a French businessman who paid me to go to Paris and review an aspect of his plant operations. Then I happened to call my mom, and she happened to be off work for the weekend. You know I haven’t seen her in years. You won’t believe how much money I made us.”

She retrieved her phone from the bathroom counter, pushed buttons as she walked to the bed. “I’m setting an alarm. I have an early class tomorrow.”

“So, those were friends from the institute.”

She set the phone beside her wedding ring. Turned out the lamp and slid under the comforter. She closed her eyes.

He switched the light back on. “Are you going to let me apologize?”

She was so still he barely saw her breathing.

“Angelina. Please.” He touched her shoulder, and she batted away his hand.

“*Angie.*”

She threw aside the covers and got in his face. “You don’t get to ask me for anything right now. Not one single thing. And if you think a bouquet of trashed flowers is going to undo the damage you’ve done, you’re in for a very rude awakening.”

“I said I was sorry.”

“No, you didn’t. You want me to be happy you didn’t come home for Valentine’s Day and our anniversary. You want me to be excited with you about making us more money when we already have plenty. You knew if you called and told me, I’d be upset. So you didn’t call—”

“Does it really matter that much when we celebrate our anniversary?”

"You took another job so you could be someone else's hero, then you called your mother." She stomped to the closet to turn off the light. "While I was here—"

They both saw the lingerie on the floor.

"Angelina. I had no idea what you had planned … You won't even look at me now."

"Are you really this relationship-challenged? What do you think people do on their anniversaries? You're so smart, Nick. You're great with people, great with ideas." She switched off the light. "Well, that's the problem, isn't it? You're smart about those things because you actually think about them. I, on the other hand, am not even on your radar. Out of sight, out of mind, huh? First, you forgot my birthday, now this."

"I was working out of state on your birthday."

"As I said, out of sight, out of mind. No phone call, no card, nothing."

"Angie." He reached for her, and she pulled away.

"Don't." Her voice went low. "Touch. Me."

"I haven't seen or touched you in two weeks."

"Two weeks and four days," she said. "And counting."

"I have to leave again on Thursday. I'm flying to Florence, Italy, for another two-week trip."

They stared at each other.

Nicholas felt his heart jerk. "Don't you love me anymore?"

Her bottom lip quivered.

"I'll die if you stop loving me," he said.

She firmed her chin. "I'm not going to tell you how to fix this." She climbed back into bed and again closed her eyes.

"You have to tell me where to start."

"No. I don't. You think long and hard, Nicholas. You knew what to do, but you didn't do it. Put that brilliant brain of yours to work for us for a change and figure out why." Tears slid down her cheeks. "I was so worried, I *prayed* for you."

"Don't cry. I can't stand it when you cry."

It hit him then, this was no tiny spat. He hadn't hurt her feelings, he'd deeply wounded her and in so doing had put a large dent in their young marriage.

He'd been distracted. Careless. And had considered of little or no value what was obviously terribly important to her.

Idiot! What was he working for if not to provide for her—a gift, a date on Valentine's Day. What was he working for if not to build a life with her—making memories with her.

He'd lost focus. In concentrating on the *how* he'd forgotten the *why* and gut-punched the one he loved most.

"I'm sorry, Angie. I'll make it up to you. Tomorrow, the next day, on this trip. From now on, I'll be different. Now, please let me hold you. I'm leaving again on Thursday."

"Fine," she said. "Hurry up and take your shower. And don't you ever hurt me like this again."

"I won't. I promise."

Chapter Seven

Third anniversary, Birmingham, Alabama

The stretch, black limousine pulled to a stop at the curb, a rare dusting of snow covering its windows.

"Mrs. Rousseau, may I assist you?" the doorman asked. "The sidewalk is slippery."

"Thank you." She accepted his arm and dodged clumps of dirty snow.

"Jade is a great color for you, ma'am."

"Why, thank you, Patrick."

Choosing to wear open-toed, four-inch heels was no doubt a questionable decision, but on this special night, she wanted to feel as beautiful as she'd always been told she was. She wanted to capture Nick's attention. She wanted him to look at her, touch her as he did when they first married.

She wanted him to fall in love with her again and tell her so.

She slid into the back of the limo, careful of her silk, formal gown and long coat.

"All in?"

"Yes, Patrick. Thank you, again."

He closed the door. The glass panel between her and the driver lowered.

"Good evening, Mrs. Rousseau."

"Angelina. Please."

"How's the temperature back there, ma'am?"

"It's fine. Thank you."

Nicholas had told her he was going all-out for their third anniversary, but she hadn't expected this level of extravagance. She couldn't have been more nervous if today was the opening of her first art show.

"I'm to tell you the evening starts with what's under the seat."

"Oh, really?"

"Yes, ma'am."

She reached down to find a large, Valentine's Day red envelope. She didn't know whether to be flattered or embarrassed. He'd not only bought a card but planned ahead to have it waiting for her. This whole scenario seemed a bit ridiculous, yet terribly romantic.

They drove around. The Birmingham skyline at night appeared clean and beautiful and somehow exciting as if offering new and wonderful experiences. The gently falling snow only added to the sense of wonderland.

"When will we meet Nicholas at the restaurant?"

"Soon, ma'am."

Forty-five minutes passed. An hour. And she realized they'd circled the same city blocks a third time.

"Where are we going?"

The driver touched his earpiece. "One moment." They took another turn. "There's been a delay. I'm awaiting further instructions."

She closed her eyes. Not again.

After a horrible first anniversary and an awkward second, they'd regrouped, for lack of a better word. When he was home, they attended church together. Despite the time he was gone, they'd completed more than one devotional for couples. When he traveled, he texted, if only to say he was thinking of her. During this trip, he'd sent her pictures of the Swiss Alps and the mountain chalet in which he stayed. During this trip, he hadn't forgotten her. When he'd asked what she wanted for their anniversary, she'd responded *a real date*. And believed him when he'd promised to make it happen.

She feared what the driver would say next. A lame apology about why Nick wouldn't be meeting her at the restaurant and probably wasn't going to be home tonight. She might even get a text from him. He'd say he was sorry. That he'd make it up to her soon. That she should go ahead with the evening and enjoy herself. He might even promise to call.

She didn't want to be disappointed again.

"What's your name?" she asked.

"Titus."

"Titus, do you know for a fact I'll see my husband tonight?"

He grinned. "Yes, ma'am. That's a fact."

They pulled to the curb. Titus raised the glass panel and closed the privacy curtains.

The door on her side unlocked, then opened. Nicholas, wearing a black tux and tails, handed her a single red rose. Snow caught on his long lashes. "Are you going to leave me out here in the cold?"

She reached for him, tossing aside the rose. He dove into her arms.

Someone must have closed the door behind him.

With gentle hands, he held her face and kissed her as they pulled into evening traffic. He kissed her mouth, her cheeks, her eyelids, her throat.

He pulled back, reached into his jacket pocket, and presented a velvet box.

"I just picked this up from having it sized for you. I hope you'll forgive me for choosing it on my own. We did it, Angie. We've made it three years, and now I was finally able to buy rings I'm not embarrassed to see you wear, rings you deserve. I love you, Angelina. Happy Valentine's Day. If I had to, I'd marry you again every year on this date to stay your husband."

Her heart actually lightened in her chest. She felt it rise, expand, and fill with new love for this man as he moved her old wedding ring to her right hand and slid the new, huge, diamond-covered set onto her left.

He rested his forehead against hers. "Dear Heavenly Father, thank You for my wife. Thank You for helping us get this far, for growing the love in my heart for her. Help me love her better every day."

He kissed her. "Your hands are shaking."

"They are."

"And they're cold."

"Yes," she said. "Do you know why I have trouble accepting gifts? My father gave my mother gifts when he'd been unfaithful. They were her consolation prize."

"That's not why I'm giving you these. They're a recommitment to you and to us. Do you like them?"

"A recommitment." She looked at the rings, a new symbol of his dedication and love for her. "They're perfect."

***

She couldn't help feeling like a heroine in a romance novel. Having been swept away in a limo, given new wedding rings, then ushered into an intimate private dining hall in the most elegant restaurant she'd ever seen.

She couldn't remember the last time Nicholas had given her so much attention.

A crystal and sapphire chandelier hung over the round table flanked by cobalt chairs, a clear tribute to The Blue Room. Even the ceiling had been painted midnight blue and dotted with tiny LEDs to simulate a night sky. A string concerto played softly from hidden speakers.

A uniformed waiter pulled out her chair. "What may I serve you first, Madame?"

"Are those French doors to the balcony?"

"Yes, Madame."

"Could you open the drapes, so we can watch the snow?"

"Certainly." He moved to do so.

"And give us a few minutes," she said.

"Of course."

Nicholas took both her hands in his. He kissed her fingers below her new diamond rings.

"This is lovely and beautiful," she said. "And I almost don't want to stay for dinner. I'm desperate to be alone with you."

"I like your honesty." He grinned.

"We did agree to be painfully honest, didn't we?" She paused. "Nicholas, we can't be apart this long. It leaves me feeling so disconnected, so alone. Like I've two lives: one where I'm a single art student, then a few days a month I'm married to you. I hurt when you leave. The longer you're gone, the more I hurt. The last four weeks were awful for me."

"I know. I'm sorry."

"Then let's stop living this way. Jenkinsons has been very good to you, allowing you consulting clients on the side, but your salary is more than enough for us. Can't you cut back? Simply work for Jenkinsons and be content?"

The waiter carried in a bottle of wine.

Angelina shook her head. "No, thank you."

"Compliments of the house to celebrate your special day," the waiter said.

She looked at her husband. He knew her mother drank herself into an early grave.

"Thank you, but we'll pass," Nick said. "Go ahead and bring the soup."

"Yes, sir."

The waiter left again.

"Thank you for that." Angelina wiped her hands on the linen napkin in her lap. "I was getting uncomfortable. I don't like feeling pressured that way."

"I know you don't. Now don't worry about it."

"What are we going to do?"

"I've been praying about this. I've a surprise for you. I'm off for the next two weeks. No work. I need to recharge. We need to be together and talk about what I think God wants me to do. Tomorrow afternoon, I want us to meet with an attorney named Gavin Hawk. I met him while I was in Mobile. He has experts in his office who specialize in accounting and financial planning for independent business owners. He's driving here to talk to us.

"If you're in agreement, after my vacation I'll resign my position at Jenkinsons and focus on my own business. I can figure this out, Angie. How to set us up so I'm not gone all the time, still pay for your tuition at the institute, and provide for us long-term. But I'm not making the final decision without you."

She studied the new rings on her finger. "Then you shouldn't have bought me these. Can you return them? And we shouldn't have moved into the penthouse apartment."

"You don't want the rings?"

"It's not that. They're exquisite. But I don't need them. I'd rather have a home and time with you."

"I don't want to return them, Angie. Buying those was important to me. From now on, we come first, you come first."

"All right, then."

Their soup was served.

Angie took her first taste of lobster bisque. "This is wonderful. I hate cooking, and I'm so terrible at it. Maybe all I need is a great cookbook."

"No cooking this weekend."

"Because you don't want the new apartment to smell like smoke?"

"No, because I want you to relax and not have to do anything you don't enjoy."

"Nicholas. Can we stay like this? Together? I need us to be close and stay close."

"I know what you mean. We're a team. That's how we have to look at our life. I'm working, doing my part. You're finishing school, doing your part. We're both heading in the same direction toward a common goal. If we both work hard, we'll get there."

She waited to speak again until the waiter had cleared away their bowls and placed their pasta with shrimp and scallops before them. They ate.

"Nicholas, happy Valentine's Day."

"I love you, Angie. And it won't just be a happy Valentine's Day. We've got two weeks that I'll be right here with you."

He stood. "Dance with me?"

She went into his arms, rested her cheek against his. "When I'm done at the institute, I want to move back to Rowe City."

His grin was huge. "So do I. Can you imagine? Being close to Daniel and Kay and all the great people at The Barn Church?"

"It'll be wonderful. Maybe we can even start a family. You're really taking time off now?"

"My only meeting is with the attorney."

"I'm blown away. You thought of everything."

"I was thinking, maybe we could take a trip during your summer break."

"I'd love that. Where?"

"Pick a place. Tell me what you want to do this weekend."

"Go with me to church Sunday morning. I hate going alone."

***

Nicholas kept his eyes closed. He knew if he opened them, he'd start moving. He'd shake the bed. Which would wake Angelina. Which was not what he wanted to do because he'd promised to stay in bed with her this morning and hold her while she slept.

"I want to wake with your arms around me," she'd said last night. What man didn't want to hear that from his wife?

So there he was. Eyes closed. Trying to be still. Not even glancing at the time, but fairly certain if he did look the first number on the digital clock would be an eight or a nine.

Even on a Saturday, how could she possibly sleep this late?

He almost sighed, then caught himself. She turned in her sleep and nuzzled into his chest. After weeks of sleeping alone, he couldn't resist kissing her.

She responded, they made love, then laid askew on the bed as the clock struck double digits.

"I'm hungry," he said.

"I bet you are." She giggled. "I can make toast or burnt toast."

"I'll make breakfast."

She fell silent. She didn't move. Still, he felt her tense.

"What'd I say?" he asked.

She rolled to her side. "You really don't know, do you?"

"No."

"When we moved up here, you said you'd cook breakfast before you left for work each day. You said we'd eat together."

"You sleep in every chance you get."

"Only on the weekends. I get up for school most days."

He thought back but couldn't remember. "What happened?"

"You went into work earlier and earlier, stayed later and later. Then you started traveling. Off you went."

"Ouch. Is that some of the brutal honesty we're embracing?"

"I suppose so."

"Maybe I should teach you to cook. Although there are a million cooking websites on the internet."

"Ooooh." She growled and hit him with a pillow. "I don't care about learning to cook. I can make burnt toast just fine."

He grabbed her. Pinned her beneath him and looked down into her beautiful brown eyes.

They shone with a spirit of play. Her face was still slightly flushed, her hair mussed. Her skin was soft. Her unique scent, amazing.

He scanned her stunning face, determined to commit to memory the slope of her cheek and the curve of her eyelashes. He studied her neck, then measured her collarbone with kisses.

She'd often accused him of forgetting her. *Out of sight, out of mind,* she'd said.

How—in a million lives—could he forget her? Forget this?

"I thought you were hungry," she said.

"I am." He raised his head. "For every moment with you."

"Charmer."

"Is it working?"

She wrestled to suppress a grin, then gave up and laughed. "I suppose."

"Good. Get used to it."

She ran her fingers through the curls on his forehead. "Don't we have to leave soon to meet that attorney?"

"Yes. But first, I'm making you breakfast."

"Why? I can make do with toast."

"Because I promised you I would before, and I never did." He turned his face into her palm. "I'm sorry, Angelina. Forgive me. I'm still learning."

Chapter Eight

Enter His gates with thanksgiving And His courts with praise. As Nick walked into the sanctuary behind Angelina, he couldn't help thinking of the verse in Psalms and agreeing with it. Being at church with his wife made him happy.

The steel and glass structure was nothing like The Barn Church back in Rowe City, except for one thing, the most important thing: God's Spirit was present. Nick recognized it, had come to depend on the knowledge that His presence would meet him and others as they worshipped, listened, and learned.

About halfway down the aisle, Nick and Angelina slipped into a row, sat. On video screens over the stage, announcements scrolled.

"Look." Angelina pointed.

Marriage Retreat, the screens read.

"I'd forgotten to mention it to you," she said. "It's next weekend. Let's go."

"Okay. How do we sign up?"

She flipped over the bulletin in her hand. "Five minutes until service starts. Supposedly we can register online. I'll try."

She used her phone, finished as the worship team walked onto the platform.

"Done." She smiled. Kissed his cheek. "Thank you. Nicholas, I feel like we're finally in sync. I love you so much."

"I love making you smile."

The band and singers started the first song. Beside him, Angelina hummed. He wasn't much of a singer, but he appreciated the lyrics posted on the video screens, encouraging him to count his blessings.

His wife, of course.

His relationship with God.

His career.

The prospect of a financially stable future, even if he chose to resign from Jenkinsons. Before his vacation was over, Gavin Hawk would get back with him and Angelina with options, possible investment and savings plans.

He knew God had been helping him with job tasks. Giving him ideas. Helping his mind stay clear and alert. Infusing him with energy when he was so tired he almost couldn't see straight.

Dear Heavenly Father, You reached for me and met a need I didn't know I had. I didn't know my spirit yearned for You. I want to grow. I want to learn even more about You and about being a good husband. Please guide me into the next season of my life.

The singing stopped. The ushers proceeded down the aisle with offering plates in hand.

His phone vibrated in his pocket. "Let me step out."

"Can't it wait?" Angie asked.

"I'll only be a minute."

He walked into the lobby and quickly returned the call, explaining to the client he was unavailable for the next two weeks.

"Nick. How ya doing, buddy?"

Upon hearing his name he turned, ended the call, and strode across the lobby to shake his friend's hand. "Hey, Ryan."

"You've been gone a while."

"Yeah. I was in Switzerland, then Mobile."

"That's a contrast, right?"

"For sure," Nick said. "How's Kristen?"

"She's good. Due in a couple months."

"That'll be quite a change for you two."

"And Angelina?"

"She's good. She signed us up to go to the marriage retreat next weekend. You guys going?" Nick asked.

"Planning on it. You know there's a workbook to download and complete first, right?"

"No. I better mention that to Angie."

"You home this week?"

"As a matter of fact, I am. And on vacation. Why?"

"I remember you saying you might be interested in getting into real estate, flipping houses and such. My brother's a realtor. He called me about some properties coming up for auction. I want another income stream with the baby coming. You want to go with me to see them, maybe catch a bite to eat? Just to see how it all works."

"Maybe." He wouldn't actually buy anything that would demand time away from Angelina. "Give me a call."

***

List three promises you've kept to your mate.

Nick tapped his pen on the kitchen table and read on.

List three promises you haven't kept to your mate.

He really didn't want to look at the first rocky years of his marriage when he'd pretty much failed at being a husband. He didn't want to think about them.

What was the writer getting at? Wasn't there a Scripture stating once someone gave his life to God, he was a new creation? The old had passed away?

Why talk about the past?

He had all day to sit there and work on this thing, then pack and meet Angelina for the marriage retreat. She'd be going straight from the art institute after classes. But he didn't want to do the workbook. If page one asked these types of questions, what would page five or ten be like?

His cell rang. The number flashed on caller ID.

"Hey, Ryan. Thought you forgot about me."

"No, man. It's been a busy week. You free today? I've got the day off, a full tank of gas, and a list of addresses. Want to look at some properties?"

He glanced at the workbook. He'd do it later. In the hotel room tonight if he had to. "Sure."

"I'll pick you up in an hour."

"Deal."

He pushed back from the table, looked toward his office. Hadn't he kept the real estate investing DVDs he'd bought right after he and Angelina married?

He searched through the cabinets and boxes in his office closet. Found the case holding all ten DVDs, the forms guides, the checklists to use when viewing properties.

This might not have been a bad investment after all.

He made copies of the forms and checklists, stuck them in a folder. When the doorman buzzed Ryan's arrival, he hurried down, folder in hand. He opened the car door to the smell of fresh coffee and donuts.

"Fuel." Ryan pointed to the large coffee in the cup holder, then pulled onto the street. "There are three I want to look at, four if we can squeeze it in. Last one's a block of ten duplexes, twenty units in all."

"How much monthly profit would there be? How much taxes, insurance—what do they call it?—carrying costs?"

"You been reading up?" Ryan glanced at the folder.

"I remember from a course I bought years ago. Brought the

checklists, just in case."

"Man, you are the most organized dude."

"Gotta be, in my line of work."

They toured a three-bedroom ranch in a Birmingham suburb. The house had been trashed. All plumbing and electrical had been ripped from the walls. The cabinets were gone, the windows smashed. They agreed too much money and time would be needed to get it rented before Kristen delivered.

The second home mirrored the first. The third, a two-story frame on a large plot, had potential.

"Termites." Nicholas pressed his thumb against a doorjamb.

"How do you know?"

"See the brown dusty stuff on the floor? That's their droppings. I have a client who lost a bunch of product in a warehouse when termites ate through the second floor. It crashed down on the first."

Ryan shone a flashlight along the baseboards. "It's everywhere. This whole house looks infested. Let's hit the duplexes. I'll text my brother."

They grabbed lunch, drove to the last property.

"You sure this is it?" Nick asked. The buildings looked to be in good condition.

"There's my brother, David," Ryan said. "He always wears that Crimson Tide cap."

They parked. David motioned them over to the curb.

"You will not believe this." David led them to the first building while adjusting his cap. "The owner called me this morning to make an offer on a home I have listed. He mentioned this property, which I thought was being auctioned next week. Anyway, the auction company bungled the dates on their website, didn't update them until a little while ago. This thing's being sold in an hour, and hardly anyone knows. The owner's made his money and wants out. This unit's empty, the others are rented. I can show you the numbers, profit/loss statements. This place is a goldmine."

The unit was dated. 1970s colors. Linoleum flooring. Only two bedrooms, one bath.

But it was also concrete block construction with stucco. The cabinets, all wood. Plumbing and electrical had been updated within the last decade, and central heating and cooling installed in all units. All the costly work had been done. With paint and a little decorating, the property would bring a much higher price.

Nicholas looked at the spec sheet David had given Ryan. "What's a bonus room?"

"It's at the back. A second living area, oddly shaped. Could be an office."

"Ryan." Nick motioned with his head. "Let's check it out."

"What are you thinking?"

"I might have an idea."

The bonus room was long and narrow, with a peculiar alcove to the side on one end.

Nick spread his arms in the alcove. "Six, seven feet, don't you think?"

David pulled a tape measure from his pocket. "Let's see. Five by eight."

Ryan crossed his arms. "You're acting like you're the one looking to buy. You want to go in with me?"

"Hold on." Nick scanned the space, walked back into the main room. "Is each unit like this one, with the funny jut out in the back?"

"I believe so," David said.

Nicholas tapped his thumbs against each other. "Three bedroom units make a lot more than two bedroom ones, right? Take the alcove, make it a master bath."

"I knew I was supposed to bring you along," Ryan said. "You're a genius. But I couldn't renovate them all before the baby comes. People live in all the others."

Nicholas shook his head. "We do this one first. Use the increase in rent money to do the next one that's vacant, and so on."

"We?" Ryan asked.

"He's right," David said. "A few years from now, this place would make twice as much as it does now."

"I'm going to look at the outside." Nick walked to the front door, leaving the brothers behind.

He wanted these duplexes. He wanted them so badly his hands itched.

He thought of his bank account. If he and Ryan made an offer together, he wouldn't deplete all of his reserves.

What about Angelina?

Being a property owner and managing long-term renovations would take a lot of time.

You told her you were a team. That means working together. Not making decisions without her.

He walked around the building once, twice. He strode to the others and scanned the exteriors.

As David had said, this place was a gold mine.

Call her. Don't do this without calling her.

He took out his cell. His finger hovered over her number.

Angelina wouldn't want him to do this. He knew she'd say he was quitting one job—Jenkinsons—only to take on another, investing in real estate.

Don't make a decision like this one without talking to your wife.

"Nick!" Ryan walked toward him. "David's on the phone with the owner. He'll lower the price by five percent if we put money down today. We can meet with my banker this afternoon about the loan and have the contract signed by morning. You in?"

Nick grinned with excitement. But ..."What about the marriage retreat?"

"There'll be another. Opportunities like this come once in a lifetime."

Inside, he braced as if someone nudged him and he struggled to stand his ground. No way was this a bad decision. The profits were guaranteed. He'd be sharing the minimal risk with a friend and fellow believer. Worst case scenario, they would sell it to break even. No harm, no foul.

"I'm in."

***

At the hotel's front desk, Angelina checked her phone. No missed call, no text from Nick.

"Hi. I'm Angelina Rousseau."

"Good evening. I have you down as attending the marriage retreat."

"Yes."

The desk clerk processed her payment, then he returned her credit card. "Please enjoy our complimentary made-to-order breakfast in the atrium each morning."

She almost laughed, then realized, no, he didn't know about her lack of cooking skills.

"I absolutely will enjoy your breakfasts. Has my husband checked in?"

He consulted his computer. "I'm afraid not."

"No matter." She scanned the monochrome lobby with its typical tile floors, benches, and ferns.

"Enjoy your stay."

"Thank you."

She took the elevator to the room. The door was thick and wide; when it sealed behind her, she heard nothing of the outside world.

Almost giddy, she called Nick but got voice mail. "Hey. Considering we haven't spent a night in a hotel together since our honeymoon, I thought you'd like to know this one's much nicer. I'm tempted to skip the classes and workshops and lock us in. Call me."

She unpacked her toiletries on the marble bathroom counter. Hung her clothes on the rack beside the door.

Her cell chimed, an incoming text. Kristen's name shone on the screen.

I'm in 305. Where R U? Ryan says they got a great rate and already have the keys. He just bought a drill and a saw. I hope Nick knows how to use them. LOL

Angelina texted back. *312. Keys to what?*

Be right there.

Dread rippled up her throat, pushing her to rise and open the door.

Kristen waddled toward her. "Ryan's so excited. He's absolutely tickled to work with Nick."

"I don't understand."

Kristen's pixie face furrowed in concern. "Didn't Nick call you …"

Angelina heard the words duplex, loan, and investment.

"I guess it's just you and me." Kristen shrugged. "But that's okay. It'll be girl time."

She felt the punch to the heart. Tasted the gall of disappointment.

"I'm not gonna stay. Sorry, Kristen."

"But you already paid for the room."

"I don't care about the money," Angelina said. "I never did."

***

Angelina arrived at the apartment door, fumbled her keys, then hesitated. She still wasn't ready to see Nicholas, still wasn't ready to talk to him. But she had classes tomorrow. She needed her books, her work in progress, and her notes.

The door opened. "Nice of you to finally come home," Nicholas said.

She entered, pulling her suitcase, and walked to the laundry room. He followed and stood watching her load her dirty clothes in the washing machine.

"You could have called," he said. "Or at least answered your phone. Kristen told Ryan you didn't even stay the first night."

The way they'd been living the last year. Then, the limo, the dinner, the meeting with the attorney, going to church on Sunday, had all convinced her he'd finally changed his behavior. The idea to resign Jenkinsons had been his. *From now on, we come first, you come first*, he'd said. This time, he'd actually planned to permanently change their lives so he could spend more time with her. Live a life with her.

That's what hurt so bad—this time he'd changed for more than a day.

She added detergent, closed the lid, and turned on the machine.

In times past when he'd broken his word to her, disappointed her, she'd gotten angry. They'd fought. He'd say he was sorry, she'd believe him, and open her heart again, hoping that time was the last.

Now she understood he would only keep his word until a reason not to came along. Until he chose to forget what he'd promised, like not making a big decision without her. And like going to a marriage retreat.

She couldn't police that. No amount of communication, connection, anger, or hurt from her would keep her in the forefront of his mind.

"You're not speaking to me now?" he asked.

"I can't figure out what to say to you."

"If you weren't going to stay at the hotel, why didn't you come home?"

"Unlike Kristen, I didn't want to stay there without my husband. I go alone to church most of the time. I'm not going alone to a marriage retreat."

"Where'd you go?"

"To another hotel."

She stepped to the door, brushed past him. She walked to the room she used as a studio and loaded her backpack for the next day.

A storm grew inside her. The wind of blame. The thunder of harsh words. The lightning of fury. She had to get them out.

Angelina lifted a fresh canvas onto the easel. Selected a brush and loaded paint onto a palette. She swirled blacks and grays across the white, added an angry red under a hazy moon.

"Angelina." Nick entered the room.

She didn't answer.

"Angie."

"I can't talk to you right now."

"Can't or won't?"

"What does it matter?"

He moved to stand beside her easel. "Then will you please put down your brush and listen? I can explain."

She continued painting, swirling blues into the blacks as her vision blurred with tears.

"I can't believe you're shutting me out because I bought some property with Ryan. Did you stop loving me?"

A tear escaped and slid down her cheek. She stood her brush in an open jar of solvent.

"You couldn't hurt me if I'd stopped loving you! This has nothing to do with Ryan, and you know it. Once again, you promised me one thing, then did another."

"This last year that has not been the case."

"Did you consult our new lawyer before you bought the property?"

"I ... No."

She turned away. "That's what I thought. Do you truly have that little control over your impulses? What am I saying? Of course you don't. You quit Denny's for both of us, bought the real estate course without telling me. Talked me into leaving Florida—"

"You can't hold stuff from years ago against me. Wait a second. You did the workbook, didn't you? All these memories were already stirred up, waiting to come at me."

"I don't have to be reminded of what the early days of our marriage were like."

If she were honest, yes, the workbook had agitated painful memories.

It had also encouraged her to forgive non-abusive offenses. To consider her own struggles and try to find common ground with her mate. A perspective they could share as each related to God.

Regarding what area do you frequently have to ask God's forgiveness? How has this weakness affected your marriage?

But I haven't hurt Nicholas near as much as he's hurt me, she thought.

She wasn't the one always needing forgiveness.

"We would have had to quit Denny's anyway," he said. "Because I did get a new job, right here in Birmingham. It all worked out, see? Like this property will. Just listen for a minute. Buying this property doesn't mean I can't quit Jenkinsons. It better not—I already emailed my resignation. Don't you trust me?"

Angelina took a deep breath. No, she didn't.

She couldn't. She couldn't depend on anything he said today being true tomorrow.

"Angie. I wouldn't have done it if doing so would significantly change our plan. Having property here gives me even more incentive to stay close."

"You're going to stay home more because of a piece of land? Wow. That says a lot about how much you value me."

"That's not what I meant. You're twisting my words."

"I don't have to twist your words. I don't want any more excuses."

This time, she wasn't going to forgive so easily.

"I'm not the one who's wrong here," she said. "You ditched me at a marriage retreat. There's no excuse for that."

He left. Obviously, hurt.

An hour later, he came in quietly, placed a single sheet of paper on the table beside her, and walked away. She continued painting, then finally read the note.

Dear Angelina, I'm sorry I hurt you. I do value spending time with you, and I want to spend more. I told you a long time ago, when we had the money and schedules allowed, I'd take you to Paris. Hoping we can do that this summer on your break from school. Love, Nick.

P.S. Trying to keep another promise.

Part of her wanted to believe him. Part of her thought he'd only written it because he knew seeing Paris was one of her heart's deepest desires. Still, she dare not dream, because the right distraction would supersede his word.

Go talk to him. Reach for him and let Me help you find a new understanding. For where two or three have gathered together in My name, I am there in their midst.

She gritted her teeth.

Give first. Give everything. Give all. Like Me.

No. This time, she would not give in. She was tired of being the only one to fight for their marriage.

She chose a clean, dry brush, and returned to painting.

Chapter Nine

Seventh anniversary week, Birmingham, Alabama

Angelina crumpled her to do list and tossed it back into her purse on the front seat. Not quite 10 A.M. and she'd already planned for lunch, boiling eggs for egg salad before she left the apartment. Then she'd gone to the dry cleaners, turned in a project at school, and visited her favorite art supply store. The back of her SUV now contained paints, brushes, and three new large canvases for her final assignments.

Twelve weeks of school remained. In less than three months, she'd complete Mitchell Art Institute's master's program. She couldn't wait to create whatever she pleased. Who knew? Maybe one day she'd have a solo exhibition at a prestigious gallery.

The crisp winter air had chilled the car while she shopped. She zipped her hoodie, pulled onto the busy street for the stop-start drive home through town. She turned on the heat and the radio.

"This is QFUN, Birmingham's best station for all the songs you love. We've got folks on the line to enter our Valentine's Day contest. Don't forget, the prize is an all expense paid weekend for two in sunny Florida. You're caller nine, what's your name and best Valentine's Day story?"

"I'm Delia. Last year I took my husband on a safari in Kenya."

"Thanks, Delia. We'll post your story on our Facebook page where our listeners can vote. Bye."

A safari in Kenya. Nick could afford that or any other trip, yet despite her summer breaks and his promises, he'd taken her nowhere.

"This is QFUN, you're caller ten."

"Hey. My name's Glenn. We don't have a lot of money to spend big for

Valentine's Day, and going out to eat is kind of tough because my wife has food allergies, you know? So last year I called a bakery and had a vegan, allergen-free cake made just for her."

"That's sweet, Glenn." The DJ laughed at his own joke. "We'll post your story."

"You've got it all backward," Angelina said.

The couple with the best Valentine's Day story shouldn't win a trip away for Valentine's Day. They'd had their moment and probably were continuing to have great moments together year after year.

The contest should be for the worst Valentine's Day story. A couple for whom the holiday represented hurt feelings and fights. A couple whose special times were historically disastrous. That's who needed help with Valentine's Day.

Don't think about it, she thought. *He hasn't even called this week, so don't get your hopes up.*

She stopped at a light where her favorite boutique sat on the corner. A banner with the words BIGGEST SHOE SALE EVER! was draped across the glass windows, blocking view of the merchandise within.

She didn't need more shoes, but …

I'm right here with you. Talk to Me. Let Me help you. You don't have to be alone.

But she was alone.

An hour later, she was shoving bags onto the front seat. Ten pairs. She'd bought ten pairs. And she felt better. She felt relaxed yet happy at the idea of going home and arranging all her new shoes in her closet.

Angelina scanned the street. A specialty gift shop sat directly opposite the shoe boutique. They always had new things, beautiful things, unique collections of pottery, glassware, and elegant statues. She looked both ways again and scooted across.

The bell on the door jingled as she entered. And she saw them—

new copper napkin rings and chargers, a matching ice bucket and tongs. Mugs, challises, a colander, even cookie cutters. All of that same shiny material, all in the same lovely shade.

You don't need them. You'll probably never use them. Find comfort in Me, instead.

But these were things she could see, touch, feel, and enjoy. Wouldn't they look stunning some day on a long, mahogany table set for twelve, no, fourteen, for a New Year's Day celebration?

Whipping out her credit card, she strode to the cashier. She signed the receipt without looking at the total. What good was her personal account if she didn't enjoy spending it?

Aren't you sabotaging your goals by spending money on unnecessary things, knowing Nick will have to work harder to pay for them?

"Can someone help me load everything into my car?"

"Absolutely," replied the clerk. "If you can pull around back, we'll load it for you."

"All right."

She hummed all the way home. She might have to move a few things, but she believed there was a clear spot in the china cabinet that would accommodate the copper.

She turned into the parking garage, pulled into her designated space.

They'd lived in the penthouse for four years now, having moved up shortly before Nicholas left Jenkinsons. And she could count on one hand the number of special days he had actually spent with her. There was always an emergency with a client or property that took precedence over their plans, over her wants and needs.

She'd told herself to be grateful Nick was a conscientious, hard-working businessman. His being in demand meant job security for him, in a time when nationwide unemployment ratings continued to climb. She'd told herself if he didn't work the way he did, she would have had to work part-time upon entering the master's program at the institute. She couldn't spend money on things she loved.

Don't think about being alone. Don't think about it, she told herself as she exited her car.

But you don't have to be alone. You're choosing to be alone.

She pulled the blank canvases from the back of her SUV and carried them to their private elevator. She wanted to move them first, so they'd remained undamaged. But she almost couldn't wait to again try on every pair of her new shoes.

The elevator arrived. She hit the STOP button and carefully propped the canvases against one wall, then input the code for the penthouse. The car rose, then gave an uncharacteristic groan and jerk. An alarm sounded.

Angelina's stomach fell. She did not like this feeling.

"Are you all right, Mrs. Rousseau?"

Thank God. The male voice over the intercom came from someone obviously watching on the video camera.

"I'm fine, thank you. What's going on?"

"The power company is switching grids today. I'm sure that's what caused the backup generator to try to kick in. The elevator will restart momentarily, ma'am. You're safe."

"Thank you." She glanced at the camera and hoped whoever watched knew what they were talking about.

She knew what to tell herself. If something were wrong with the elevator, they wouldn't restart it, they'd come get her.

She hit the emergency call button. "Excuse me. Will the elevator kick back on soon?"

The car rose. She held her breath, paying careful attention to any unusual shift in its movement. Finally, the doors opened on their private floor. Angelina lifted the first canvas and walked into the apartment.

A wall of smell hit her—burnt eggs.

"No, *no*, no!"

She knew what had happened even before she set down the canvases. She'd forgotten to turn off the boiling eggs … three hours ago?

The stench was amazing in the worst possible way and almost made her gag.

She didn't want to look but knew she had to. Although at this point, one more minute wouldn't make that much difference in the mess, would it?

Angelina scurried through the apartment, opening windows. She sprayed air freshener. She lit candles in the living room.

Taking a deep, fortifying breath, she walked into the kitchen.

The six-burner, double-oven stove was covered with chunks of egg. The pot, charred beyond salvaging, smoked. She turned off the burner.

Baked on, caked on yellow crust dotted the underside of the range hood, the nearby cabinets, and the tile floors. A white powder, probably disintegrated egg whites, lay thick on the nearby countertop, along with pieces of egg shell.

This kitchen disaster being one of her worst, she considered taking a picture, then decided against it. Some catastrophes shouldn't be remembered.

To clean up, where should she begin?

She picked up the in-building extension and dialed for maintenance.

"Hi. This is Angelina Rousseau. In the penthouse suite? I kind of burnt something again, and I'm not sure what to do about the smell."

"I'll send someone up."

"And maybe have them bring those cleaning supplies? I have a couple, but I'm afraid this is going to take something with a little more power."

"Sure thing, ma'am."

"Angie, what is going on?"

She hung up as Nicholas joined her in the kitchen.

"You left your car open. You left the front door open. And this place smells like someone tried to have an indoor bonfire."

"I forgot to close the hatch. I was going to go right back down and unload my car."

"You can't leave it open like that."

"I didn't mean to. I got distracted trying to get my new canvases up here without damaging them. Then the elevator got stuck. I got flustered."

"What about the front door? Yes, this place is secure, but you can't take that for granted. Close and lock the door when you come home."

"I opened the door"—she waved her arms—"smelled *this*, and forgot about the door."

Then she really looked at him. "Why are you even here? Aren't you supposed to be in Texas? Or Nevada? I can't keep it all straight."

He laid his briefcase on the dining table and rolled up his sleeves. "Thanks for the welcome home."

"That's not what I meant, and you know it."

The door buzzed.

She walked around him to answer. "I am handling this. I called someone. He's here now. And I will handle it. I handle everything around here by myself ninety-nine percent of the time. You just happened to walk in on one of those times."

She opened the door. "Hey, Ralph. Oh, you brought fans and cleaning solution. Perfect. Just set the fans in the door. I'll take the cleaning caddy. Thanks. I'll call you when I'm done."

"I can stay and help like last time."

"Nope. I'm good."

"You remember how to use the steam cleaner?"

"Yes, I do. Thanks."

She practically shut the door in the uniformed man's face, but she didn't care.

"Angie, how often do you do this?" Nick asked.

Often enough, she thought but didn't want to share that particular fact.

She carried the caddy and the steam cleaner into the kitchen, sat them on the clean end of the counter.

"Do you want to help me? Unload the car. If the private elevator isn't working, you can take the main elevator up to the twentieth floor, then use the stairs for the last three, like I have to sometimes. It's great exercise. By the time you're done, I'll be half-done. We can order takeout, or you can go pick up something for lunch. Egg salad isn't on today's menu."

He turned to go. "All right. I'll unload."

"Wait. Did you close the car?"

"Of course. And I locked it, too."

She thought of the shoes. The bags from the art supply store and the specialty boutique.

"Maybe I could use help cleaning up here. Or better yet, maybe call for some Chinese takeout?"

***

"I still smell something," Nicholas said.

Angelina didn't throw her last wonton at him, but she thought about it. "I'll light another candle in a minute."

They continued eating.

She didn't want to feel irritated with him. Didn't want to be irritated that he had caught her in one of her standard kitchen disasters. She knew her embarrassment was overriding any joy she might have at his unexpected return home. But she couldn't seem to set aside the event. If he would *just* stop talking about it.

"You know, you can call one of the doormen to meet you in the parking garage and help you. You don't have to do that all by yourself when I'm not here."

You're never here. By a millisecond, she stopped the words from jumping out of her mouth.

"I don't like doing that," she said. "They're busy, and it seems a bit ridiculous."

"As opposed to leaving your vehicle open for an extended period of time? That's not only inefficient, it's dangerous."

"Don't you *inefficient* me. I'm not one of your clients."

"Forget I said anything." He tossed his napkin onto the table, then carried it and his containers to the garbage can. "I'm telling you I still smell something over here. Maybe we need to pull out the stove and clean under and around it?"

"I cleaned up every speck." She threw away her garbage and joined him near the stove.

But a funky smell lingered in the air.

She looked up to check the ceiling. All clear.

She peered under the range hood, just to be sure. Again, all clear.

Nicholas opened the top oven.

"Nothing could have gotten in there," she said. "I boiled the eggs on the stovetop."

"I think it's in here."

"No. These are clean and empty." She slammed the top oven shut and opened the lower one. She shut it quickly. "Oh, my goodness!"

They both backed away, hands over their noses.

"What is in there?" Nick asked.

"The eggs couldn't have dripped down inside, they simply couldn't have. I haven't even opened the lower oven since Christmas."

She stared at the lower oven.

To go with the spiral cut ham they'd purchased, she'd baked potatoes in the top oven. Between the timer and Nick being home, she knew she couldn't mess up baked potatoes.

But she'd also prepared baked beans. A surprise for Nick, because he loved them. She'd cooked them in the lower oven on a lower temperature.

And forgot about them.

Nick had helped her carry the food to the table. He'd probably turned off the ovens without realizing the second one was on.

"It's baked beans. From Christmas," she said.

"We didn't have baked beans at Christmas."

She explained what had happened, wet a dishcloth, and held it over her nose. "I'm fairly certain they've grown a rare fungus."

"We should throw the whole dish away. Where do you keep the garbage bags?"

"I can wash it."

"Not without that smell permeating our apartment. I don't know how you're going to clean the second oven."

"It's not that bad."

"It smells like something's dead in there."

"Then go take a walk, let me clean up and take care of the smell. I'll light another candle. You'll never know."

He huffed. "Angie. Lavender-scented rot still smells like rot. Spray a disinfectant and antibacterial in there."

"Don't tell me how to do something better." She clenched and unclenched her jaw. "I'm getting tired of you treating me like one of your clients who needs improvement. You're supposed to come home to spend time with me. To live life with me. Not correct me."

"When I do come home, all we do is fight! You act like you don't want me here. You won't even open the gifts I bring."

"I don't want consolation prizes." She faced him. "You only give gifts to try to appease me. You started your own company so we could spend more time together. Attend church together on Sundays. I don't want jewelry, I want you."

"I can't win with you, can I? I never do anything right. I've worked to support you, to provide a lifestyle like you were used to having. One like I never had, like my father never gave my mother. Do you know when I was growing up, she sometimes worked three jobs, did without things she needed, and still she managed to be my biggest cheerleader?"

"She wasn't married to you," Angelina whispered and immediately wished she could take back the words.

He looked at her. "I think I will take that walk."

"You do that."

"When you act like this, you make me not even want to come home." He walked away.

She held her breath to keep from saying something else she'd regret and exhaled after she heard the door slam. She waited long enough for the elevator to return, and while he was gone unloaded her car.

***

Nicholas couldn't sleep. Not because he was working late on a productivity problem or finishing a proposal for a client. Not even because of the sulfuric scent still hanging in the apartment.

He couldn't sleep because he was alone in his and Angie's bed.

He couldn't figure it out. When he traveled, sleep never eluded him.

Staying in a hotel or even a short-term efficiency apartment seemed to switch something in his brain. He knew he was alone. He knew he'd sleep alone, and he had no difficulty with it.

But tonight, when she should have been beside him, she wasn't here, indulging in her favorite pastime of sleep.

He threw aside the duvet. Walked through the living room and found the canvases gone and the bags of art supplies also gone.

She hadn't left; he would've heard her leave.

He checked her studio. The door was closed but unlocked. He knocked and opened it.

She wore an old T-shirt over frayed cut-offs. She'd tossed aside her shoes. She'd pulled her hair back into a ponytail and was slashing paint onto the canvas as if she were gutting it.

He watched silently from the doorway, feeling like a voyeur, as she feverishly mixed colors on her palette. Her eyes were dull, her movements full of desperation as if her life depended on creating a specific shade.

Was she punishing him? Did she not care about how much time they had together before he traveled to see his next client?

What could he do to reach her? What else could he possibly try?

He wanted to tell her about the newest property he'd acquired in Montgomery. A small strip mall of eight units, all of which were occupied and flourishing. His lawyer had told him about the opportunity and helped him with a plan to hold, then resell in three short years, as values in the area were expected to double in that time. Surely she could be happy with him about that.

He walked away, located his briefcase on the dining table. Removed a Valentine's Day card and noted the date. Two days early, what could it hurt?

He walked again to where she worked.

"I want to give you this." He laid the envelope on the table holding her paints and brushes and cloths.

"Why?" She shifted her brush to the hand that held the palette. "Why do you want to give me this? Why do you want me to open it?"

"I came home for our anniversary. I didn't forget. I bought you a card, and I came home."

"You want me to open it two days early? What, are you leaving again tomorrow?"

He turned away. Swung at an invisible foe and clenched his fists. He turned back.

"No. Unless you really don't care that I'm here. I feel like you don't care that I'm here. Did you stop loving me?" He grabbed her shoulders. "Why do we do this almost every time I come home? How do we hurt each other? Say all the wrong things? Do all the wrong things?"

"I don't know! But it scares me worse than I've ever been scared before."

"It scares me, too," he said.

"I read some articles—no, you'll think I'm stupid."

"I won't. Tell me."

She looked at him, and he felt a twinge rather than the jolt he used to feel when their eyes met. If he looked closely enough, would he still see himself in her eyes?

"Some experts say marriages go through phases, almost like seasons. Looking back, I think we've been in sync maybe three times: when we first married, when we met Daniel and Kay, and before you bought your first properties. The rest of the time? I don't know."

"Don't say that!"

She flinched, and he let her go.

"I'm sorry," he said. "I'm *sorry*. I wasn't yelling at you."

She trembled, and a tear ran down her face.

"And now I've made you cry. I can't stand it when you cry." He paused. Thought. "Do you cry when I'm not here?"

"Sometimes."

"Because?"

She shrugged. "Because I'm lonely. I miss you. Don't you miss me, even a little?"

"Well, yeah."

Her mouth firmed. "Until you forget about me."

"It's not like that. When I'm on the road, I'm in a time warp. I'm gone for a while, then I come back. I guess I expect to pick up where we left off."

"Your time warp has lasted almost seven years; meanwhile, my life goes on. I'm almost finished with school. We've aged. You don't notice, I know, but other than a shared address and our wedding rings, there's almost no evidence we're married. I don't even have to walk around your dirty socks on the floor. I live alone, and once in a while, my husband visits me. I don't have pictures of us. No silly trinkets we picked up somewhere."

"Trinkets?" He felt his blood pressure rise. "Like all the things packed in your car today? All the stuff you *stuff* into this apartment? You spend money faster than I can make it."

"Money is all I get from you! The last time you came home, we didn't even make love."

"Yes, we did. You wore a frilly white thing."

"I wore it, all right. Your phone rang, you took the call, and I went to sleep alone, as usual."

He'd thought he'd always want her. Thought he'd never get enough of loving her. Looking at her now, he felt little of the attraction and none of the craving that had consumed him when they married.

"Do you keep a list of everything I do wrong? To clients, I'm a genius. At home, I never do anything right." No wonder when he came home, they always derailed.

That's not what she's saying. Listen to the loneliness—you feel it, too. Look at her face. She's desperate to be loved.

But how could he love a woman who held every past transgression against him?

Cut back your work. Sell some assets. Give her you.

The solution hit him in the usual way, with a thought that gently knocked him back. A whoosh through his mind, as the perfect, illuminating idea bloomed. Immediately, he saw the next steps backward and forward and knew he'd figured this one out.

"We always talked about moving back to Rowe City. What if, after you graduate, we do it? Buy a house."

"A real home? For a family?" Her face shone with hesitant hope. "We'll be near Daniel and Kay."

"And The Barn Church."

She dabbed her brush back into the paint. "I'll go when you go, but I'm not going alone anymore."

"We'll go together, I promise."

"Like we went to Paris a few years ago?"

He felt it—the temper threatening to rise over yet another way he'd supposedly failed her. The resulting push to busy himself in work.

"I really can't win with you, no matter what I give you. I think I'll pack and go early to my next job. We can use the extra money to buy the house."

He waited, hoping she'd ask him to stay as she had earlier in their marriage.

He wanted to touch her, just one caress or kiss before he left. But rejection had spurs. He was tired of being stabbed.

Reach for her. Reach for Me. I'll help you both.

No. When Angelina got like this, she wouldn't listen.

Don't go. Stay. Try. Love her like I love the church.

"I'll call when I get to Rome."

PART II

Chapter Ten

Present day, Las Vegas, Nevada

The handsome usher offered a white handkerchief from his pocket. Angelina accepted and dabbed at her ruined makeup—a lost battle. Was it too much to ask to feel connected to someone in this world? To a husband after almost ten years of marriage? To God, after years of attending church?

"I'm not sure what I need," she said.

He commented, but she couldn't understand him amidst the din of ringing slot machines and nearby conversations.

She sniffed. "Pardon me?"

He stepped closer. "Maybe some quiet, yes?"

She nodded.

With a gentle hand, he guided her farther around the corridor, away from the fray of anxious gamblers and clanking glasses. Within moments, they strolled down a long, bricked hallway of restaurants and storefronts, decorated to mimic a quaint European street.

She held out the handkerchief to return it, but her eyes continued leaking. She reconsidered and dabbed again at her face.

"By the way, I'm Angelina, and I never cry in front of others. And you are?"

"Lorenzo."

"How do you know Rita?"

"Thomas and I are—how do you say?—step-brothers." He smiled. "His mother married my father last year before Thomas met Rita."

They continued walking. He seemed perfectly content to do so.

"I don't know why I can't stop crying."

He didn't seem embarrassed by her emotional display. What would it be like to have someone wipe her tears instead of expecting her to squelch them? What would it be like not to cry alone?

They traversed half the length of the hotel and arrived at an isolated bank of elevators on the same wing as her suite.

He caught her hand in both of his. "It hurts to be lonely, no?"

She looked into his dark, European eyes. Yes, it hurt. She always hurt. How did he know what she felt?

He took the cloth from her. Turned it over, found a clean side, and blotted her tears with such tenderness she almost leaned into him.

He bent to her ear. "Maybe we can fix that."

If only that were true. Could it be?

She let her head rest back against the wall and looked at his sweet smile. Tonight, just for tonight, she could feel something besides loneliness. And what happens in Vegas …

"Will you take me to my room?" she asked.

"Of course."

They rode the elevator in silence, his hand at her elbow as if he knew she needed to compose herself. Angelina watched the digital numbers above the door, a countdown in reverse.

"You're shaking," he said.

"What?" She dropped her evening bag. "I'm such a klutz."

"I'm sorry?"

With fluid grace, he retrieved her bag and offered it to her. His deep brown eyes—so like her husband's—locked onto hers. Then, she couldn't help looking at his mouth. The corner rose slightly, and he winked at her again.

There were reasons she shouldn't be doing this. Like breaking God's laws. Breaking her marriage vows. And breaking Nick's heart.

Who was she kidding? Nick's heart had been wrapped in Teflon-coated Armani for years. When he kissed her, his body went through the motions, but his mind and heart were absent. On the rare occasions they made love, he barely looked at her. She could have been any woman, any body there with him. After, Nick always quickly went to his home office to "check his email," leaving her to stare at the dark and fall asleep alone.

She took her bag and dropped her gaze to the marble tiled floor. "Thank you."

If hooking up with another was so easy, maybe Nick had been unfaithful to her for all these years on all his trips. Maybe that's why he'd never wanted her to accompany him to Rome, to Japan, to Milan, or Paris, or any of the other dozens of cities he frequented.

The elevator stopped smoothly, the brass-plated doors opened without a sound. Her heels were silent on the thick, royal blue carpet. Still, she was certain her companion could hear her heart pounding and the tight gulps in her throat.

But this man, Lorenzo, had reached for her. Pursued her. If the attraction and feelings between two people were instant and mutual, if they needed each other, if they connected …

They stopped at the door to her suite. She reached into her evening bag and retrieved her key.

"You're missing the rest of the ceremony because of me," she said.

He took the key from her hand. "But I prefer to be here with you."

They stepped inside. The door closed behind them with a decisive click, shutting out the world. His fingers barely grazed her skin as he helped her remove the organza wrap. He was maintaining a respectful distance. Giving her time.

Oh, to be pursued by a sensitive, patient man. Wouldn't that satisfy the need for companionship clawing inside her?

He strode to the full kitchen and lifted a glass in her direction. "Would you like something to drink?"

She was about to say she didn't drink alcohol when he shook his head.

"No. You're right. Wine is not the answer. Water." He grabbed a bottle from the fridge, set it on the breakfast bar. "Are you fighting a headache?"

"What?" She hadn't noticed her right temple was throbbing, but now that she thought about it, yes, she was. "How did you—"

"It is in your eyes. If you don't have something for it, I will call the concierge."

So this was what an instant connection with someone felt like. The other person simply read your mind, knew your needs, and met each one.

Maybe she *could* have a close relationship with someone, just not with Nicholas.

She stepped toward him, placed her hand near his on the counter. Her heart raced as she measured the last ten years against the few inches separating their fingers.

"I'd rather stay here than go to the reception," she said. "Will you stay with me?"

"If that is what you want."

A delicious tingle traveled down her spine.

"Yes, Lorenzo, I think that is indeed what I want."

Her cell phone chimed from inside her purse. The caller ID showed *Unavailable*. When she looked back at him, he held her gaze.

"Should you answer?"

"It's not important."

Nothing was as important as the way he was looking at her, scanning her face, her hair, her shape.

"You are very beautiful," he said.

She smiled at him, unable to hide her pleasure. "Thank you."

She eased her right hand beside his. Her heart sputtered, and for a moment, she couldn't breathe. Was she really going to do this?

The phone finally stopped ringing, but her wedding rings seemed to pulse on her left hand. Lorenzo had already discarded his jacket, left the unhooked bow tie hanging over an open collar. Would he remove the pins from her hair, watch it fall to her waist, and run his hands through it?

Being focused on by a man would feel so good.

She watched his rich brown eyes sparkle as he raised her trembling hand to his lips. Warmth—wonderful, delicious warmth swam up her arm.

If his lips on her hand made that one limb feel this good …

Angelina laughed and stepped around the bar to stand directly in front of him. She'd not felt this happy—no, optimistic—since, well, she didn't remember. Being desired felt so good.

He released her hand, gently cupped her chin, and raised it, the look in his eyes so intense her heart leapt in her chest. Was he going to kiss her?

Oh, yes. Please. Right here. Right now.

"You are feeling better, yes?"

"Yes. I am."

"Then I have done a good thing." He released her chin. "You're lovelier than the pictures Rita showed me."

"Pictures?" Angelina gulped. "Rita. She showed you pictures. Of me."

"Of course. She predicted your husband would not change his mind and come with you—she was right, yes? She is the bride so she cannot play hostess. She made me promise to watch for you, be your escort so you would not be alone here, and see to your needs. Even on her wedding day, Rita is very thoughtful, no?"

Her phone rang again, an electronic laugh at a cosmic joke.

"Yes. Rita's always been thoughtful."

She'd been set up, so to speak. Rita knew Nicholas had refused the gift of the ticket to attend the wedding, and she didn't want Angelina traveling all this way to attend alone, so she'd persuaded Lorenzo to watch for her, show her kindness. And he did, as a favor to his future sister-in-law.

None of the imagined romance was real.

She turned away, reached for her insistent phone. "Excuse me."

"Of course."

Her balcony doors opened. Lorenzo watched the sun shine down on Vegas.

Angelina choked down her own mortification. "Hello. Um, hello?"

"Angie," Nicholas said. "Where are you?"

She could have told him she was anywhere—shopping in New York, at the local salon, standing in line at Disney World. Somehow the truth was so sad.

"Rita's wedding. You really don't remember, do you?"

"Who? You have to come home. I need you to come home."

"Nicholas, please." She sighed. "What can't you find? Whatever it is, just go buy a new one."

"Angie."

"Hurry it up, sir," a male voice said in the background.

"I know. I know." Nicholas' voice was strained.

"Where are you calling from?" she asked.

"Angie. Call Gavin Hawk."

"You want me to call our attorney?"

"Right after my plane landed, I was arrested for real estate fraud, and I don't know what else. I don't understand the charges. You've got to call Gavin for me. You're my one phone call."

She heard his voice quiver and felt a fleeting blip of compassion, then she glanced out at Lorenzo and thought of what she would've done had he truly been interested in her. Her stomach twisted with the nausea of the profoundly embarrassed. Maybe there never had been love, not the lasting kind, between her and Nicholas. Maybe she'd been holding on to a dream that wasn't real.

Maybe she and Nicholas were both members of the not-cut-out-for-intimacy crowd. And life had just hammered the final nail into the coffin holding their marriage.

"I think they're going to search the house, Angie. I don't know what you'll find when you get home."

Their house? The police were going through her things? Of course he'd think she'd obsess about the house, she'd filled it to bursting with the loveliest things she could find. But he hadn't been home in months. He didn't know she'd been unable to bear their too quiet, too empty home over the recent holidays. He didn't know she'd been living in, sleeping in, the recently renovated carriage house above the stables, where she painted.

Her paintings. Her first solo art exhibition and sale would be held in two weeks. Had the police searched the carriage house? Damaged her work?

Her marriage was definitely pathetic when she worried more about her paintings than her husband.

"Angie? Did you hear me? I'm in the county jail."

"Nicholas, what have you done now?"

She couldn't say she was surprised. His impulsiveness had derailed her life more than once. Envisioning him bending the rules and crossing legal lines wasn't a stretch. What, exactly, would his actions cost her this time?

"I'll call Gavin and catch the first flight home."

She hung up.

"Was that your husband?" Lorenzo called through the French doors.

She walked to the doorway, looked at the handsome stranger relaxing on the balcony. And closed her eyes against her lonely heart's pathetic mirage.

"I'm calling the concierge for a car to take me to the airport. I need to leave as quickly as I can."

He smiled. "Ahh. He misses you after all, no?"

She cleared her throat, trying to dislodge the knot stuck there. "Not exactly."

"To have you, he is a very fortunate man."

She made her way to the bedroom, closed the door behind her, and retrieved her monogrammed suitcases from the closet.

"I used to think so," she said.

Actually, she used to look at Nicholas and think she was the fortunate one.

***

County jail, Rowe City, Alabama
Nicholas Rousseau returned the heavy, sticky receiver to its cradle. The black, wall-mounted device was obviously older than him and had the scars to prove it. In the tiny alcove, he turned, faced the armed officer, and met cop eyes—no emotion, not even disdain, despite overhearing Nicholas' pleas for Angelina's help.

The nametag read "Franklin." The officer was built like a defensive lineman—his round face protruding over a bulging neck as if his uniform were one size too small. He was twice as wide as Nicholas, and if provoked, could probably snap a suspect's neck without popping a button. He placed a club-like hand on Nicholas' shoulder. Nick fought not to flinch and lowered his cuffed hands.

"Will I be spending the night here?" He still couldn't believe he'd been arrested.

"A likely possibility."

To their right, twenty feet across the processing area, two cops hauled in a man bigger than Franklin.

"I'll kill you, cop!" Red-faced, hands bound behind his back, he head-butted then kicked the officer facing him. The officer fell.

The partner fired a Taser at the suspect. The behemoth went down, smashing through a wooden chair, and writhed on the floor.

Nicholas froze. He really hoped he wasn't put in the same cell with that man.

"Come along, Mr. Rousseau. Just a typical Friday evening." Franklin took his arm to lead him onward. "You're going to a holding cell."

They passed through a series of metal doors, each buzzed the same jarring tone. Bare concrete replaced tile and absorbed the fluorescent glare from fixtures suspended at least ten feet above the floor. The corridor seemed to slope down into the depths of the earth. The cells weren't barred like he'd seen in old westerns. Rather, their steel doors lined one narrow hall. Through the tiny peep window in the first, the concrete room looked maybe eight feet deep.

And he was about to be sealed in one of those rooms, behind one of those doors.

Chilled sweat dampened his palms. "Officer Franklin, exactly how long will I be detained here?"

"You hungry?"

"No." Who could eat right after being arrested?

"Good thing. Next meal's at eight tomorrow mornin'."

"But—"

"You looking to confess anything, Mr. Rousseau?"

"Of course not. I'm innocent."

Franklin huffed. "Everybody is."

The officer stopped beside the fourth cell and ran a key card through the slot, punched in a code. The locks hummed and clicked. Franklin opened the door.

"I don't understand why I was arrested."

"You've been Mirandized, Mr. Rousseau. You might want to be quiet until your lawyer gets here."

Nick raised his hands to chest level. "Will you remove these now?"

Officer Franklin motioned with his chin. "Inside. Put 'em through the tray slot below the window."

He crossed the threshold of the empty cell. The door snapped shut. Hands shaking, he offered his bound wrists to the officer as instructed. Franklin didn't look at him as he unlocked the cuffs and walked away.

He leaned back against the nearest puke-green, block wall, breathing through his mouth against the room's pungent stench. Quivering with dread, he lowered himself to the edge of the long concrete bench spanning one side of the windowless room.

The seat was cold. No, it was wet.

With … urine? Soaking into his prison-orange scrub pants.

But there was so much of it, he knew if he stood whatever it was would run down his legs.

He stood anyway. Bile rose in his throat, and he gulped it down. He stripped off the pants—they'd taken his underwear—and used the pants legs to blot dry, then removed his shirt and covered himself with it.

There he was, naked and locked in the county jail.

He took a deep breath, let it out slowly. Gavin would come and get him out before the night's end, right?

Think. Think!

He glanced at his wrist. No watch. He'd been taken from the airport in handcuffs by two policemen. Brought here and photographed and fingerprinted. His watch and other belongings had been taken, bagged, and were somewhere in this building with a case number attached.

Somewhere in the corridor another door buzzed, opened, and closed. Nicholas peered through the thick glass window. Officer Franklin's thick body paused outside the door. Nicholas knocked on the glass.

"Officer? Officer Franklin?"

The cop's rotund face filled the window. "Step back, Mr. Rousseau."

He complied.

Franklin opened the door, glanced at the soiled clothing at Nicholas' feet, then gave a bland look. "Put the scrubs back on."

Nicholas cleared his throat, squared his shoulders with as much dignity as he could muster. "Officer Franklin—"

"I didn't peg you as a troublemaker, Mr. Rousseau. I'm not usually wrong," he said. "Guess I'm losing my touch."

The air conditioning kicked on. Icy fingers crept over Nick's bare skin. Yet he felt sweat break out along his spine.

His brain went into overdrive. Officer Franklin was a man used to facts, figures, reports, the kinds of information Nick used when presenting a proposal to his more intimidating clients.

"Sir, I mistakenly sat on the bench without first checking its condition, and sat in urine. So I removed the pants. Attempts to dry myself were only partially successful. I would sincerely appreciate clean scrubs. I apologize for the inconvenience. If cuffs are protocol, you have my full cooperation."

Franklin looked at the scrubs again, then sniffed.

"Had a couple of drunk and disorderly gentlemen in here earlier." Those cop eyes narrowed. "Guess the cleaning crew didn't get here before you did. Don't move."

"Yes, sir."

The officer left, again locking Nick inside. He exhaled a tight breath but stayed where he was. Franklin returned with clean scrubs and four antibacterial wipes. Nick used the wipes and dressed quickly.

"Hands through. Cuffs go back on for your trip to the interview room."

"My lawyer's here?"

"Ask your questions in the interview room. Wrists, Mr. Rousseau."

Until moments ago, he'd half-thought this was a mistake. When he hadn't been immediately questioned upon arriving at the jail, he'd figured someone had determined his innocence and was even then processing his release.

Despite his willingness to bring the clean scrubs, Officer Franklin's face showed the last sands of patience had just trickled through the hourglass. Nick had no allies here. He was on his own.

Chapter Eleven

"Miss?" The airline counter attendant looked hopefully at Angelina. "Have you chosen a flight?"

She had two options, with almost identical outcomes. Take the red-eye at 12:05 A.M.—with two stops and layovers she'd land at 1:00 P.M. tomorrow. Or she could take the 6:30 A.M. flight in the morning with one stop in Atlanta and arrive in Montgomery at almost the same time.

She should have called the airline before leaving the hotel, but her brain was addled from misinterpreting Lorenzo's actions. Instead, she'd spent the ride there calling the attorney's office and leaving multiple messages on his voicemail.

Nick said they were going to search the house. Not the carriage house. Still, with Godiva close to delivering a second time, Angelina was glad she'd made arrangements to board her horses with her vet.

"Miss?"

"I'll take the six-thirty tomorrow." Spending the night on a plane would do her no good. She paid, gathered her belongings, and hailed a luxury car service SUV outside the terminal.

As the driver stowed her bags, she slid into the back. A news clip of Rita and Thomas enjoying their first dance as husband and wife flashed onto video screens embedded in the front seat headrests.

"Today Rita Dade, the world famous designer, married for the fourth time," the commentator said. *"She and Thomas Mastrangelo of Italy started the new year by tying the knot today in Las Vegas . . ."*

The driver climbed in. "Where to?"

She turned off the screens. She couldn't go back to her room at the wedding venue. She might run into Lorenzo.

"Take me to the Paris Hotel." She closed her eyes.

She felt them pull away from the curb, glide smoothly into traffic.

"Lots to do in Vegas," the driver said. "Take one of my cards from the back in case you need a nice, clean ride."

She caught his gaze in the rearview mirror. "Actually, I'll need to be back here at five tomorrow morning."

"I'll pick you up at four-thirty."

"All right." One less thing to worry about.

"Just here for one night, huh? Meeting someone? You're in Vegas, lots of options out there. You don't have to be alone if you don't want to, and I might know some people."

Did she look that desperate? Like someone reduced to paying for companionship?

"Not that you'd need help finding a date. You're a looker, that's for sure." He shrugged. "You know, if you wanted something kind of anonymous, it being New Year's and all."

"No," she said. "No."

She stared out the window. *A looker.* What good did beauty do if your husband was never around to look at you?

She called ahead to the Paris Hotel. Upon arrival, she checked in quickly and went straight to her suite. Looking across to the Bellagio, she saw the 8:00 P.M. fountains show burst to life. She could cross the street, spend the remainder of the evening strolling through the Richard MacDonald exhibit of his Cirque de Soleil-inspired sculptures. She wanted one. She'd admired his work for years but couldn't seem to choose.

A white-haired couple stopped on the sidewalk and shared a long kiss. Arm-in-arm, they watched the lighted water show.

They've probably been married fifty years or more.

Angelina turned away. She'd fallen to bitter depths, lower than she thought she could ever go.

What was wrong with her? Was she destined to make the same mistakes as her father? Even after the humiliation of revealing her attraction to Rick and being gently rebuffed a year and a half ago, now she'd been willing to hook up with a random stranger for the weekend.

Shame rose inside her. If she'd actually cheated, if no one knew but she and Lorenzo, would she have been able to keep the secret and maintain a façade of innocence? Or would she have been driven to confess her guilt?

She sighed, thought of Nicholas, and dialed Gavin's number again.

Whatever Nick had been accused of, was he guilty or innocent? How awful she didn't immediately think *innocent.*

Either way, after what she'd almost done today—for better or worse—their marriage would never be the same.

***

Franklin walked Nicholas back the way they'd come down, up the corridor of cells, through the thick doors. Down another short hall of offices, and past the row of cop desks cluttered with laptops, radios, stacks of paperwork, mugs, and cups. They turned left and entered a room smaller than the cell he'd just left. Drab-gray walls, a metal table sat centered on the longest wall flanked by two metal stools bolted to the floor.

"Sit," Franklin said.

Nicholas sat on the small seat. Franklin unlocked one wrist, looped the chain around a metal bar at the end of the table, and re-cuffed him, leaving Nick with both arms locked to his right.

Another officer, a little older than Franklin but smaller, appeared at the door. "What took so long?"

"Wardrobe mishap." Franklin spoke beside Nick.

The new officer's tag read "Detective Reedy." He sat opposite Nick. "Leave us alone for now. Mr. Rousseau, are you willing to talk to me without representation?"

"For the moment. My wife's contacting our attorney. I hope to hear from him soon."

"That would be your personal attorney, Gavin Hawk. He isn't a criminal attorney, is he?"

"No." But maybe he'd know what Nick should do.

"Tell me about this key, Mr. Rousseau." Reedy slid a safe deposit key across the table.

"Is it mine?"

"Removed from your key ring moments ago. What's it for?"

"My safe deposit box," Nick said.

"At People's Bank in Mobile?"

"You already knew?"

"Of course we knew."

"Then why ask me?"

"Just checking your level of honesty." Reedy paused. "When did you rent the box?"

"Last year."

"For?"

"Keeping documents I didn't want to keep at home."

"And why is that?"

Because he didn't want to deal with Angie's disapproval or anger, or even silence over his latest investment, even though he'd done the deal with her in mind.

"I wanted to surprise my wife."

Reedy smiled a plastic smile. "Really?" He pulled out a photo from a folder and held it to study. "She knows nothing of your business dealings?"

"No."

"Hard to hide things from a beautiful woman. You travel a lot, don't you?"

"For business. I'm contracted by companies all over the globe."

"Ever take your wife on those trips? Hard to leave a beautiful woman." Reedy leaned forward. "Ever take her along to soften up clients? Socialize with customers? Persuade investors?"

"No." Nick clenched his hands on the table. "*No*, and I'll ignore what you're implying. My wife has nothing to do with my business. She doesn't travel with me. She knows almost nothing of what I do. I barely—"

See her.

Reedy smiled slowly as if he knew Nick's thoughts.

"We'll get back to your wife. Now, about your personal business. Did Gavin Hawk set up your LLC for your consulting firm? What about your real estate purchases? Was he involved in those in an advisory capacity? Did you consult him regarding all your real estate purchases? How many properties do you own?"

"You're asking questions too fast. I've been traveling. I've barely slept the last day and a half. I can't remember everything, in order to answer." He squeezed his eyes, straining to keep up. "I no longer own properties."

"But ..." Reedy prompted as if he and Nick were sharing secrets.

Nick swallowed. "I'm an investor in a large project."

"Where's your wife?"

He shook his head. "What difference does it make where Angelina is?"

"Your personal business attorney, Gavin Hawk, isn't answering his phone. We've called several times. How do you know she didn't run off with him?"

"Because I know her."

"Do you? You're never home. You never take her with you. Where is she, Mr. Rousseau?"

His breathing came fast. "She's at a wedding—I was supposed to go with her, but I didn't—in, um, Las Vegas."

"That's right. She's staying at the Paris Hotel, and she's booked on a morning flight to return tomorrow. Will she tell me the same things you are? I've already confirmed you traveled alone. Pretty Mrs. Rousseau was always left behind. What I can't figure out is, did you do that because you didn't want to share the money you hoped to make?" He looked again at the picture in his hand, then back at Nick. "Or are you just plain stupid? Any man who would leave a woman like that alone for months at a time is either an idiot, blind, or both."

Nick almost reached for the picture, just to see if Reedy was messing with him.

"She's making a name for herself in the art world, isn't she?" Reedy asked. "Wonder what kind of contacts that gives her."

"Are you going to arrest my wife? I'll tell you anything you want to know, just don't arrest my wife."

Reedy tilted his chin. "You care about her?"

"Of course I care about her. She's my wife."

"Hmm. Maybe it's better you kept her out of the loop. Whether you did it out of care or selfishness remains to be seen." Reedy stood. "I'll be back."

"Wait!" Nick rose, his bound wrists jarring him to a stop. He sat. "Are you going to arrest Angelina? Do I need to get her an attorney, too?"

"That's up to you." Detective Reedy let the door slam behind him.

Nick looked at his cuffed hands hooked around the bar on the table. At the orange scrubs he now wore.

Never in his life had he been in a police station, let alone been arrested. Aside from when he and Angie had first visited southern Alabama right after they married when a cop bought them a meal and gave them directions, getting a speeding ticket was the only contact he'd ever had with law enforcement.

He caught himself bouncing his leg and stopped. He clasped and unclasped his hands. Drummed his fingers on the table.

Think. *Think.*

He'd been charged with real estate fraud, which was impossible. With the exception of his home, he no longer owned properties.

He could only sit and wait until his attorney arrived or the detective returned and gave him more information. To figure out what was going on, he definitely needed more information.

And something told him the worst news was yet to come.

***

The door on Nick's left opened and a dark-haired man in blue jeans and a knit shirt entered. Nick knew those blue eyes and that face.

His shoulders relaxed. "Pastor Crane?"

"Pierce, please." He waved away the formal title.

"What are you doing here?"

"Dad volunteers weekly as chaplain with the Emergency Responders. He's on vacation, so I took his shift. I heard about your arrest." He sat on the stool opposite Nick. "Are you all right?"

"No." Nick motioned at his cuffed hands.

"Have you been told anything?"

He wasn't sure how much he should say. "I'm charged with real estate fraud, but I don't know exactly what that means." He paused. "I just flew home today. I've been working in Spain for over three months. I haven't been in the country a full week in almost a year."

"Did you tell them that?" Pierce asked.

"I think they already know it. They know I've been in Spain." A thought occurred to him. "Did they let you in here hoping I'd confess?"

Pierce sat back. "No. Can I do anything for you? Where's Angelina?"

"A wedding somewhere—Las Vegas." He let out a breath. "I can't think straight. I called her. She's flying home, but she probably can't get here until tomorrow. Could you call her again? Ask if she reached our lawyer?"

"Sure."

He told Pierce Angie's number. "Can a police detective lie to a suspect?"

"I have no idea. You think you're being lied to?"

"I don't know. I've been on and off planes for the last twenty-plus hours. I don't even know what day it is."

"You said Angie was trying to call your lawyer. So, you already have representation?"

"Sort of. He specializes in corporations, trusts, and wills, and long-term estate planning."

Which meant even if Gavin got Angie's messages, he couldn't defend Nick.

He adjusted his hands in the cuffs. "Do you know a criminal attorney nearby? I need someone right away."

"I do. Julius Floyd, Deacon Floyd's son. I'll call him right after I call Angie."

"No," Nick said. "I need you to call him first. And Pierce? If Angie's spoken with our personal attorney, I need to know that as soon as possible."

"Will do."

Pierce left.

Franklin returned. "Comfort break." He freed Nick's handcuffs from the security bar. "Follow me."

"Where are we going?"

"I figured you could use a bathroom about now."

"Oh. Yeah."

Franklin walked him to a single-person restroom with a steel sink and urinal bolted to the wall and no toilet paper in sight.

"That work for ya?" Franklin asked.

"Yes. Thank you."

"I'll lock the door from the outside. Knock when you're done. I'll expect that knock in about sixty seconds."

"Yes, sir."

It was the shortest sixty seconds of his life.

He knocked.

Franklin opened the door. "Follow me."

They walked back to the interview room. Franklin re-secured his wrists to the table.

"Preacher man said your new attorney will be in to see you tomorrow morning. Sit tight, not sure what we're doing now."

"Thank you."

Alone again, Nick stared at the dingy tile ceiling.

How had this happened? It couldn't be real.

Fear—like a dark, open mouth—swallowed him feet to throat. He'd been worried about the tax implications of selling off his properties so quickly. But the opportunity of a lifetime had presented itself right at the end of the year. Had his hasty decisions inadvertently led him into breaking the law?

***

Angelina's cell rang. The ID read *Rowe City Emergency Services.*

She answered. "Hello?"

"It's Pierce Crane. Pastor at The Barn Church? My dad rotates as chaplain with the emergency responders here in Rowe City. I'm covering for him as he's on vacation. I've just spoken with Nicholas. He wanted me to call you."

She almost said she didn't care what Nick had to say. That she hadn't seen Nick in almost four months, and before that, only for a couple of evenings after a fourteen-week business trip, which had been the pattern for many years. What was the difference if he were in prison?

"I'll fly out in the morning and arrive by two," she said.

"Do you need someone to pick you up at the airport?"

"No, thanks. I left a car there in the garage."

"I've called a criminal attorney for Nick. Julius Floyd—from the church?—will see him as soon as possible tomorrow." Pierce paused. "Nick wanted me to ask if you've heard from your personal attorney?"

"All I get is voicemail."

Similar to when she called Nick during his many trips.

Something rose in her, like lava burning its way to the surface.

"Do you know why Nick and I don't attend church together very often, Pastor Crane? Why I have all but stopped attending? Because my husband was home maybe three Sundays last year. Maybe that many. I grew tired of going alone."

"I can understand that. And call me Pierce."

"Why are you being so nice? You barely know us."

He chuckled. "My wife would say it's because she's rubbed off on me."

From her sporadic visits to The Barn Church, Angelina knew Pierce had a sensitive, emotional radar similar to his wife's. Hence Angelina envisioning his sermon on adultery when she'd stupidly thought Lorenzo was the solution to her loveless life. But she hadn't known he could pick up vibes from the other side of the country across phone lines.

"And," he continued, "I don't think I'd be wrong in saying Nick's not the only one who's hurting right now."

"You have no idea." She reddened at what she'd imagined doing with Lorenzo.

"What's happening with your husband is pretty serious. One way or another you'll be affected."

"That's the nature of marriage, isn't it?"

She hated sounding so cynical but couldn't seem to stop herself.

"Sorry," she said.

"No offense taken. Laurie and I are available if you need us. No expectations. I'll text you our cell numbers."

"Thanks. I'll let you know."

She ended the call. Laid her phone on the antique writing desk beside the bed.

A text came, instructions for those who wanted to line up outside her previous hotel and blow bubbles at Rita and Thomas as they left on their honeymoon. They'd looked so in love when they'd said their vows. So in tune with each other.

She remembered that feeling. When as newlyweds she'd thought she and Nick would never drift apart. When she'd thought nothing could wedge itself between them.

When it seemed they'd barely go an hour without saying *I love you.*

With painful clarity, she realized Nick had spoken more words to her today than he had during his previous trip. And despite his arrest, neither of them had spoken the words *I love you.*

Chapter Twelve

Nick didn't know how long he sat before the door opened again. Officer Franklin carried leg shackles into the room.

"We're transporting you to the state prison in Troy. Stay seated, Mr. Rousseau."

Nicholas obeyed as his cuffs were removed from the restraining bar and re-applied.

"Turn this way." Franklin knelt before him, snapped a cuff around each ankle, and secured a chain up to his wrists.

"Suspect on the move!" he shouted out the door.

Another officer stepped in, sandwiching Nick behind Officer Franklin. The shackles required he shuffle in small steps. They escorted him through the maze of desks. They rode an elevator and stepped out onto a ground floor loading dock. A police van waited.

"Down the ramp, Mr. Rousseau. Duck and climb in the back seat."

They chained his shackles to the metal floor, secured a seatbelt around his waist.

The van pulled away, its big engine humming as the old Buick's he'd owned when he and Angelina married. He thought of his humble honeymoon. Of wanting to provide for Angie and drawing one of his first big ideas on the steamed bathroom mirror. Maybe this time his big idea would claim his freedom.

They rode on in the dark, down unlit rural roads that seemed to stretch forever. Then, up ahead, a haze of light shone like a beacon. Nick thought it a small town until he realized they'd slowed at a security gate.

"Don't move until we tell you to." Franklin spoke from the front passenger seat.

The state prison facility in Troy was enormous, a rigid brick building lit from all directions by wide lights on tall poles. A high fence topped with razor wire surrounded the complex. As the gate closed behind the police van, Nicholas shook his head to clear it.

"You all right back there?" Officer Franklin asked.

"As good as can be expected, I guess. Thanks for asking."

The other officer's radio beeped.

"Conley," he answered. "We're pulling into the loading dock now. ETA five minutes. That was the State Prosecutor. He wants to talk to Rousseau."

Franklin shot Nick a glance. "You willing to answer questions again without an attorney?"

"I don't know. Maybe. I can listen."

That would give him more information about the charges and the evidence supposedly compiled against him.

He was taken to a small room that held one table, two chairs, and had what appeared to be a one-way mirror along one wall. Officer Franklin removed his leg shackles. This time, he didn't secure Nick's cuffed wrists to the bar on the table, but rather let him rest them in his lap.

"I'll be handing you over to the state," he said. "Stuff works a bit different here than at the county. You want a sandwich?"

"Yeah. Thanks."

"Be right back. You stay put, and they won't hook you to the table."

"Got it."

There was no clock on the wall. No music filtered into the room. He heard footsteps in the hall, voices, and random laughter.

The door opened. A man dressed in a suit entered and took the seat across from him.

"I'm State Prosecutor Darrin Simon."

Instinctively, Nick started to offer his hand, then caught himself and lowered them back to his lap.

The prosecutor's cool eyes studied him, his angular face twitched once. "Are you willing to talk to me without representation?"

"For the moment. I've another attorney coming tomorrow. Mr. Simon, there's been a mistake."

"Oh, there have been lots of mistakes. And I think you made many of them."

Nicholas opened his mouth, then shut it. He recognized that tone, the I'm-not-going-to-believe-what-you-tell-me tone he encountered from so many clients—CEOs and company owners who doubted Nick's input on increasing their business's productivity. He'd learned when to rephrase his ideas, when to push, and when to simply let the numbers speak for themselves. If a potential client didn't want his expertise, there were ten more lined up who did.

But the man sitting before him wasn't a potential client.

Simon blinked once, twice. "You've been charged with four counts of real estate fraud." He paused. "Nothing to say?"

Nick didn't know how much he should say without his attorney present. He only knew he was innocent.

"I don't understand what you think I've done. I've never committed fraud or stolen anything in my life. I'm not guilty. I've been out of the country for over three months."

Simon glanced through a file he held. "That's right. You've been in Spain. You've made many trips to Spain over the years, haven't you, Mr. Rousseau?"

Nick's heart skipped; he felt his blood pressure rise. "Yes. I have clients all over the world."

"You've also been investing in real estate for many years. When was the last time you spoke with Gerald Barker?"

His old boss from Jenkinsons?

"Is Gerald all right?"

"If one can be all right after losing over five million dollars to a scam."

"What? Five million?"

"You should know, Mr. Rousseau."

Simon reopened the file. He laid papers on the table like a casino dealer revealing a poker hand card by card. Each document bore the PGI logo of a black pyramid with gold letters.

"He lost the money to you and your phony investment scheme. Where's the money, Nick?"

Nick looked at Simon, and his throat went bone dry. "You're serious."

Simon pointed to the first document. "As serious as five million from Gerald Barker."

"I haven't spoken with Gerald in half a dozen years."

"Six-point-two million from Frances Sweeney." Simon moved his hand to the second document.

"I don't know anyone by that name. I don't know what you're talking about. Where did you get these?"

Simon slid the third stack of papers in front of Nick. "A whopping eleven million from Jeremy Jenkinson—president of Jenkinsons in Birmingham."

"I've never even spoken with Jeremy Jenkinson. His father ran the company when I worked there years ago."

"Are you sure about that?"

"I've never stolen from anyone. I've never taken a dime that wasn't mine in my whole life."

Simon gathered his papers and stood. "I think I'll let you sit there and think about that. Sometimes simply being in this room for a bit will jog a person's memory."

"Wait! You said there were four charges."

So far, Nick read on Simon's expression. "Or maybe your wife knows where the money is."

The State Prosecutor walked away, closing the door behind him.

Nick raised his bound hands to his face. Angelina. Whatever they thought he'd done, they thought she was involved.

Officer Franklin arrived with a sandwich and bottled water.

"Stay there, and eat it quick. Not long before lockdown. We've got to get you to your cell."

"Thank you."

All the saliva had dried up in Nick's mouth. He could barely choke down the peanut butter and jelly sandwich amidst gulping the water.

Franklin led him down a series of halls. They took an elevator up to the fourth floor, and Nick's knees nearly buckled. Bare concrete stretched between two rows of metal doors facing each other for the full length of the building. The smell of disinfectant over grime and sweat made the sandwich curdle in his stomach. They walked halfway down the row of doors on the right, and Franklin unlocked a cell.

Nick went inside, put his hands through the tray slot so the cuffs could be removed.

"It's a light weekend, no roommate for you yet. Hang in there, buddy." Franklin left.

Nick looked at the metal toilet, sink, and the small cot. He sat.

"Lights out!" Nicholas heard, and his cell went pitch black. A thick, dizzying darkness that removed every point of reference. If he hadn't already been sitting, he might have fallen over.

Someone screamed. Others cursed. Profanity and sneering chuckles lanced the air.

"Lights out!" A booming voice came over the loudspeaker. "You all know the rules. Last warning."

His eyelids drooped; his shoulders sagged into the lumpy mattress. He should have been too scared to sleep, too bothered by the eerie silence interrupted by the occasional drip of the sink bolted to the wall. But his body was on Spain time. To his body, it was six hours ahead, almost tomorrow morning.

Then, wariness churned. Simon planned to question Angelina about millions Nick had supposedly stolen from others. *Maybe your wife knows where the money is.* But there was no money to find.

Detective Reedy had speculations of his own about Nick and Angie's marriage. *How do you know she didn't run off with Gavin Hawk? You're never home.*

But Angie would never …

He opened his eyes to utter darkness. Had something been missing in Angie's voice today?

In the early years, she'd often asked to accompany him abroad. They'd had some rocky patches since; then at some point, she'd stopped asking.

When, exactly, had that happened? And why had he not noticed until now?

***

Between traveling from Europe, the time differences, and being arrested without going home, Nicholas hadn't showered or shaved in two days.

He'd been given a small toothbrush and a travel-size tube of toothpaste, which he'd used twice this morning. As he watched his metal tray and used plastic silverware be slipped from the slot in the

136

door, he swallowed down the lump of runny eggs and dry toast he'd devoured almost without chewing.

Officer Franklin had warned him last night. *They distribute breakfast, delivering trays down one line of cells, then up the other. Eat fast. They'll come right back around picking them up. Three, five minutes tops.*

God's truth, he thought, rising from his bunk. He'd never eaten so quickly in his life. The small container of juice hadn't been nearly enough liquid to wash the food down. Now, he cupped water from the faucet in his hands and drank heartily, despite its sulfur smell and hard-water taste. Dasani, this was not.

He sat again.

He had no books. No work. No internet. Just four concrete walls and a small window in the door, in a room twice as big as the twin cot against one long wall.

With the exception of plane trips, when was the last time he'd been this still? Even while flying, he always worked. He wasn't comfortable having nothing to do.

This situation was simply a gross misunderstanding. PGI wasn't his company. In a couple of days, a week at most, the prosecutor would realize the truth, and Nick would be absolved, released, and could go on with his life.

He raised both hands to his face, lowered them as he again thought of Angelina and his latest investment she knew nothing about. That deal could be the reason behind his arrest. If the worst happened—if he learned the investment was less than legal, and Angelina didn't forgive him for making yet another financial decision without her—exactly what kind of life would he be going home to?

Chapter Thirteen

Someone was following her.

Angelina had vaguely noticed the dark sedan as she'd paid her parking fees when leaving the airport. The car had nudged up behind hers rather than taking the other open lane.

Now it followed at a distance as she passed the red water tower, Benson's Hardware, and the Downtown Diner.

She crossed the railroad tracks at the east edge of town. Turned toward home. About five miles out, she approached The Barn Church. The familiar horse silhouette in a front loft window made her smile. But as she glanced again in the rearview mirror, the sedan closed the gap, and her smile faded.

She reached into her purse for her cell. Placed it on the seat beside her. Located the panic button that would immediately place a call to 911 if necessary. Maybe she should turn around and head straight to see Nicholas. Cops would be at the jail, right? If she needed protection, she'd have it.

But she needed to stop by the carriage house above the stables first. Nicholas had said the house might be searched. The police wouldn't have damaged or seized her paintings, would they?

And she needed to steel herself before seeing her husband. She didn't want him seeing on her face what she'd wanted to do yesterday in Vegas, because she didn't yet know how to explain herself, even if she wanted to.

She'd realized some things during her solitary night in the Paris Hotel and earlier today as she'd flown across the country. She refused to live the rest of her life lonely and alone and married in name only.

Never again would she feel ashamed of or embarrassed about her wants and needs, or be left to search elsewhere for companionship.

And she wasn't going to let Nick's current situation sway her into staying in a loveless marriage. If he'd gotten into trouble, it was his trouble.

She deserved a life.

She reached the long stretch of white cross-fencing marking their property and slowed before her driveway. The sedan slowed as well, then drove on.

Angelina took a relieved breath. She turned onto their quarter mile lane. Drove between the front pastures. At the stand of pine trees shielding the house from the road, she took a fork to the right.

She continued to the back of their thirty-five acres. Past the stand of pine trees, the land opened again to more pasture. She pulled up to the stables, complete with carriage house, which had sat unused until last fall when she'd had it renovated. The classic barn-red siding with flat black crisscross braces on Dutch doors held such a welcoming sweetness, she sighed inwardly at the sight.

She parked, carried her luggage up the metal stairs to the apartment, and laid it on the sectional sofa in the center of the room, which doubled as her bed. The cool, open space with its white-washed vaulted ceiling boasted sightlines out windows lining both walls.

The end-to-end tables she'd placed below the windows for brushes, palettes, paints, solvent, rags, and other supplies appeared untouched. Her paintings, thankfully, were unmoved. Both those carefully stacked at the end wall and the unfinished works on easels.

She needed a few minutes to compose herself and maybe eat something before going to see Nicholas. And, yes, she might call Pierce and ask if he'd meet her there.

Angelina walked to the bank of windows at the front and opened one for fresh air. Normally she felt perfectly safe out here by herself, but after believing that car had been following her …

She heard tires on the gravel driveway and peered up the lane. The dark sedan had returned, taken the fork, and now parked beside her car. A man and a woman, badges clipped to their belts, got out and climbed the stairs.

She grabbed her phone and dialed Pierce.

The visitors knocked as he answered. "Hello?"

"It's Angelina. I'm home, and I think there are two cops at my door. Would you stay on the phone with me? Until I'm sure who they are?"

"Sure."

Holding the phone at her side, she cracked open the door the length of the security chain. "May I help you?"

The woman held up a badge. "I'm Detective Jernigan." She motioned with her head. "My partner, Detective Niles. May we escort you to the state prison where your husband is being held? The State Prosecutor would like to ask you some questions."

"What kind of questions?"

"He will decide that, ma'am."

Angelina looked from the female officer to her partner, then back again. "Do I need my own lawyer?"

"That's entirely up to you."

"Angelina?" Pierce's voice called from her phone.

"They want me to go with them. To the state prison. I guess Nicholas was moved last night?" she asked the female and received an affirming nod.

"Hold on," she told Pierce.

"Are you arresting me?" she asked the officer.

"Not at this time," Detective Jernigan said. "You can drive yourself. We'll follow."

Angelina heard, then saw, more cars arrive.

"We have a warrant to search all your and Mr. Rousseau's property, including this carriage house and stables," Niles said.

"Excuse me a moment." Angelina lowered her phone and closed the door in the officers' faces. She unhooked the security chain and leaned back against the doorframe, scanning her work area, her sanctuary.

What had Nicholas done? And why would he implicate her?

She'd long since accepted he rarely considered her feelings, but had he become hostile? Vengeful toward her now?

She'd never have thought him to be the kind of person who would hurt another to deflect from his own pain. Or had he somehow learned she'd moved out, and this was payback?

"They'll follow me to the prison," she told Pierce.

"I helped Nick secure another attorney. He should be there now talking with the authorities before he sees Nick. Call me if you need a lawyer, too."

"Thank you." She ended the call and opened the door.

"We need to go, Mrs. Rousseau." Detective Jernigan spoke into the radio clipped at her shoulder. "Jernigan and Niles en route with A. Rousseau. ETA fifty minutes. Alert State Prosecutor of same."

"Roger, Detective Jernigan," the voice on the other end said. "Upon arrival, proceed to interview room 3-B."

"Copy that," Jernigan said.

Angelina looked at the people now lining up behind the officers on the stairs.

"They must be careful with my paintings." Her breath came fast. "My first solo exhibition is in Mobile in two weeks. They cannot destroy my work. I'll show you anything, just don't damage the paintings. I use oil on canvas. I've several that aren't dry."

Niles looked over at Jernigan. "What kind of timeline did Simon want?"

"ASAP, I was told."

Angelina thought of Nick. How could he do something that threatened her work? "I'll stand to the side and tell you how to handle them, but you must not damage them."

"Ten minutes probably won't matter," Jernigan spoke to Niles, then looked back at her. "You can show the technicians how to handle the paintings, then we'll be on our way."

"Thank you."

Niles and Jernigan entered. A half-dozen others followed.

"Quick demonstration, Mrs. Rousseau." Niles motioned the others forward. He pulled aside a man her age who gave her a lingering look. "Go through her luggage."

Angelina told herself not to be embarrassed and went straight to the wet canvases so the officers could examine those first. Then she showed them how to safely move and re-stack the others.

"Anything else in here we need to be careful of?" Jernigan stood at the door.

"No. We can go now."

Angelina got back in her car, then lowered her window as the detectives passed by. "I don't know the address of the prison. For the GPS?"

Jernigan rattled off the location, repeating as Angie input the information.

"Thank you," she said. "Can't you ask me what the State Prosecutor wants to know?"

"He wants to ask his own questions. Are you willing to go, or will we have to come back with a warrant?"

"I'll go," Angelina said and waited to lead the detectives off her property.

***

Angelina wished she'd followed the officers instead of the other way around. She didn't like them behind her, and at each stop sign, at each red light, she worried she'd pulled up too far, or not far enough. She tried to keep her speed below the limit, and more than once caught herself readjusting her hands on the steering wheel.

At the security gate, she was given a pass to display on her dashboard and directed to visitor parking. The attendant was friendly enough, but Angelina didn't like watching the gate arm lower behind her and the dark sedan.

They parked.

"This way," Detective Jernigan spoke as she passed.

Angelina needed something to do with her hands. Something to hold. She braced against the dusty breeze and grabbed her purse.

The building exterior was putty brown. The door, metal of the same color. It closed behind them with a buzz and a thud, opening to a lobby of dirty yellow walls and flecked, worn terrazzo tile.

At once, she wanted to turn around and leave. Drive back to the carriage house, lock herself inside, and lock out the world. She should have refused to come. She should have stayed with her paintings, moved each one herself and made arrangements to talk with the State Prosecutor another day, another time.

They reached a metal detector, complete with armed policemen strolling up and down the line of those waiting to enter.

"Empty your pockets into the tray. Place your purse or other belongings on the conveyor belt. When directed, step through," the attendant stated and repeated the instructions.

"Always busy on a Saturday," Jernigan said to Niles.

"Right. But if you visited someone here on a regular basis, wouldn't you get used to the routine? Most of these people act as if they don't know where they are or why they're here. Our country's doomed."

Angelina scanned the folks in front of her. If Nicholas were convicted of a crime, he could spend years here. She'd go through this process every time she visited him.

Wouldn't that be a switch? Nick waiting on her to come see him.

Still, the thought brought no satisfaction, only sadness.

They reached the front of the line. Niles and Jernigan went ahead. Angelina passed through the metal detector. Her purse was confiscated, and a policeman motioned her away from the line where he emptied her purse into a plastic box.

"Is something wrong?" Angelina asked.

Finally, he held up her keys with her metal Eiffel Tower keychain.

"Here's the culprit," he said. "Cute. You can reload."

"Thank you."

Angelina didn't take the time to re-organize. She simply dumped the contents into the center pocket and continued on.

She followed Niles and Jernigan until they arrived at interview room 3-B, a small gray space on the third floor, complete with what she believed to be a one-way mirror. A dozen people could be watching and listening.

How she disliked being made a spectacle.

"The State Prosecutor should be with you momentarily." Niles and Jernigan closed the door as they left; immediately, it reopened.

"Mrs. Rousseau? I'm State Prosecutor Darrin Simon." He wore a tailored suit, a strategically charming smile, and no wedding ring.

He stood across the table with arms crossed, looking down at her. She didn't know whether to hold his gaze, look away, or stare straight ahead. She'd never before been inside a prison, let alone into an interview room for questioning.

"Thank you for coming so quickly," he said.

"It seemed the wisest decision. How can I help you, Mr. Simon?"

"To the point. I like that. When was the last time you spoke with your husband?"

That was easy. "Last night. He called me."

"You were at a wedding? In Vegas?"

"Yes. Should I get myself a lawyer?"

"Do you need one?"

"I don't believe so."

"What do you know about your husband's investments?"

She looked in his expressionless, gray eyes. "I don't know anything about my husband's investments."

"What do you know about his business?"

"I don't really know anything about my husband's business, other than he travels extensively. He's an efficiency expert in high demand."

"And you never travel with him?" His slight grin was both mocking and flirtatious.

She thought of the first years of her marriage when she'd asked Nick to let her accompany him during summer breaks. When she'd counted the days of his trips, anxiously awaiting his return. The later years that had passed; the birthdays, holidays, and anniversaries he'd been absent, despite his promises to one day take her with him.

She blinked slowly. "I have never accompanied my husband on any trip, business or otherwise. Although I did meet him once in Gatlinburg right after I graduated from the art institute. The location was convenient for both of us." They'd spent a few days there before traveling to Rowe City to look for a home.

Simon sat on the corner of the table, leaned forward. "And why didn't you ever travel with him?"

Because he didn't want me to—she gulped back the words. *Because what I wanted wasn't important. Because even though he married me, he didn't care if we ever spent time together.*

Simon pulled back, his expression sobering as if he'd read her mind.

"He never took you anywhere? Never shared his business dealings and accomplishments? His long-term plans?"

The flash of confused pity in his eyes made her look away. In another time, another life, she probably would've thought him handsome despite his fair features, in a young Kenneth Branagh sort of way.

"He did not."

"I'm told you didn't go to your home. You went straight to the carriage house over the stables with your luggage. It appears you not only paint there, you live there. Am I correct?"

She wanted to lie. For some inexplicable reason, she didn't want a State Prosecutor to be one of the first to know she'd left her and Nick's enormous bed for a sofa.

Simon laughed. "He doesn't know, does he?" He rubbed a hand over his face. "Wow. I'm … wow. Either he really is an idiot, or he's the best con I've ever seen."

He stood again. "You can go home, Mrs. Rousseau."

"I don't understand."

He laughed again. "Just don't leave town."

She blanched. Their gazes locked. Both of them knew she'd be going to the carriage house.

"Don't worry. I'm a prosecuting attorney, not a divorce lawyer. I won't tell him."

Her heart went numb. She actually felt it stop hurting, stop yearning, and completely disengage from any concern for Nick as the last glimmer of care for her marriage burned out.

"You can tell him anything you like," she said.

"One more thing."

"Yes?"

"I was serious about you not leaving town. It's quite possible I'll need to speak with you again."

"I don't know anything that could help you."

"What about convicting or clearing your husband? Charges of real estate fraud at the amounts Nick is accused of are very serious. The FBI is involved."

She didn't know if she could trust the man before her to be completely forthcoming. Still, she needed to ask. "How much money are you talking about?"

"Over twenty-six million and counting."

Angelina caught herself before she gasped. She'd always known Nick wanted more financial stability than most. While she understood the cause for his obsession, she couldn't imagine how he might try to justify his need for that much money. Surely he hadn't used wanting to provide for her as an excuse.

"I assume you have some sort of proof," she said.

"We do indeed. His signature is all over documents for his dummy corporation Paragon Group Investments, or PGI. Did he ever discuss PGI with you?"

"No." She'd never heard of it.

She folded her hands on the table, stared ahead as she realized. He was trying to trip her up, telling her she could leave, then asking more questions. He was watching her reactions, her body language, searching for signs she was lying. Waiting for her to add details or an explanation. How much longer would he continue?

"Do you know where or how he hid the money?"

"You're making me wish I had a lawyer here with me."

"Other than Gavin Hawk, of course." He paused. "We know you

met him a few times, with Nick. The question is: How involved were you in Nick's plans? How much did he tell you?"

The backs of her eyes stung but she willed away the tears. She swallowed a decade of hurt over what little time she'd actually spent with her husband, how little she actually knew about his life apart from her. "I told you. I know nothing about his business or his investments."

"All right. Have you seen your husband yet?"

"You know I haven't."

"I can't let you see him yet." He thrust his hands into his pockets, cocked his head. "I'm not satisfied you aren't involved. I wasn't joking about the FBI's interest in this case. If I gave you time with him, would he tell you the truth about his deals? About the money?"

Simon might be interested in justice. Or, he might be interested in getting a conviction. However, the way his expression was changing from interest, to flirty, to lust, he might hope she'd be willing to bargain anything to get what she wanted—be it her freedom or Nick's.

If she agreed to seek answers from Nick for the prosecutor, she might be playing with fire. But frankly, she was beyond sick and tired of seemingly every man except her husband noticing her. Talking with her husband might be the only power she could use in her favor, in the impossible position his actions had put her in. If Simon wanted to, he might misconstrue or even ignore evidence supporting her innocence. She might have to get Nick to say she wasn't involved.

"Will you be watching?" she asked.

"Watching?"

"You and others." She motioned with her head. "Standing behind the one-way glass, watching everything Nicholas and I do, listening to everything we say?"

She—they—were probably being watched and recorded right now.

"That's an interesting question. Do you have something to hide?"

She refused to look away first. If this man caught any hint of fear, hurt, or the fact she wanted nothing else at that moment except to be back at the carriage house checking the condition of her paintings—he would, no doubt, exploit any and all of them to get what he wanted. His entire demeanor was probably an act to manipulate her.

"How long until I can see him?"

"A day. Maybe two."

"And I can leave now?"

"You may."

She rose and opened the door. "Then I'll await your call. You obviously know how to find me."

Chapter Fourteen

"Hey, Nick. I'm Julius." The man who entered the interview room where Nicholas sat had both his father's dark skin and intimidating size, along with his little mother's quiet smile.

"I've just been told the State Prosecutor questioned your wife but has now let her go home."

"Even if I'd known she was here, they wouldn't have let me see her, would they?" Nick asked.

"Not right now. Why did you talk to the State Prosecutor without an attorney present? Why would your wife?"

"I didn't do anything wrong. I thought if I listened, I might be able to clear up this entire misunderstanding. As for Angie, she probably thought the same."

"From now on, you say nothing to Simon or anyone without me there."

"I understand. I really thought this was all a big mistake."

"Let's not get off on the wrong foot," Julius said. "I'm on your side, but I need you to be straight with me. Does Angelina have reason to worry about being arrested?"

"No. No, I can say with absolute certainty I kept my professional life and my married life completely separate."

Julius placed his briefcase on the table and withdrew an iPad. He used it to take notes. "Can you think of anything that might help us prove your innocence?"

"I don't even understand the charges. Real estate fraud? I no longer own any properties."

"What about PGI?"

"Paragon? It's not my company. I'm an investor. My attorney—my other attorney, Gavin—told me about them."

Julius looked at him over his silver-rimmed glasses. "PGI was a scam."

Nicholas felt his heart sink all the way to his feet. He let out a long sigh and closed his eyes.

Paragon Group Investments, known as PGI, had been the answer Nick had been looking for. Dividends from The Group should have provided for him and Angelina for life.

He'd had it all planned. Secretly retiring, surprising her, and finally starting a family. He wanted to be present in his children's lives as his father had not been in his.

He looked at Julius. "How was PGI not a legitimate company? I've seen board meeting minutes. Preparations were being made to have publicly traded stock once the resort was finished."

"The scheme surrounds a particular stretch of beachfront property down in Mobile County which suffered greatly when Hurricane Katrina went through," Julius said. "The owners are thought to be deceased, as they never filed an insurance claim or paid property taxes. No living relatives can be found."

"I've seen that property. PGI called it Paragon Beach. They're building a billion-dollar resort there."

"You saw the property, or you saw the resort building itself?"

Nick's hands started to sweat. "I saw the land this time last year."

But he hadn't been down there since. As far as the resort was concerned, he'd only seen videos of the progress, sent via e-mail from Gavin Hawk, his trusted attorney who knew he was anxious to retire and looking to invest.

"You mean nothing's built there?" Nick asked. "Nothing?"

"A shell of a building is there. Cheap framing covered and camouflaged to look more substantial. There is no interior. No plumbing, nothing. Braces hold up the exterior walls.

"A utility company employee noticed the beginnings of the structure and realized no power had been run for the resort. He spoke to his boss, started asking questions. Turns out not one permit had been pulled. The building isn't real."

"No. You must be mistaken. Gavin and I talked about the land, the resort. I know all about top-secret phases two and three. I've known Gavin for years. He wouldn't do this to me."

"I'm sorry, Nick. Apparently, not even the land belongs to PGI. Someone using your name paid the back taxes to get access. The outstanding mortgage was never addressed. Even if the utility worker hadn't discovered the façade, this scam couldn't have gone on much longer. The property is coming up for foreclosure auction next month."

"My name? That's not what happened. I invested in PGI. I thought I was getting in on the ground floor of a life-changing opportunity. I saw the deed."

Gavin had shown it to him.

"Did you verify it was legitimate?"

A fake deed? Had Nick believed what he wanted, seen what he wanted, that day in Gavin's office when his lawyer had leaned in as a friend and shared with Nick the deal of a lifetime?

"Who was listed as owner?" Julius asked.

"PGI."

"Do you have a copy of that deed? The State Prosecutor believes PGI was yours and yours alone. That you used the bogus opportunity to persuade others to invest millions. I've seen the documents, Nick. They all have your signature on them. The incorporation papers. The silent partner agreements with other investors."

That's why Simon had spread documents on the table last night. He'd hoped Nick would notice his own handwriting as representative of PGI.

Nick thought back over the last seven years he'd known Gavin. What had he missed? Had he been so focused on the brass ring that was PGI, he didn't question Gavin the way he should have?

"Julius, I admit I signed everything Gavin put in front of me. I trusted him, and I'm still not ready to throw my friend under the bus. But I'm not guilty. I have copies of my investment agreement in my safe deposit box. I even have a document giving Gavin Hawk my POA."

Julius smiled. "Now we're getting somewhere. Where's the key?"

"In evidence? Detective Reedy questioned me about it yesterday at the county jail."

"Did Gavin have access to your safe deposit box?"

"Never."

"Did he know about it?"

"No. Although I did use People's Bank near his satellite office in Mobile. It seemed a good choice."

"The original warrant didn't list the safe deposit box in Mobile. Now, the State Prosecutor wants you to voluntarily reveal its contents. Is there any reason we shouldn't do that? My counsel to you is, if you haven't been forthcoming to me, tell me the truth now. If we cooperate, I believe the court will consider that at the hearing."

"Why doesn't Simon use my key and take what he wants?"

"He can't without a warrant. He's giving you the chance to prove yourself innocent, or—for lack of a better term—hang yourself. He could be starting to believe you're a victim, too. Understand you're still a suspect, but cooperating could help you in the long run."

"You mean like when an accused murderer says *I'll show you where the body is if you reduce my sentence?"*

"Something like that."

"But I'm innocent."

"I know this is a horrible place to be. I need to ask you to trust me to do my job. One of the investors, Frances Sweeney, lives in Mississippi. The fact the fraud was perpetrated across state lines, combined with the dollar amount, resulted in the FBI being notified. Feds don't like surprises. Even though tomorrow's Sunday, the FBI is prepared to make arrangements to have the bank opened and ask for their own warrant. Simon will be happier if I tell him we'll cooperate."

"I'll cooperate." Anything to clear his name and protect Angelina. "Julius, I can't believe they questioned my wife. They might even still be searching our home. When you leave, will you call Pierce and Laurie, and ask them to check on her?"

***

At the carriage house, Angelina thoroughly inspected the first stack of paintings. Magnificent waterfalls from around the world.

She'd visited each one two years ago when Nick's two-month trip to Baltimore stretched to three. She'd spent days at each location, taking photos and recording video. He probably didn't even know she'd gone.

In truth, unless he'd snuck into her old studio on one of the few occasions he was home, she doubted he'd seen these or any other of her paintings.

The corner of one canvas had been slightly damaged. The gouge would be covered by framing. Still, she'd have to disclose the imperfection to Mr. Fairchild, the show's facilitator.

She moved to the next stack, a set of eight, each showing a different, yet overlapping view of the same beach inlet of the Seychelles Islands

155

by East Africa. When hung in a circle, they'd create a panoramic view. In person, the sight had literally taken away her breath. The horseshoe-shaped beach contained sand so white it could have been mistaken for confectioner's sugar. The water, a study in a flawless transition from clear to turquoise to cobalt, and back again as it edged a center island of jutting stone.

She'd agonized as she mixed the colors, intent on perfectly matching the hues in her photos and video files. Success had come after hours of work and sparked instant joy and laughter, followed by acute loneliness. She'd had no one to rejoice with. No one to brag to.

At that moment one year ago, she'd felt the first snap of bitterness toward Nicholas. Was that better or worse than the numbness she'd felt today on the drive home from the prison?

In her purse on the floor behind her, her phone rang.

She didn't want to answer. The caller could be the police detective wanting her to come back in for more questioning. Or that horrible Darrin Simon, intent on intimidating her, or manipulating her, or whatever his game was.

She looked out the bank of windows into a blue Alabama sky streaked with pulled cotton candy clouds. Better to face the dragon than have it sneak up on her.

"Hello?"

"Angelina? It's Laurie Crane. Pierce's wife?"

She pictured Laurie's round, freckled face and her blonde-brown hair with short, straight bangs. She'd often thought Laurie resembled a typical college freshman rather than a pastor's wife and professional decorator in her early thirties.

"Hi, Laurie. Can you, um, hold on for a minute?"

"Sure."

Angelina lowered her phone. For the first time in years, she thought of her dad and his comments about churchgoers being nosey and flocking to catastrophe just so they could feel better about themselves.

She didn't need fake sympathy or Christian-speak clichés. Or to be questioned why she hadn't attended church the last several Sundays.

She could only guess why Laurie had called, as she and Laurie had exchanged only a few words since Pierce took over The Barn Church. They weren't close friends as Julie Matthews—Rick Matthews' wife—and Laurie were.

Julie and Rick. Of course. Knowing Angelina's husband was now in prison, if Laurie also knew of Angelina's history with Rick, she'd want to protect her friend and more prominent church member. Hopefully, Laurie would ask her questions, then offer a quick, generic prayer and hang up.

Angelina shook back her hair and lifted her phone. "Hey. Sorry about that."

"No problem. Wondering if I could come by for dinner."

She checked the time and thought of the microwave meals in the kitchenette fridge. "Well—"

"That didn't come out right. I brought dinner. I'd like to stop by." She paused. "Oh, I don't abide subterfuge and secrets. Look, Nicholas asked Julius to ask me and Pierce to check on you. Rather than subjecting you to a very busy two-year-old, I volunteered Pierce for daddy duty and snatched the chance to leave home alone and go somewhere that isn't the grocery store. So there. I'm about five minutes away."

Terrific. First, half of the Rowe City police department, then the State Prosecutor, and now her pastor's wife would know she moved out of her and Nick's home. Then again, why did that matter?

"Actually, I'm in my studio in the carriage house above the stables. When you approach the house, you'll see a driveway to the right.

Follow it to the back of the property."

"All right. I'll be right there."

She restacked the Seychelles set and listened for Laurie's approach. She heard the car door slam, Laurie's footsteps up the stairs, and opened the door as Laurie raised her hand to knock.

"I hope you like chicken and dumplings," Laurie said. "Because I made a mess of it."

"A mess?"

"Sorry. A bunch. A big pot." She blew her bangs off her forehead. "I mean we've got plenty."

She looked at Angelina without judgment, without a dozen questions in her eyes. She held a foil-covered dish like it was a chunky infant. In her other hand, she held an insulated bag, which she handed over.

"That's biscuits. Piping hot. I'm envisioning rivers of butter dripping down the sides and hope you'll overlook it if I lick my fingers."

The image of Laurie licking dumplings off her fingers further caught Angelina off-guard.

"We can sit over here." Angie carried the bag to the round glass-topped bistro table in the kitchenette.

"Oh, I love these. Pierce and I had a table almost exactly like this in our first tiny apartment." She pulled large disposable plates and plastic silverware from her large purse. "I didn't want you to have to clean up. I figure you've got enough on your plate, so to speak."

She prayed a simple prayer over the food and served Angie.

"I can't remember the last time I had a home-cooked meal," Angelina said. "I'm a terrible cook."

She hadn't meant to say that aloud, yet found she was more uncomfortable hearing her own voice in the space than the fact she'd actually said the words.

Laurie's eyed filled with sympathy. "I'm sure you're not."

"I assure you, I am."

She felt herself smile and immediately squelched it. For a moment, she'd forgotten about Nicholas, and the prison, and why her pillow and a blanket waited on the end of the couch.

"Laurie. This was kind of you. And thanks for being honest about why you're here. But you've done your duty checking on me. Julius already filled me in. You've no obligation to stay and—"

She'd almost said *pretend to care about me.*

She pasted on what she knew from her beauty pageant competitions to be a perfect smile. "Thanks for coming."

"I'm not here out of duty. I'm here to offer friendship and a listening ear if you need it. If Kay and Daniel weren't out of town, I dare say they would have beaten me here."

At the mention of Kay, Angie swallowed against old, hopeful memories of having friends and feeling accepted.

"Your mother-in-law is a very special lady."

"Don't I know it? I'm not sure where Pierce and I would be without her and Daniel. She kept me from the edge when I was pregnant with Hope, and Pierce all but left me."

Angelina remembered a service shortly after Pierce had come to pastor The Barn Church, in which he said he'd recently almost walked away from the church and everything he believed in. He'd asked the congregation to forgive him and to pray for him and Laurie. At the time, Laurie had indeed been pregnant with their daughter. Angelina had envisioned them having the perfect life with the perfect, storybook marriage. So, she'd thought he was giving an illustration and hadn't taken his confession or his request seriously.

She lowered her fork. Laurie was a compassionate, obviously mature and stable woman. Pierce, a pastor, with Daniel and Kay for parents, and the support of The Barn Church's entire congregation—the perfect mate for her. Still, he'd almost single-handedly destroyed their marriage.

"This was kind of you, but I can't eat any more," she said.

She pushed away from the table, walked to the bank of open windows overlooking the back of the property. She picked up a nearby paintbrush and squeezed. It snapped in her hands.

She and Nicholas never had a chance. They'd been doomed from the start.

No, even before they'd married, their relationship had been destined for failure. She saw that now.

Angelina—who grew up with a domineering, philandering father and an absent, alcoholic mother. She'd been so young and inexperienced, terribly naïve, believing her fledgling yet strong love for Nicholas would carry them through trials and be the foundation on which they could build a life.

And Nicholas. A young man with no example of marriage and fatherhood. A poor, latchkey kid, who was smart and highly ambitious but had no clue how to stay connected to another person.

"The State Prosecutor questioned me today," Angelina said.

"Pierce told me. How awful for you."

"He thinks Nick confided in me about his investments." She shook her head. "I never wanted money and expensive things. I grew up with that. I know wealth won't satisfy a person."

"What did you want?"

"Him and his attention. I wanted him to think of me and spend his life with me."

"I think that's what every woman wants when she marries. At least, the woman who loves her husband."

"When he first started his consulting firm, we'd been married three rocky years. Setting his own schedule was supposed to allow him to spend more time home—kind of a new start for us. Instead, his time home shrank to less than what it had been before, and money I thought we'd spend on me traveling with him went into real estate—Nick was always looking for a great deal.

"When I graduated from art school, we moved here. Another new beginning that wasn't. If I had a dollar for every promise he made me …"

"That must have hurt you very badly. When I believed Pierce wasn't going to keep his promises to me, well, that's the worst pain I've ever felt. Worse than when my parents died."

"I wanted children with him. I wanted to make a home with him, have a family. Instead, he left me over and over again without ever looking back."

Angelina turned to face Laurie.

"I'm so sorry." Tears slid down Laurie's cheeks.

"So am I. I sleep here. I moved out of the house weeks ago. Being there hurts too much."

And she wanted to be alone. There, in the quiet of the small carriage house, with the smell of solvent and oil-based paint. She wanted to finish checking all her paintings and curl up on the couch and sleep. If she couldn't sleep, she'd paint.

Although she dare not turn off her phone. Having the police, or worse, the State Prosecutor, show up at her door would heap even more disruption into her life.

"I'm supposed to be preparing for my first art show in Mobile."

"Angelina, that's wonderful. I've heard the advertisements on the radio. Fairchild's Gallery in Mobile has quite a reputation." She scanned the dozens of paintings throughout the space. "This is an incredible amount of work."

"No kids, and really, no husband, remember? You and I have nothing in common. You must know I haven't attended a service at The Barn Church in weeks. I'm not active in the church. Your kindness is touching, but I'm sorry, you being here doesn't make sense."

"My offer of friendship was real. And I see I should've done it long before."

"I don't have women friends. I don't have any friends, really."

"I know Kay and Daniel would consider themselves your friends."

"Why would they? When we lived in Birmingham, I didn't keep in touch. Aside from a few months right after we moved here, when—once again—Nicholas and I were making a fresh start, I haven't seen them except from afar. I've barely spoken to them at church."

Laurie cocked her head. "Forgive me, Angelina. Didn't you love Nicholas even when you didn't see him?"

"Why are you so determined to, to, *connect* with me? I'm not friendship material. I'm not marriage material. I'm not even churchgoer material."

"Why would you say that?"

"Because God's supposed to be perfect, right? Anyone who can't maintain a relationship with a perfect being must have something terribly wrong with them. I'm not cut out to be close to anyone, deity or otherwise."

She lifted a canvas. One of a series she'd done of Paris after she'd traveled there alone, months ago. Each painting depicted a different Parisian scene or landmark as if the viewer looked over the shoulder of a woman who stood taking in the sight. The woman was actually her—long, dark hair flowing down over a red cape. She'd entitled the series *The Lonely Woman*, and she considered them her highest quality work.

She removed her wedding rings and laid them aside. "Nicholas and I aren't like you and Pierce."

***

She couldn't paint fast enough. After Laurie left, Angelina had been unable to sleep, so she'd set up a fresh easel. Listening to the rhythm of the cicadas, she swirled and dotted blacks, yellows, and grays across the canvas—a rare storm brewing over a barren desert.

The varied terrains of the world had always fascinated her. But deserts? They spoke to her.

Empty, dry, isolated. If the storm brought rain, it wouldn't be absorbed. The land was too parched, too hard. The desert would remain what it was by nature, a desert.

She added stones, sprigs of solitary grass, and tumbleweed. Hour after hour passed, her own words echoing in her head. *I'm just not cut out to be close to anyone, deity or otherwise.*

At dawn, she stopped. Her hands were cramped, her eyes gritty, and the painting about two-thirds complete. She warmed a bowl of Laurie's chicken and dumplings, ate, then fell asleep face down on the couch.

Her cell chimed, an incoming text. Sweeping her long hair behind her shoulder, she checked the message from her vet.

Godiva delivered around 8 A.M. She's fine. New filly fine, as well. Come visit any time after you return.

She'd forgotten about her horses. Godiva and her year-and-a-half old twins born when Angelina had boarded Godiva at Matthews Stables. There, the night of Zeus and Apollo's birth, she'd revealed her unrequited feelings to Rick. Embarrassed beyond words and worried about the repercussions from Rick's wife, Julie, Angelina had moved the horses to the never-used stables here on the property.

Now she had a fourth horse, another girl, and honestly, she couldn't care less. Having boarded them with Dr. Bohannon for her trip to Las Vegas less than a week ago, she'd already emotionally disengaged.

Pete hadn't expected her to have returned home yet, as she'd told him she'd be gone at least a week. Nicholas' actions might very well mean soon, she'd no longer have the stables or any home. What would Pete say if she called and asked if he knew someone who might want the horses?

She'd want them to go to a good home. Someone who would love them and keep them.

Rachel. Julie and Rick Matthews' daughter. She'd be at the end of her sophomore year in high school now and might be more interested in boys than horses. Would Julie let Rachel have Angelina's horses?

She took a chance and dialed.

"Hello. Matthews Stables."

Julie's voice gave her pause. She'd expected Rick to answer.

"Hello? May I help you?"

"Hey. This is Angelina Rousseau."

"Hi, Angie. How can I help you?"

She couldn't read Julie's demeanor. She didn't sound irritated or angry or even impersonal. Maybe Angelina had caught her in a good mood.

"I'm looking for a good home for my horses."

"Really?" Julie's voice lowered. "May I ask why?"

Call her a coward, but she wanted to keep the whole nasty truth about Nicholas private for as long as she could.

"Several reasons, some I'd rather not go into. Suffice it to say I've recently realized I'm not wired for long-term horse ownership."

"I suppose Rick might know someone in the market. Are you looking to sell them quickly?"

"There are four horses, now," Angelina said. "Godiva delivered a filly this morning at Dr. Bohannon's. Actually, I was wondering if you'd let me give them to Rachel. Unless she's no longer interested in horses."

"That's incredibly generous of you. I'm afraid she's not here right now, either. She and Rick have gone to Kentucky for college days at a university that offers equine studies. If you're certain, I'm sure she'd be thrilled to have your horses, although I will have to speak with Rick about it first. I know he'd want to give you something for them. I heard about your upcoming art show. I didn't realize you were such an accomplished artist. Congratulations."

"Thanks." It was true, after returning to Rowe City she'd shared her love of painting with no one, not even Rachel during all the time she'd spent at Matthews Stables. Just more evidence she tended to more surface relationships.

"Why don't I call you after Rick and Rachel return on Friday?" Julie asked.

"That would be fine. I appreciate it."

She hung up and felt nothing. No sense of loss, no remorse. Even though she'd thought she loved those horses as much as any human could love an animal.

CHAPTER FIFTEEN

They transported Nicholas to the bank the same way they'd moved him to the county jail—by van. A three-plus hour drive that made him think of his first trip through southern Alabama, when he'd gotten lost from the detours and stumbled upon The Barn Church.

Julius followed, as well as several other vehicles, one of which carried State Prosecutor Simon. No sirens blared. The officers in the front seats—whom Nicholas had not seen before—gave repeated instructions regarding procedure upon their arrival. Under other circumstances, Nick would have been bored out of his mind. But after spending yesterday evening alone in his cell, he was grateful for even this small amount of human interaction.

They parked. Waited while the others went inside. Still handcuffed, wearing leg shackles and sandwiched between the officers, Nick shuffled his way to the back employee entrance.

The door opened from the inside.

"A moment with my client." Julius spoke to Nick's escorts.

The officers looked at each other.

"I'll wait outside the door," one said. "My partner will be ten feet down the hall. You've got two minutes."

Julius shielded him from the officer in the hall.

"In a moment, we'll walk down together, accompanied by these officers," Julius whispered. "Don't stop. Don't engage in conversation. Watch me for a nod before you do anything, before you say anything, even if you're desperate to explain yourself. Do you understand?"

"Yes."

"Answer only what is asked, but I can't stress enough that you be completely honest when you answer. You probably won't get a second chance to answer truthfully."

"I've nothing to gain by lying."

"Remember that. And don't stare at the federal agents. I'm not sure they're human."

Nick nodded. "Thanks."

"We're ready." Julius spoke over his shoulder.

The path down was a familiar one. Marble floors, wide steps, and a sterile bunker quality.

Escorted by the officers, they bypassed the small private rooms he'd previously utilized when visiting this area and arrived at a large conference room that contained an enormous table. The two officers flanked the door, joining four federal agents and two bank security guards already present.

Darrin Simon stood beside Nick's drawer. "When you said safe deposit box, I pictured something smaller. I'm told these have space comparable to a small trunk."

Julius nodded. Nick took the cue.

"I didn't mean to be unclear or deceptive. It's simply a larger option."

"Agreed. Mr. Floyd, you may hand Mr. Rousseau the key."

The bank manager approached. "Hello, Mr. Rousseau. I'm sorry for your troubles."

Nick glanced at Julius, who nodded again.

"Thank you," Nick answered.

Together, they unlocked the drawer; Nicholas pulled it open.

The documents Simon wanted were in a manila envelope at the back. Nicholas reached for them.

"Gentleman," Simon said.

Bank security guards nudged Nick aside and lifted the drawer onto the table.

"Empty the contents, Mr. Rousseau."

Nicholas swallowed.

"Everything out."

He removed the envelope first, laid it before the State Prosecutor. He could barely make himself look at the other items but knew if he didn't do as he was told, Simon would willingly misinterpret his inaction.

Julius peeked inside. He stepped back, his eyes filled with questions.

Nicholas braced himself and lifted the long gold box on the top—a gift Gavin had helped him choose. He placed it on his far right. He did the same with the next item and the next until three gifts lined his end of the table.

Finally, he produced a leather legal document satchel and laid it directly in front of where he stood.

Without turning away, the State Prosecutor nudged the manila envelope to one of the federal agents. "Let me know if these match the others."

Simon lifted the leather satchel, then cocked his head at Nick in calculation. Everyone waited. "What will I find in here?"

Nick looked first to Julius for a nod, then met the State Prosecutor's gaze.

"Customs and tax documentation on all foreign gifts I bought for my wife. You'll see I disclosed each item and paid applicable taxes, although most items were below the limit and without penalty."

"Are these the only gifts you purchased for her?"

"No."

"So, there are others. Where are they?"

"I believe in my home."

"All are unique, I assume?"

"Yes."

"I bet you know where and when you purchased them, even how much you paid."

"That's correct. I can match each item with its appropriate paperwork."

"Two opened, one unopened. These belong to your wife, yet you kept them here. Why?"

Nicholas glanced at Julius, then set his jaw at Simon's smirk. The man knew something about Angelina, was rolling it around in his mind, savoring it like a fine, aged Italian wine. Nick could almost picture him fantasizing about her.

Julius cleared his throat. "Do we need to confer before you answer the question?"

Nick shook his head. "Yes, these belong to my wife. I keep them here because—"

Every pair of eyes rested on him. The starched security guards', the stoic FBI agents', even the sympathetic bank manager's.

"Be completely honest when you answer," Julius had said.

Why not? What good would pride do him now?

"These are gifts I bought my wife. At the time they were given, she didn't want them. I saved them for her, hoping one day she would indeed want them. Their presence in our home caused unwanted tension. I felt it best to remove them."

"Take it all," Simon said to his associates.

Nicholas watched as each item on the table went into an evidence bag.

"Julius, how long before I can talk to my wife?" Nick asked.

The prosecutor stared at him as if studying a puzzle, then motioned with his head. "Take him back to the prison."

Nick rose. Simon turned away, speaking into his phone.

As he was led out, Nick thought he heard the prosecutor say "Angelina Rousseau."

***

Two trips to the state prison in two days was bad enough. Being escorted both times by an officer to an interview room, even worse.

Angelina took a fortifying breath as she heard masculine voices murmur outside the dingy space. She feigned her default, non-committal smile, the one she'd learned to use in beauty competitions. She turned away from the wall of glass, pretended to search for something in her purse, and prepared to see her husband.

Simon and others would undoubtedly be watching, listening. To the State Prosecutor, their interaction would be like a reality show episode, to be enjoyed or picked apart.

On her right, the door to the interview room stayed closed, and she realized Simon might keep her waiting for a while to mess with her. Just because he could. Nicholas might join her in two minutes or two hours.

She turned to see Darrin Simon enter the room and close the door behind him. Once again, she met his icy gray eyes.

"Good afternoon, Mrs. Rousseau. Thanks for coming in again so quickly." His half-grin mocked her, and his eyes scanned her face and torso above the tabletop.

He sat, while asking the same questions he'd asked her yesterday. She even thought they might have come in the same order as if he were reading a script.

Now he stood again. "The last time you saw your husband, what was he wearing?"

Angelina startled. "Wearing?" She had to think. What difference did it make?

"A tailored black suit, a plum-colored silk dress shirt, and a black silk tie. He called it his Uniform for Success and often wore it to important meetings."

"That was over three months ago, correct?"

"Yes." He'd given her a quick peck on the cheek, mentioned Gavin and the airport.

"So, this important meeting—did he tell you where he was going? Who he was going to see?"

Now she understood this line of questioning. "Our attorney, Gavin Hawk."

"Did he tell you why he was meeting with Gavin?"

"No. I assumed to discuss his investments, properties, and business."

His phone beeped, an incoming text he read silently, then re-pocketed his phone. "Your husband requested a shower before seeing you. Of course, I granted his request."

The door opened. Nick entered wearing orange scrubs and rubber flip-flops. His curly hair was wet, in need of a trim. He wore handcuffs, and on his face were several specks of blood as if he'd cut himself shaving.

At that moment, she despised Simon for enjoying Nick's humiliation. Her love for Nicholas was all but dead, but she could never be that cruel to him.

Simon nodded. "I'll leave you two alone to talk."

"Thank you for this, Mr. Simon," Nick said.

"Sorry, but the cuffs stay on."

The State Prosecutor wasn't sorry, but at least he left. Although she was certain he would soon be watching from behind the glass.

Nicholas looked at her as a man might a rare treasure. She wished she believed he felt that way even when he wasn't looking at her.

Finally, he spoke. "Angie, I did what I did for us, for our future."

She remembered early moments in their marriage, the two of them dreaming together of what their life might be like in five, ten, fifteen years. All the plans and promises he'd pushed back time and again. In Nick's mind, the future was always, well, in the future. It meant nothing to her now.

"What exactly did you do?"

He hung his head. "I mortgaged the house."

"What?"

"And I sold my business and properties."

"When?"

"And I invested all the money in PGI—along with other investors—because it was going to set us up for life without me having to leave you to work ever again." He lifted his eyes to hers. "I was going to surprise you."

She wanted to slam her fists on the table. She wanted to scream.

She wanted to smack his face.

But she knew they were being watched.

Nick inched his bound hands toward hers. She pulled back, clasped hers in her lap, and steadied her breathing. If she didn't rein in her emotions, these minutes would be a live freak show, which would no doubt be talked about for years here in the state prison.

"Is what you did legal?"

"Yes. Although I see now I should have told you about the house so you wouldn't be upset."

"About the house?"

"You love it. You decorated it and filled it with everything you love."

"I don't love the house. I loved …" *You* she almost said and pressed her fingertips to her lips.

Stay on task. This isn't about how I feel. It's too late for that, too late for us. And he has no idea.

"So," she said. "You invested all your money with and through Gavin."

"Our money. Not my money, ours."

"I don't know how much time they'll give us," she said. "Quit picking apart the details and look at the big picture here. I need to know how the money was invested with Gavin."

"Why are we talking about this instead of talking about us? Angelina, how are you? You must have been so scared when I called. When you flew home and then came here for questioning. I'm so sorry for that. I begged them to leave you alone. Did they mistreat you?"

"Nicholas. Were you in business with Gavin and I didn't know it?"

"I don't understand." His brow furrowed. "You never cared about my business. Never cared about our investments for the future. Why all these questions now?"

"Because you were arrested. Because they're asking me about the business arrangement between you and Gavin."

He sat back. She saw the light bulb go on in his mind.

"I have to prove to them you knew nothing about what I did with Gavin."

"That's right."

"So my first priority is keeping you out of here."

"I've never been your first priority." The words escaped before she could stop them.

"Angie?"

She didn't want to talk about this now. She wouldn't.

"Look, let's set aside the part about us," she said. "Can you prove you didn't steal millions through PGI?"

She saw the shock hit him as it always did when the weight of a moment finally caught up with him. Hurt followed.

"You don't believe me, do you? You think I'm guilty."

"What I think doesn't matter. Does Julius believe he can prove your innocence?"

"He's taking my case, even though I'm not sure how we'll pay him. Unless you still have money in your account. We could use that. We could live on that while this gets straightened out.

"What am I saying? If you don't believe me, I don't have a chance."

She swallowed as she realized she might indeed be starting over, and starting over with nothing. Nick, however, didn't know she'd spent almost every cent he'd ever given her. Her most recent expenditure? Renovating the carriage house.

Should she tell him about the money, that most of it was gone?

Grief bubbled in her stomach like acid. Nick's freedom, and very likely their marriage, were about to end.

And neither of them would have anything to show for the last ten years of their lives.

Still, even if divorce meant starting over on her own, going back to living in a one-room apartment and more often than not, dining on boxed macaroni and cheese—she'd rather live single and alone than married and lonely. She'd rather live single and alone than live in a mansion constantly reminded of what could have been, swimming in bitterness toward the one she'd once loved the most. She could support herself with her art if she had to.

"I need to go." She braced her hands on the table and stood.

Nick stood, too. "Angie. Angelina," he whispered. "You're leaving?"

She turned away. Pressed her lips together in an effort to keep the accusations and questions inside.

Then she figured, *Why not ask?* If Nicholas went to jail for the rest of his life, if this was the last time she saw him or spoke to him in person, didn't she deserve a real answer?

"Why didn't you ever take me with you?"

"I can prove you had nothing to do with the business. Don't worry about that."

"No. *No.* No!"

She turned back and looked into those deep brown eyes with lashes only a girl should have. Into the face of the only man she'd ever slept with, ever loved.

"I gave you the best ten years of my life. I gave you my youth, my love, my time, everything. Why didn't you want to spend time with me? Why didn't you ever give me you?"

"Please say you didn't stop loving me. Don't leave me now, Angie."

She scanned his face, this man whom she'd once loved as deeply as a woman could love a man. She didn't have the energy to hate him and certainly wouldn't waste the time.

Still, the grief over what could have been—and wasn't—weakened her knees. So this was what the death of a marriage felt like.

Cold. And dark. And sad in your very bones.

"When this blows over, I'll be different," Nick said. "Even if we have to start over financially. I promise I'll be different."

She thought back to when he'd quit their jobs at Denny's without telling her. To when he'd talked her into moving to Rowe City, only to change that to Birmingham after the job offer at Jenkinsons. To all the new strategies and plans he'd suggested to address their marriage problems.

"Nicholas," she said. "Stop making promises you never intend to keep."

***

He'd lost her.

Nicholas watched Angelina leave the interview room, quietly clicking the door closed, and he knew—he'd lost her. He felt the severing as he imagined one would with the death of a spouse. The life that had pulsed from the nearby mate, their essence, their spirit had been removed.

Hollow, he thought. This Angelina was hollow and empty and looked at him without expectancy, anticipation, or connection.

How had that happened?

One of his skills was viewing a task or problem from multiple angles. He could assess a company's inner-workings from both macro and micro perspectives, find the glitches, the breakdowns, the minute yet influential details others missed.

What had he missed in his relationship with Angelina?

Stop making promises you never intend to keep.

He thought back over their marriage. He had to concentrate to forget who she was, how he felt about her. He had to work to separate how he felt when she walked into a room, the memory of the first time he saw her, touched her, from the Angelina he'd just spoken with.

After sifting through the emotions and external circumstances of each memory, he looked deeper. He replayed conversations and conflict. Her expressions. The way her tendency to reach for him at every opportunity had changed to crossed arms, then to clenched fists, and finally, to the clasped hands of today.

She'd gone from rebuttal.

To rage.

To resignation and retreat.

The truth stared him in the face: Angelina had never been happy in their marriage, at least, not for long.

Her smile—her killer, knock-your-feet-out-from-under-you

smile—had only appeared at random intervals. Was always quickly replaced by worry, fear, frustration, or even disappointment. And each instance had been farther and farther removed from its predecessor.

Why didn't you ever take me with you?

His mind convulsed with insight. She hadn't asked the question in relation to the possible charges he now faced, or the fact she'd been questioned, as well.

She'd asked because she'd needed to know how he could leave her so easily.

He doubled over in his seat. His stunningly beautiful, insecure Angelina had indeed stopped loving him because she no longer believed he had ever loved her.

To her, he'd told one lie after another. How could she think otherwise when his intentions, though good, never resulted in her getting what she asked for, even if he promised it?

If he could go back in time and talk to his younger self, he'd say, "Keep your word to her or one day she won't believe you."

Chapter Sixteen

"Nick?" He raised his head as Julius entered.

"Are you all right?" Julius asked.

"I just realized what I've done to my wife."

His attorney handed him bottled water. "I'm sorry. Drink. Try to relax. I've got good news."

"Tell me. I need you to explain everything." Although right then he almost didn't care what happened to him.

"I will. What's the whole story about why those particular gifts were at the bank? Why hide them in a safe deposit box?"

"I wasn't hiding them. I told you. I was saving them for Angie. The last several years, she didn't want gifts from me, especially expensive ones. She left one unopened, remember? We often fought about them, so I didn't want them in my home. I figured I'd keep them in a secure place, and maybe one day, she'd change her mind."

Julius stared at him, then sat back and shook his head. "You're serious."

"Completely."

"Why not use a bank here in Rowe City rather than People's in Mobile?"

"Gavin suggested People's for the mortgage. I figured if I needed more investment capital, I could use some of the jewelry as collateral. I had enough after mortgaging our home, so the jewelry sat there, and I forgot about it until now."

"You worked with Reuben Marx at People's. He processed the loan, correct?"

"Yeah."

"Did Gavin suggest that bank and Reuben?"

"Not directly. Although I think I called People's from Gavin's office. Funny, now that I think of it. The call went straight to Reuben's direct line. He said to come on down, so I did. Could Reuben be involved?"

"Possibly. Frances Sweeney used People's Bank to refinance her home and borrow against several of her assets. Reuben helped her as well, but so far all of the related documents look credible."

"I should have known something was up," Nick said. "Getting the money was too easy."

"Because your home is in your name only. Why wasn't Angelina on it, too?"

"She had no income when we bought the place, so she wasn't named on the purchase contract or the original loan."

Nick had neglected to add her name on the county records. If he had, he would never have been able to borrow against their property without her signature.

Again, he kicked himself for all he'd failed to do for her over the years. Angelina probably would have refused to sign, or at least made him think twice about it. Then none of this would have happened to either of them.

"So far, the FBI is unable to locate Gavin Hawk. To them, that could mean several things. One, he's hiding in fear of you, having discovered what you were doing. Or two, you and he were in this together, and he was smart enough to skip town. You get the idea—FBI agents get paid to be suspicious, and they are. Based on the information you provided them this morning, they're open to postponing the initial hearing to allow us time to prepare a defense. That is if you're in agreement. It means another night here, but it might help my efforts to get you out on bail."

"You think it's best?"

"I do."

"All right. I trust you, Julius."

"Great. Tuesday morning, you'll appear before a judge in a courtroom here on property. I'll be with you. The charges will be read. I'm going to push the judge to declare there's not enough evidence to hold you for trial. Brace yourself. I'm going to portray you as a clueless guy who happened to be in the wrong place at the wrong time."

"Thanks."

"Don't mention it." Julius smiled. "I'll commit our full cooperation and agree to them keeping your passport, in good faith. And I'll ask for bail to be set."

"Even if they release me, it won't be over, will it?"

"I'm afraid not. I think the investigation is going to take several months and hundreds of man-hours. Unless you know where we can find Gavin Hawk, and he confesses."

"We always met at one of his offices. Sometimes here, sometimes in Mobile." He didn't want to believe his long-time attorney, a man he'd thought a friend, would do this to him. But no one else could have. "Have they searched his house and offices?"

"No. And they probably won't any time soon. It's up to us to raise suspicion about Gavin. The more evidence we gather, the better. Let me know if you think of anything, any detail. Okay? Day or night."

"What am I up against here?" Nick asked.

"A long-term battle. I need to hire a private investigator."

"When will my wife's gifts be returned to me?"

"Slow down. I don't know about the gifts, but I'll ask. First, we deal with the hearing and bail to get you home."

"Where I'll live not knowing if I'll be arrested again, as until we find Gavin or more evidence, I'm still a suspect."

"Sorry, Nick. Right now, you're the only suspect. We have to prove your innocence."

"And in the meantime, I have no company, no income, a huge mortgage due, and probably no hope of recovering the money I invested with Gavin."

"Unfortunately."

"If I'm released, can I liquidate our personal possessions? Antiques? Collectibles?"

"Possibly. If you can prove they were purchased before the scam and prove you use the money to fund your defense and to pay living expenses."

By this time Tuesday night, he might be back at home with his wife. Unless a miracle happened between now and then, she'd look at him with the same disconnected expression he'd seen earlier today.

And he thought being in prison was hard. That look on her face, knowing she didn't love him anymore—he'd die inside every time she looked at him.

"Even if all goes well at the hearing, how am I supposed to pay bail?"

"We have to ask Angelina for it. First thing in the morning, I'll go talk to her."

"She'll have to pay to get me out?"

"Yeah."

Nick laid his forehead on the table at the unbelievable irony. Angelina would have to use money he'd made when leaving her alone, to give him the opportunity to come home to her now.

***

Angelina dumped half a bowl of uneaten cereal in the garbage. If Julius

182

hadn't called asking to see her, she'd still be asleep, blissfully unaware of the possibility the State Prosecutor might want to talk to her yet again.

She showered and dressed, then stood at the window watching through the morning haze for the attorney's arrival. Then she thought, *Why waste the time waiting when I could be painting?*

She turned to the nearest easel, set aside the incomplete stormy desert painting, and lifted a blank canvas into place. She left the background white, gave a light gold shading to the corners. Across the middle, she sketched in pencil. Two hands—one masculine, one feminine—met in the center, their corresponding forearms disappearing at the edges. Their fingers didn't quite touch. Their positions were opposite so the viewer would decide which one offered and which one received.

A knock sounded at the door. She dropped the pencil.

"A moment." She glanced out the window. Surely, the Volvo parked below belonged to Julius rather than a state or federal government employee.

She opened the door.

"Thanks for seeing me." He entered, carrying a briefcase. "This where you work?"

"For a while now."

He glanced at the couch where her pillow and blanket rested. "I wouldn't have known this building was back here if you hadn't told me."

She crossed her arms. "I don't mean to be rude, but what's so delicate it can't be discussed over the phone?"

"First, I have a bit of good news. Unless State Prosecutor Simon is lying to me, he's mostly persuaded you're not involved in the real estate scam."

"Since when?"

"Yesterday."

"He questioned me again yesterday."

"Yes, while new evidence was reviewed by his team. He received their report last evening."

"What new evidence?"

"Angelina, I know you're really upset with Nick right now. I know there's been strife between you two for some time."

"He confided in you about our marriage?"

"Not exactly." He lowered his voice. "I need you to tell me the truth about something."

"So you'll know if Nick is lying?"

"So I'll know what facts I have to work with."

She needed to do something with her hands. She walked back to her easel, added an orange shimmer to the edges of gold. "Julius, just ask. No matter the condition of our marriage, I won't lie simply to hurt Nicholas."

He stayed silent, looking at the floor.

"Oh, I see," she said. "Nick's not the one you believe will be hurt. Well, it wouldn't be my first wound."

"Did you know Nick had a safe deposit box?"

"No."

"Did Nick regularly try to give you gifts?"

"Yes."

"Did you accept them all?"

She switched brushes to one with a fine-tip point and lined the nail beds of the feminine hand. "No, I did not."

"Where are the ones you didn't want?"

"I don't know. He might have kept them; he might have returned them. I couldn't tell you. Why do they matter?"

"Did he ever give you a sapphire and diamond bracelet?"

She remembered how delicate it seemed and stopped her work. She couldn't paint and talk to him about this at the same time.

"He tried to."

"A ruby choker?"

"I handed it back to him."

"Do you remember a long, gold box?"

She placed her brush in a jar of solvent, wiped her hands on a rag. "I refused to open that one."

The last time Nick had returned home from a long trip. When they'd fought over yet another unwanted gift. When she'd told him she didn't even want them in the house.

"So, they were all gifts for you."

The unspoken *as opposed to someone else* hung in the air between them.

"Yes. I was the intended recipient."

"And you knew nothing of the safe deposit box?"

"Is that where he put them? I didn't know."

"Angie, yesterday we put a serious dent in the prosecution's prospective case, but I need Nicholas out of jail and free to help prepare his own defense. I need him to think and work with me, rather than concentrating on surviving each day in prison. I need to know if you have the money to post bail. At the hearing tomorrow, I'm going to ask for bail in exchange for concessions Nick is willing to make. But I won't waste a bargaining chip asking for bail if you can't, or won't, pay it."

"I don't know how bail works. Can't the court consider the jewelry as an asset and use that?"

"It's not that simple."

"Even if I give my permission? After all, they're technically mine."

Again, he looked at the floor. "Technically, they're evidence."

"As proof of what? Our arguments?"

"Simon sees them as proof Nick would use whatever means at his disposal to get the money needed to invest in PGI. He didn't have to put them up as collateral, he was able to get the money without them, but he was willing to. It goes to motive and shows his determination. It's a strike against Nick, and you. One of Simon's theories is you told Nick to use them to secure the loan."

"Which makes me what, an accomplice?"

"The official charge would probably be that of a co-conspirator."

"So, I won't be cleared of all suspicion unless Nick is."

"Something like that."

"And you need Nick out of prison and available twenty-four-seven to prove his innocence, and therefore mine, as well."

"Yes. And I'll have to hire a private investigator, as the state is so focused on Nick—and you—I don't believe they're looking at anyone else."

"Then, as usual, I really don't have a choice, do I?" She turned back to her painting. "Go away, Julius. Tell your client I'll post his bail tomorrow if necessary."

"I'm sorry." He walked to the door.

"Julius? What was in the gold box?"

He handed her a picture from his briefcase. "This multi-layered necklace with a very large blue diamond. I'm told it's valued at about one million."

She remembered a younger Nick, standing in a cheap hotel room and making promises on their first night together. *I'll buy you expensive jewelry. A dozen new necklaces to wear all at one time, like you like to do.*

She gave him back the photo. "Call me after the hearing."

Julius left. She heard him tromp down the metal stairs, heard his car drive away.

She chose silver, then blue, and traced the edges of a multi-layered necklace dangling between the hands, its blue stone turned into the light.

<h1 style="text-align:center">CHAPTER SEVENTEEN</h1>

Nick was going home.

Five days later than he'd expected. Unsure if he'd get to keep his limited freedom, while he tried to convince Angie of his innocence and begged her not to end their marriage.

As he sat in his cell waiting while the appropriate paperwork was processed, his predicament seemed so unreal, he expected to wake on a plane to find the day was last Friday, and he'd not yet landed in Alabama.

Now, the officer opened the main door from this block of cells with the customary *buzz*. Nick thought that might be one of the most beautiful sounds he'd ever heard.

They walked to what looked like an old-fashioned teller window, complete with visible black lines running through the glass. Bulletproof?

The officer signed for a plastic bag full of Nick's belongings and escorted him to a nearby table.

"Go through it, Mr. Rousseau. Check off the list, make sure everything's in there."

"My luggage?"

"Guess that wouldn't have fit in a bag, huh? Eloise!" He called to the woman behind the counter. "We got his luggage back there?"

"Come get it. It's standing in here by the door. I'll buzz you through."

While the officer retrieved his luggage, Nicholas dumped the bag's contents onto the table. His clothing. Wallet, watch, cell phone. Half a package of mints.

His wedding ring. He slipped it on, then shoved the rest back into the bag.

The officer returned. "You can change in the restroom there. Send your scrubs and sandals down the chute."

Nicholas entered the restroom and closed the door behind him. He hadn't had a private bathroom moment since last Friday.

Come to think of it, normal privacy—no, anonymity—might soon be a thing of the past. Until now, both the State Prosecutor and the FBI had kept Nick's involvement and the investigation a secret. But today's hearing would be a matter of public record. Soon, Nick might be contacted by the media to "give his side of the story." Julius had urged him to make no statements. Not to watch the news or pay any attention to the outside world.

So Nick changed quickly into his wrinkled suit and dress shirt, his dirty socks, and joined the officer.

"If it's all there, sign the inventory sheet and give it to me."

They rode the elevator down to street level. The doors opened.

Pierce greeted him with a handshake. "Julius said you could use a ride. Hope you don't mind sharing the backseat with a two-year-old."

"I don't mind. I'm grateful to be going home."

Even though he didn't know what he'd find when he got there.

***

"Ree-ries! Ree-ries!" Hope yelled from her car seat beside Nick in the back of the car.

Laurie turned to Pierce. "Hear that? That's Hope-speak for French Fries. She's already learned about the beauty of the drive-thru. If she yells that, give in. The battle's not worth fighting."

"We're getting pretty close to supper," Pierce said. "Hey, Nick.

Should we grab a couple of pizzas and take them with us?"

"Pee-zup," Hope said.

"That's probably a good idea," Nick said. "My phone battery's dead. Maybe give Angelina a heads-up we're bringing food and what time we'll be there."

Laurie ordered pizza. "Done. I'll text Angelina."

They neared Rowe City and passed the bright red water tower. Pierce slowed as he drove around the city square, past the courthouse and Benson's Hardware, past the Downtown Diner.

At that moment, Nick wished he could walk the street hand-in-hand with Angelina.

"Laurie, you went to see Angelina on Saturday?"

"I did."

"How was she?"

"Not knowing her very well, I'd say she was reserved and sad. Skeptical about me being there. Pierce, here's the pizza place."

They picked up supper and continued on. The quaint town gave way to residential housing and a two-lane highway. Then, frame houses set back off the road and surrounded by fields. Fencing lined the street on both sides, sectioning off dormant farmland.

"Peez-up. Peese. Peez-up."

"Just a minute, Hope." Laurie pulled a cup with a curved straw out of a diaper bag. "Nicholas, will you hand this to her?"

"Sure thing."

He gave the baby the drink. Hope gulped it down.

"If you don't mind my asking, how long have you two been married?"

"Over nine years," Laurie said.

"You ever had real trouble? A crisis you thought might end it all?"

In the front seat, Pierce and Laurie exchanged a look.

"I think every marriage does." Pierce glanced at him in the rearview mirror. "Including ours."

"I think Angelina's going to leave me. I think—without trying, mind you—I've finally killed her love for me."

Saying it aloud left him feeling as if he couldn't breathe.

"I think she'll never trust me again. Never let me anywhere near her or her heart."

Again, Laurie's eyed locked with Pierce's.

"I think you should tell him," Pierce said.

"I don't know," Laurie half-whispered. "She didn't say it in confidence, but … Nick, after all you've been through the last few days, I can't stand the thought of you being blind-sided again."

"Did she already file for divorce?" His lips went numb on the words.

"Not that I know of. But she did move out of your home. Apparently, she's been living in the carriage house for a while."

Hadn't she mentioned renovating the space to use for an art studio? He'd listened in passing, remembered seeing for all of two seconds the loft-like, long, open room. It had been full of bugs and dust and cobwebs. Maybe that's what she'd done with some of the money he'd given her to spend last year.

"I think I've broken almost every promise I ever made to her. Except fidelity. I've never been unfaithful."

Although looking back, he hadn't exactly been faithful, either.

He thought back to the morning's hearing in the bland beige and wooden room. Much smaller, much less grand than any courtroom he'd seen on a television show or movie. Hearing the prosecutor's accusations, then Julius' defense statements, while Nick sat listening to the results of his bad decisions. If his behavior in his marriage were under the same scrutiny he'd endured since being arrested and during the hearing, would he even try to defend himself?

"Can a couple rebuild when they've messed up ten years of marriage?"

Pierce slowed and turned in at Nick's driveway. He stopped and looked back at Nick.

"My parents would say marriage seldom works well without both spouses listening to God. I'm inclined to agree. And I'd add, listening to God and being obedient can be the hardest thing you'll ever do, even when you love someone. There are those who keep score. Those who suffer in silence. Those who keep trying, then one day wake up and believe they have nothing else to give."

"I think that last one's Angelina. Partly, anyway."

He surveyed the fenced pastures, the slope of land to the pines. He'd risked it all, might have lost it all, including his wife.

"Nick, would you describe yourself as a practicing, growing believer?" Pierce pulled forward down the long driveway.

Nick shrugged. "No. It's like every promise I made to Angie. I'd start out consistent, get distracted or committed elsewhere, and stop. I never stuck to faith or any of the things I knew I needed to do to know God and grow spiritually."

"Then that's where you start," Pierce said. "Right now, above all else, you need God's wisdom. To know what to do for yourself and for Angelina. Whatever your first instinct is, don't follow it unless you know that's what God wants you to do."

"My relationship with Angie is completely broken. No magic formula is going to repair it."

"It's not a magic formula," Laurie said. "Asking God for wisdom and being obedient is the only way you'll have a hope of sowing good things into your marriage."

"Hope! Hope!" The toddler beside him obviously recognized her name.

"Yes, that's my girl, Hope." Laurie reached back and took her child's cup. "Angelina texted me back. She'll meet us at the main house."

"Can you guys stay for a bit?"

"If you want us to," Laurie said.

Nick remembered when he'd come home for their seventh anniversary, and Angelina's prickly demeanor had made him feel unwelcome and unwanted. *Cut back your work. Sell some assets. Give her you.*

The gentle thought had come so quietly, he'd easily brushed it aside, telling himself he had to make money first. There would always be time to do all the things Angie wanted him to do with her. He'd had no clue ignoring that Voice would lead him where he was today.

***

Angelina walked the lane to the main house. She wanted to keep her space exactly that—hers. She didn't want Laurie or Pierce, or especially Nick, plopping down and staying until they were good and ready to leave. So, rather than inviting them all to join her, she was going to them.

You're paranoid, she thought. Always expecting to be left behind or left out. Yet no one could argue with her experiences.

Yes, Laurie had seemed nice enough on Saturday, but Pierce hadn't been around. Laurie could change in a second, especially if she felt threatened by Angelina.

She pulled the collar of her jacket tighter around her neck against the evening's gentle breeze. In the flickering twilight under the canopy of pine trees, a squirrel scurried across the ground in front of her. For safety's sake, she removed a flashlight from her jacket pocket, scanned the earth around and ahead of her. Snakes shouldn't be wandering; the night air was too cold for them. Still, one couldn't be too careful in the south.

She approached the front door and realized she hadn't brought her keys. She rang the doorbell.

Nick answered. She could tell by the look on his face he wanted to reach for her but chose not to. Because Pierce and Laurie were here? Or because he knew she wouldn't want him to?

"I didn't have Julius call you to come get me today because I figured you didn't want to be alone with me. I asked Pierce and Laurie to stay, but I can ask them to leave if you don't want them here."

"It's fine." Honestly, she didn't want to be alone with him.

He opened the door wider. "It's chilly out there. Come in from the cold."

She stepped into the two-story foyer, stopped, and braced her heart. She hadn't been inside since mid-November. Seeing the glossy floor, the ivory damask-covered walls, the twin Louis XVI secretaries, and the carefully selected artwork was more a shock than she'd expected. She couldn't begin to count the hours or dollars she'd spent with Rita creating the perfect balance of light and dark, new and old.

Avoiding his gaze, she entered the formal dining area, complete with three-tiered chandelier and custom ceiling medallion she'd designed. She proceeded to the kitchen. She'd chosen the hand-scraped floors, French Country cabinets, and hardware with a dark patina. *Ignore it,* she thought. *Ignore it all.*

Nick followed. "That burnt smell is because I turned on the heat."

"As opposed to because I cooked."

This was how she'd play it. Simply be cordial to all, keep him at arm's length, keep her walls intact.

She wouldn't be cruel, couldn't be. She'd be upbeat and pithy and treat him as if he were a somewhat likeable acquaintance. She'd be polite and mature. One of those people who bragged about having an amicable break-up or divorce.

"Laurie, you're feeding me twice today," she said. "I finished off your chicken and dumplings at lunch. Now you've brought me pizza."

Angelina took a plate from a stack beside the pizza boxes on the large island and served herself. She sat at their oversized table.

Pierce entered carrying Hope. "Someone's diaper is changed, and she's ready to eat." He handed the child to Laurie. "I'll be double-bagging this one; we'll take it home to throw it away."

"That bad, huh?" Laurie asked.

"It's ripe." He looked at Nick. "Okay if I wash my hands in the kitchen sink?"

"You never ask me that at home," Laurie said.

"We're not at home, are we?"

"This kitchen's too elegant for that," Laurie said. "There's a perfectly good powder room back in the direction you came from. Go use it."

Angelina motioned with her head. "Compromise. There's a butler's pantry with a sink right there. Nick, show him."

Her husband looked both startled she'd spoken directly to him and chagrined, as he obviously hadn't remembered the swinging door behind him or what it concealed.

She almost felt sorry for him, her clueless, embarrassed, absent-minded professor of a husband. Brilliant in all things beyond their house and marriage. Completely inept at long-term bonding and love.

Pierce followed Nick into the pantry. Laurie carried Hope to the table and sat across from Angelina with the child on her lap.

"Peez-up."

"Yes, pizza." Laurie tore pieces of crust into small bites and laid them on a plastic plate she'd obviously brought with her. "On Hope's plate."

Hope reached for Laurie's pizza. Laurie turned, making it more difficult for Hope to reach Laurie's food.

"No, ma'am. This is Hope's plate." She pointed. "Hope's plate. Now you eat."

Hope obeyed.

Angelina felt a twinge of sadness at not yet being a mother. No, she wouldn't dwell on that disappointment. With Nicholas gone all the time, if they'd had children, she would have basically been stuck being a single parent. Not to mention he knew less about being a father than she knew about being a mother. How awful life would have been for any child they might have had.

Nick and Pierce returned, brought their plates and the pizza boxes to the table. Pierce sat beside Laurie. Thankfully, Nicholas left an open seat between himself and Angelina.

As Pierce prayed over their food, she stared at the table. Then, they ate.

Angie felt her emotional strength weaken. She couldn't sit here much longer with Nicholas near and the perfect family—everything she'd wanted—staring right at her.

"Obviously, I posted bond." She looked at Nick. "Julius explained some of the legal aspects of the investigation to me. Maybe you could fill me in on the rest? About the house and our finances?"

Nick looked at Pierce and Laurie, then at Angelina, his concern obvious.

"I don't care if they know." She looked away from those brown eyes she used to lose herself in.

"For now the charges are dropped," Nick said. "That doesn't mean new charges won't be filed. I could be arrested again. I'm not allowed to leave the county on my own while I work with Julius to figure out what really happened. As far as our finances, the mortgage is paid through the end of the month, which is another few weeks. Unfortunately, I borrowed more than the actual value."

She looked at the ceiling. "Oh, Nicholas."

"I'm sorry, Angie. I thought I was providing for our future—"

"You always thought you were providing for our future." She took a breath. "What's done is done. What are our options?"

"Julius verified we can sell some personal possessions in an effort to keep our home. And to pay my defense costs."

"You mean sell our furniture and other belongings to hold on to a building. A structure you hardly ever visited, let alone lived in, and one I no longer want."

"I'm sorry."

She raised both hands at him. "Stop. Apologies help nothing and are unnecessary at this point."

"No, they're not. I owe you hundreds of them."

"It's too late, okay? Sorry, Pierce and Laurie, this is what people who don't have a healthy marriage sound like."

"Da-da-da." Hope lunged at her father; Pierce took his daughter from Laurie.

"Angelina," Nick said. "I know what the house means to you. You spent months decorating, working with Rita to get every room just so. That I've jeopardized it all is breaking my heart."

Keep calm, she thought. *Keep calm.*

"I don't care about this house like I used to." She paused as the implied *I don't care about anything or anyone like I used to* hung in the air. "So, we need to sell everything to be able to pay Julius and probably a private investigator, as you try to prove your innocence."

And, consequently, hers.

"I'll call Rita," Angie said. "I don't know how quickly she'll get back to me—she's on her honeymoon—but she'll know how to find buyers. Laurie, are you available starting tomorrow to help me catalog everything? Not as a favor, I'll hire you."

"Tomorrow? I am in-between clients right now. Pierce, can you keep Hope?"

"Sure."

"I'll be here," Laurie said. "If you're sure. Rita's work is amazing. I hate to help you dismantle it all."

"We don't have a choice," Angelina said.

"My in-laws get back tomorrow evening. I'm sure they'll be happy to babysit most mornings after that."

"Great. Rita might want to purchase specific pieces or have clients who would want them. We won't get anywhere near what I paid for them, but if we take the time to catalog and authenticate the finer pieces, we'll get more than we would otherwise."

Hope lunged again. Nicholas jumped, going down on one knee to keep her from falling to the floor. She climbed into his arms, rested her blonde, curly head on his chest, and blinked her big blue eyes up at him.

"Cup," she said.

"That child's memory is too good," Laurie said. "She'll want one every time she sees you now."

"All I did in the car was hand it to her," Nick said.

"It only takes one time." Laurie gathered her daughter, carried her to the diaper bag sitting on the counter, then refilled her cup at the refrigerator. "Here, baby."

Angelina froze. She'd never seen Nicholas interact with a baby.

Maternal longing rose inside her heart and spilled out. Over the years she'd kept the desire deep inside, acknowledging it only when she thought she had Nick's full attention.

She had that now, but only because his newest plan was ruined, his business gone.

He moved back to sit two chairs down from her, and she smelled him. And somehow, she instantly knew what their child could have looked like—and if they'd had a boy, would smell like.

Anger surged, spiking her heart rate. Until this moment, she'd been looking backward through a filter of constant waiting. Only back at what they hadn't done, what she'd lost back then.

But Nicholas hadn't taken a mere ten years of her life. No. He'd taken from her what could be.

The future anniversaries and holidays. The future children who would have sat at this table and played in this house, then left it to start their own lives. A future where she and Nick grew old together, then looked back on their lives and reminisced at how much they meant to each other.

The pain blasted through her.

She rose too quickly, nearly knocking over her chair, and stumbled. Nick grabbed her elbow.

"Don't touch me!"

Her gaze locked with Laurie's. The sympathy and compassion she saw there unraveled the seam of her tightly woven cocoon.

"Do you know what it's like to have a man marry you, then only visit you, spend time with you, when he's not otherwise occupied? To have him not only promise to build a life with you, but plan it. Agree with you. Say he wants the exact same things as you, and he wants them with you.

"But he makes you wait and wait until that becomes second nature to you. What do you do with all those plans? You wait for them. What do you do with all your pent up needs for companionship and love? For someone to listen and share? To even touch you? You tell yourself to wait. Because that's what you've been trained to do. Do you know what it's like to want so badly to have a child with the man you love you ache inside as if someone beat you?"

Tears puddled in Laurie's eyes. "I do indeed know what it's like to want a child with the man you love."

Angelina rounded on Pierce. "Did you ever hurt her that way? Walk away from her because you were focused on other things?"

"I did for a time, yes," Pierce said. "I'm ashamed to say I almost single-handedly ended our marriage."

"But it's all fixed now, right?" She didn't even try to keep the sarcasm from her voice. "You've got your happy little church and your happy little girl and your happy little life with your happy little wife."

"I'm sure it looks that way to you," Laurie said. "I can see why it does."

"What's wrong with me?" Angelina beat at her chest. "Why won't a friend, a husband, even a supposedly loving God stay and be close to me?"

Shaking, she stepped back. "I have to go. Pierce and Laurie, I apologize for behaving this way in front of your daughter. She's innocent and beautiful, and you two are truly blessed. Laurie, if you don't want to come back here tomorrow, I completely understand."

"Of course I'll come tomorrow. I can be here around ten. I'll bring something for lunch."

"Well, you catch on quick. Nobody wants to eat my cooking."

"Angelina," Nick whispered.

She raised a hand. "Don't say anything to me right now. I won't forget my keys tomorrow, so if you have to go somewhere with Julius, or to pick up your car at the airport, just go."

"My car was impounded—"

"It doesn't matter!" Angelina swiped her hands over her face and turned to leave.

The cold she'd felt when she'd seen him on Sunday turned to dark ice in her gut.

The sadness tightened inside her, leaving behind misery. She couldn't imagine ever again feeling joy.

"Everything you said is true," Nick said. "But from this day on, it won't be."

"I've heard that before. How can I possibly believe you now?"

She scanned the beautiful, perfect kitchen. She'd finally learned what her dad had told her during her childhood—people don't change.

"When you wanted to move, we moved," she said. "When you wanted to start your own business, you started your own business. Everything you wanted, we bought. Everything you needed, we did. Now we're selling everything because you need us to. This time is no different than any other."

PART III

Chapter Eighteen

His wife left.

Nicholas stared at the empty doorway and wondered how many times Angelina had done the same—watched him walk away without looking back.

"Hope's getting tired," Laurie said. "Pierce, if you hold her, she'll probably conk out on your shoulder."

Pierce obliged while Nick and Laurie cleaned up the kitchen.

Laurie laid a hand on his arm. "I can't imagine how your mind must be spinning from the arrest, the conflict with Angelina, and having your home searched. Do you want us to stay while you—I don't know—check to see what's been disturbed?"

"That would be nice. Thanks."

Earlier when they'd arrived, he'd noticed the kitchen and dining room appeared to be untouched. Now, he led them back through those rooms, into the formal living room, the library. Those, too, showed no obvious evidence of disruption. Then again, how would he know? He'd barely set foot in these rooms during the past year.

Finally, they reached his office. Julius had advised him the original warrant had stated specific items would be removed, but other warrants could be issued at any time for other belongings.

As expected, his computer was gone. Only a dusty outline remained. The top of his desk was clear. The drawers, empty. His file cabinet, vacant. The heavy, pleated drapes across the rear windows had been opened to the fullest extent, revealing panes reminding him too much of prison bars.

"Nicholas, your entire house is a showpiece," Laurie said. "The woodwork in this room alone is positively stunning."

He raised his gaze. He'd never really noticed the intricate crown moldings at the ceiling, the thick baseboards, or ornate doorframes.

"I can't take credit. I chose none of it, and honestly, never paid attention. Angelina was trying to make our home nice. She probably thought if she made it nice enough, I'd spend more time here." He paused. "I didn't even pick my desk."

"Did she love this place?"

"I thought she did."

He quickly located two boxes buried in the credenza. One held the Bible Daniel and Kay had given them. The other contained several books on faith he'd read.

"I know what's wrong with me," he said to them. "Believe it or not, one of my recent clients insisted I take a personality test before interacting with mid-level staff. I'm a starter and a fixer with a twist of *if it ain't broke, don't think about it* thrown in. I start things but tend to leave non-emergency tasks incomplete. When I was home, I was always distracted with what needed fixing elsewhere. God isn't broken, so I don't pay Him much attention for any length of time."

"God's not broken, but you are," Pierce said. "We all are."

"I have started over so many times with Angelina and God." Nick lifted the Bible. "If I start again with God—for the hundredth time?—I still have to deal with this, don't I? I'm still stuck with the consequences of what I've done to myself and to Angie."

"Yes," Pierce said. "But don't forget, God knows Angelina better than you do. If you listen to Him, you won't cause new damage to your marriage, and you might be able to repair the damage you have done. God can redeem all, that's what the cross is about. No matter what we've done, God can heal and restore."

"That might not matter," Nick said. "Did you notice she wasn't wearing her wedding rings? In her heart, I think Angelina's already gone."

"She might be," Laurie said.

He might not get the result he wanted. He might still end up in prison.

Either way, he might be without Angie for the rest of his life.

"I see what I've done to myself, to Angelina," Nick said. "I don't want more regret. Even with no guarantees, if the only thing I can control is myself, this time I want to do it right."

"Your parents gave me this. God's Word is right there, telling me what to do, telling me how to live, how to love God and learn from Him. Since the very beginning, Angelina's told me how to love her. I never listened to her, or Scripture, or the Holy Spirit. I knew what to do; I just never did it." He braced his arms on the desk. "I almost can't stand this level of failure."

"Listen to yourself," Laurie said. "*God's word is right there,* and *she's been telling you how to be her husband.* Yes, you have two broken things—your relationship with God and your marriage—but you also have the tools to fix them."

"Hmm," he said. "I didn't think of it that way."

***

The next morning, he woke alone.

Even though Angelina's blanket and pillow were missing from the other side of their enormous bed, even though she supposedly hadn't been in this room for months, her scent surrounded him.

Curious, he went to her walk-in closet. As far as he could tell, her clothing was all there. A rainbow of the silk shirts she liked to wear.

Jeans—many perfect duplicates—hung together on a low rack beside two shelves of functional boots. He opened the tall jewelry armoire. Chains and charms rattled. She seemed to have left almost all the bracelets and necklaces.

Did she no longer enjoy jewelry? Had she changed so much, and he hadn't noticed? Or was there another reason to leave behind all these once-beloved possessions?

He showered, dressed, went to the kitchen to scope out breakfast. In the refrigerator, he found two eggs, the leftover pizza, and wished Angie was there, even to share a piece of burnt toast.

Carrying a piece of cold pizza, Nicholas went to his office. Figuring he'd start with what he most remembered, he opened his Bible and read John 15.

He stopped at verse four.

"Abide in me, and I in you. As the branch cannot bear fruit of itself unless it abides in the vine, so neither can you unless you abide in Me."

He continued through the passage to verse nine.

"Abide in My love."

He knew Jesus was speaking to those who followed Him, but the words were also exactly what he wanted to say to Angelina. Abide in my love. Stay with me. Stay in my love.

"Heavenly Father," Nick prayed. "I know I wasn't obedient in the past. Many times I felt You leading me to change. Sometimes I ignored the Voice. Sometimes I just flat told You *no*. Forgive me. Help me. I didn't know then the firestorm I was setting myself up for now. This time, I'll listen and *obey*. Give me ideas for showing my wife how much I love her. I'm determined to never again get distracted and forget You or her."

And he remembered. Their first anniversary. Angelina hurt and angry and—he realized now—embarrassed over sexy lingerie lying on the closet floor. *Put that brilliant brain of yours to work for us*, she'd said.

Nicholas laid aside the Bible and the half-eaten pizza slice. He licked sauce from his thumb and removed his cell phone from his pocket. He quickly programmed an alarm to ring at every hour with the message "Abide in my love."

If this kind of reminder was what it took for him to stay present, stay aware, stay engaged with God and—hopefully—his wife, he'd submit to using it every day for the rest of his life.

He returned the phone to his pocket, then, it rang.

He checked the caller ID. "Hey, Julius. Any news?"

"Not yet. I need you to make a list of anyone else you met with at Gavin's firm. Date, time of day, what you talked about, anything you can remember."

"Can't we ask them to check their scheduling records?"

"They're not talking without a warrant. Gavin didn't show yesterday or today—which I expected—so the place is in chaos. Document all you can. I plan to have the PI start tracking down things today. You good with that?"

"Yeah." He thought of his wife. "Angie might not be. Julius, I don't know how much money we have. I don't know how much she's willing to spend on my behalf."

"I already spoke with her and got a yes. She wants to be cleared of suspicion asap, before her art show. I'll touch base with you later today. Start that list."

Nick ended the call. Angie's art show. Honestly, if the detective who'd first interviewed him hadn't brought up the event, Nick wouldn't have remembered.

Dear God, I neglected and forgot and missed out on so many things that were important to my wife. How can I ever make them up to her?

The sorry-excuse-for-breakfast pizza slice caught his attention.

At once, he knew the first way he could show love to his wife.

***

Her husband was cooking dinner. She should have suspected he'd planned to do so, as earlier he'd borrowed her car and returned with groceries.

Now, the aroma of simmering, un-burned meat and vegetables drifted from the kitchen. Not once did a smoke alarm go off.

Show off.

As Angelina retrieved packing tape from the utility room, she considered flipping the kitchen breaker simply to mess with him, then decided against it. He might laugh and smile.

She'd have trouble keeping her resolve if he looked at her with his curly hair mussed, his dimple showing, and laughter in his eyes. She'd remember the good times between them, and she simply couldn't risk that because she'd remembered them throughout the night as she'd dreamed of him.

The joy they'd shared at purchasing their home in Rowe City. In the title company's parking lot, he'd actually picked her up and spun her around. He'd kissed her, and she'd felt like a heroine in a movie when the hero declares his love and the happily ever after begins.

The days they'd spent together in Gatlinburg right after she graduated from the art institute. Strolling the streets, playing mini-golf, and perusing storefronts of wood crafts, candles, and quilts. She'd thought they'd found common interest in mission-style bedroom furniture and artist Bev Doolittle.

Their wedding night.

The way he looked at her when they first met, as if he were amazed and speechless and didn't care he couldn't put two words together.

He'd smiled that disarming smile, laughed that slow chuckle, and said, "Hey." Just "hey." And they'd looked at each other for a long moment because neither of them had wanted to look away.

Nope. She couldn't have that.

No smiles. No dimples. No laughing. No long looks.

She returned to the library where Laurie stood cleaning and categorizing books by author and edition.

"I could live in this room," Laurie said. "The domed ceiling with wooden buttresses, the built-in shelves, the judge's chambers treatment on the far wall. Your entire home is a study in design and architecture. The flow from room to room, the color palettes, the high-end finishes. You and Rita did a beyond amazing job with every detail."

"Thank you." But, oh, it hurt to be there, surrounded by shadows of memories that hadn't happened.

"I really hope you get to keep this place. If you want to, that is. And maybe you won't have to part with all of your lovely pieces."

"Rita is sending someone to guide us through the cataloging process."

"We'll be glad she did. I've only done it once when I worked for a firm in Orlando before Pierce and I moved here. That task takes a careful and experienced eye."

Until now, they'd worked together without small talk. Now, Angelina took a fortifying breath. "I want to apologize again for my outburst last evening."

Laurie touched her hand. "You were hurting pretty badly. You still are. That kind of hurt can't be held inside. No apology is necessary."

Every negative thing she'd ever heard her father say about people of faith rushed through her mind. "I can't figure you out."

"Whatever do you mean?"

"You know I'm thinking about ending my marriage. I went

completely off the deep end last night—in front of your toddler daughter, I might add—and stormed off like a crazy woman. Yet you're talking to me the same way you did when you brought me chicken and dumplings. Why aren't you wagging a finger at me? Condemning me?"

"I only wag my finger at my daughter. And maybe Pierce when he acts like a child."

"And?"

"And what? What am I going to condemn you for? For being hurt? For wanting more from your marriage? For wanting to feel more loved than you have?"

"I didn't think you'd look at it that way."

"I had all those feelings back when Pierce turned away from me. So, what you'll get from me are sympathy and a listening ear. And lots of oohs and ahhs over your stunning home. And I might shed a tear or ten over you having to part with your marvelous things. I'll warn you—I don't merely cry over Hallmark commercials. I cry if I drive past a Hallmark store. Don't worry, tomorrow I'll bring my own tissues."

Angelina couldn't help but laugh. "Are you for real? Sorry. I didn't mean to be insulting."

"I'm not insulted. Look, I know you're still leery of me. But I think you're leery of everyone. Am I right?"

She nodded.

"Here's what you should know about me. I hurt when I see others hurting. Sometimes I absorb it too much, and God or Pierce, or both, have to remind me to keep my head on straight. Right now, God's directed my path to intersect with yours. You're hurting, so I hurt for you. If there is anything I can do for you, or share with you, or pray about for you to try to take away your pain, I'll do it. Providing it's not illegal or against Scripture. That's what friends do."

Were they becoming friends? With the exception of the days she'd spent with Kay so long ago, the weeks right after she asked God into her life, and a few other times at church functions in Birmingham, she'd felt alone for most of her life. She'd pretty much decided that was her lot in life. Could she be wrong about that?

"Is every woman at The Barn Church like you and Kay?"

"Some of them are. And some are like you, hesitant and on the fringe."

Hesitant. Laurie had definitely pegged her with that one. *On the fringe?* She'd have to think about that.

She only knew she didn't want Laurie to leave.

"Please stay for dinner," Angelina said.

"Oh, I don't have to. You're paying me; you don't have to feed me."

"No, I mean *please* stay for dinner."

Laurie lowered the book in her hands. "You don't want to be alone with him, do you?"

"No. I don't."

Nicholas knocked on the door. "Ladies, supper's done. Beef stew."

She met Laurie's gaze. "You want to eat in here?"

"You bet I do."

***

Nick carried dirty bowls and spoons to the kitchen, then leaned against the counter.

All day, he'd given Angelina space. He hadn't hovered, hadn't touched her, hadn't cornered her into speaking to him. Instead, he'd cleaned his office, talked twice with Julius and worked on his list, gone grocery shopping, and cooked supper.

The act of serving Angelina and Laurie—especially Angelina—

211

knowing she ate what he'd prepared and had enjoyed it, that he'd nourished her, for lack of a better word, brought a sense of fulfillment and joy he didn't remember having before. Giving her what she needed, even when she hadn't asked, made him so happy he wondered how he'd lived without this particular satisfaction.

Today, you loved her like I love the church.

In the past, he'd missed thousands of opportunities to serve her. Now, the desire to love her in whatever way she wanted, give her whatever she wanted, expanded in his heart, filling a place he didn't know had been empty and unused.

His cell chimed, an alarm marking the eight o'clock hour. *Abide in my love.*

What if for the next year, he made these two activities part of every day: Read, or study, or worship, or listen to a sermon—something to stay connected to God—and if she'd let him, do something intentional for his wife to show her how much he loved her?

How might he grow spiritually? Assuming Angie didn't immediately file for divorce, how might his marriage change for the better?

"Nicholas, the stew was delicious." Laurie entered the kitchen carrying her purse and donning a jacket. "I'm going home."

"I'll see you out."

"All right."

He watched her taillights disappear down the dark driveway.

"I'm leaving, too." Angelina approached from behind.

"May I walk you to the carriage house?"

"Why?"

"It feels wrong not to."

"I walked home last night by myself."

"I know. It's not about you being incapable, it's about my priorities."

"O-kay."

"Don't worry. I won't try to make you talk to me like I have in the past."

She raised her eyebrows. "Interesting you realize you've always done that. But I'm not the same person I used to be. You can't make me talk if I don't want to." She pulled a flashlight from her pocket to light the way and proceeded out the front door.

He stayed a few steps behind. Dry leaves and pine needles stirred in a gentle breeze, and the gravel driveway crunched under their feet. Cicadas chirped in chorus.

Close by, an owl hooted. Angelina didn't flinch, but he did. He was glad she didn't see his reaction.

They rounded a corner through the pines and oaks, into the clearing holding the stables. A motion sensor utility light activated at their approach.

"The light was a smart choice," Nicholas said.

He couldn't remember the last time he'd been back there and couldn't resist walking under the metal overhang and peeking into one of the stalls. It was clean, empty, and looked as if it had never been used.

"Where are your horses?" he asked.

"At the vet's. I boarded them for the trip to Vegas for Rita's wedding."

"Of course you'd have had to do that."

"I probably could've paid someone to come care for them here, but Godiva was about to foal again. I didn't want her giving birth alone, not after having twins last time. The vet texted me on Sunday that she'd delivered."

"Boy or girl?"

"A filly," she said. "He sent me a picture. She's gray now. She'll be black, but with a blonde mane like her mama's."

"You always wanted one with that coloring."

"Did I?"

"You mentioned it a couple of times."

"I'm not keeping them."

They reached the bottom of the steps.

"Because of my arrest? I'm sorry, Angie. I'm sorry you were questioned twice—Julius told me. I'll do everything I can to clear us."

"I don't want them." She paused. "I don't love them like I thought I did."

"What? Why?"

She looked off into the night. "I thought you weren't going to make me talk to you."

"Right."

He had about ten seconds tops before she went up the stairs. *Dear God, help me make the most of this moment.* "I'd like to give you something."

"We've been over this. I've never wanted gifts."

"I know. I know. It's not like that. Hear me out. I realized the times I brought you things you didn't want, I let my, um, anger and frustration at you ruin the gesture. I never told you why I bought a specific item for you."

"I know why. They were my consolation prizes for all the times you were gone, all the times you didn't take me along."

"No, that's not necessarily true. A couple of times, maybe, although I'd have to really think back to each time to be certain. Mostly, I bought them because I'd see something and think of you. Your smile, your favorite color, something you said you'd always wanted. Like this."

From his jacket pocket, he produced a small, carved wooden horse. Black with a blonde mane. She was perfectly proportioned, her head bent with a mischievous tilt.

"I saw her at the airport in Spain before flying home last week. From a local artisan, I presume. But she made me think of you, because, well, I remembered you saying you wanted one with these markings."

She continued to avoid his gaze.

"Please take her. She's for you."

"Nicholas, this isn't going to work. We aren't going to work."

"Thanks for letting me walk you here."

"No argument? No plan and promise for how this time will be different?"

"I know you can't believe you've gotten my attention this time, and you'll have it from now on. I'm not going to try to talk you into moving back into the house tomorrow or even letting me kiss you. I only ask for one thing: Every night, let me walk you back here and accept the gifts I'll have for you."

He backed up. "Think about it. Just consider it. You can let me know tomorrow."

He stopped. "And maybe go ahead, walk up the stairs and lock the door. I love you, Angelina. With everything I am. And I don't want you to say it back to me unless you mean it forever."

Chapter Nineteen

She'd stayed up too late.

Angelia's head pounded as she rolled away from morning's light. She knew she should have gone to sleep after Nicholas left, but the desert painting had beckoned her.

She'd let the skyline be and had worked instead on the desert floor, adding rifts and dips in the sand. She'd spent almost an hour on a lizard she placed on a large rock, his multi-colored throat bulging as he gauged the threat of the coming storm.

She opened one eye and spied the painting. The colors needed time to settle. She'd have to let it sit, let it breathe for a couple of days before she added more layers.

Her cell phone chimed with a text. *Would you like an omelet? – N*

Ha. After all these years, the man was really going to make her breakfast? Call her picky, but she didn't want burnt toast this morning.

She shouldn't let herself think this way, how nice it would be to have someone prepare her breakfast. To not eat alone.

To smell something besides smoke in her kitchen.

Eating an omelet the man prepared couldn't hurt her. And if—no, when—he changed back into the old Nick, she'd stay very far away, once and for all.

Be there in fifteen she texted back, then realized Laurie wouldn't reach the house for an hour. Angelina wouldn't only be near Nick, she'd be near him and alone with him.

Unless she carried the omelet to the library and ate while she worked. That's what she'd do.

She dressed in jeans and a long-sleeved T-shirt, pulled her hair back in a ponytail. She slipped into her sneakers by the door, grabbed her keys, and jogged to the main house.

She let herself in the front door. Inhaled deep, the scent of butter and bacon and yumminess coming from the kitchen. She went straight there, curious to see what else he'd made besides the omelet.

Pancakes. The omelets he'd placed on the warmer, while on the griddle, he flipped pancakes. He knew she loved pancakes. The jerk.

Two for two, she thought, remembering the figurine horse from last night as she watched the pancakes brown.

"Good morning," he said.

"Hi." She bit her lip against saying more, flexed her fingers against the desire to touch the damp curls at his collar. She knew, if she stepped closer, exactly what he'd smell like from a fresh shower.

She folded her arms. Turned away to set the table.

No, no, no. Danger, Will Robinson. He'll only be this way for a day. Two at the most. If she started counting with Tuesday, the day he came home, he'd be back to his old ways by tonight.

Yep. When he walked her back to the carriage house tonight, the metamorphosis would begin.

The thought made her sad. She didn't want to witness him changing back again. Then again, if Laurie saw it, too, she'd understand what Angelina had been up against all these years.

She watched him retrieve a tray from a large cabinet, arrange the food on plates like one might for a picture in a magazine. A glass of juice for each, and silverware. One place setting went onto the table, the other onto the tray.

"Enjoy." He carried his breakfast from the room, leaving her alone with her growling stomach and a plate of delicious food.

She ate. Expecting at any moment he would return and request a certain response. The Nick she knew wouldn't give her space. He'd smother her until he was assured she'd forgiven him for whatever offense, then slide back into whatever behavior had caused the conflict.

Before she realized it, she'd taken her last bite. No Nicholas.

She waited. Listened. No footsteps echoed in the marble tiled hallway leading from the kitchen.

Angelina carried her dishes to the sink. Rinsed and loaded them into the oversized dishwasher. She grabbed a disposable cleaning rag.

The doorbell rang. She walked back through the house and reached for the front door.

"Hey, Laurie—"

Lorenzo stood on the doorstep. Dressed in a Polo shirt, pleated dress pants, and men's penny loafers with leather tassels, he looked as if he might have been filming a Ralph Lauren commercial.

"Beautiful Angelina." His eyes sparkled with interest and appreciation. "How is it you are equally stunning in formal wear or blue jeans?"

He raised her free hand to his lips. She recognized the attempt and pulled back.

Still, he smiled. "Rita has told me of your troubles. We must prepare to sell your hard work here."

She stifled a sigh, wishing she'd known Rita had sent him. "Come in, of course."

She closed the door behind him. He followed her back to the kitchen.

"It smells as if you prepared a feast."

"Not exactly."

He stepped close. "Why did your husband do this to you?"

"I heard the doorbell." Nicholas carried in his tray, then set it aside.

"Nicholas, this is Lorenzo. Rita's brother-in-law—and I guess he works for her company. Lorenzo, my husband. Nick."

As the men shook hands, Lorenzo kept his gaze on her. "As I said when we met at the wedding, I introduced Rita to Thomas. I have worked with her for almost two years now. She got your message and asked if I would come since she is still on honeymoon with Thomas." He looked around the kitchen, then again rested his gaze on her. "I have seen pictures of your home, but as most photos, they do not do the subject justice."

She knew he referred to his comment in Vegas, about Rita showing him a picture of her and asking him to keep a look out for her at the wedding.

"If you continue through that door and to the right, you'll see the library," Angie said. "That's where Laurie and I started working yesterday. I'll be there in a moment."

"Then I shall go to the library." He winked at her and left.

Angelina let herself breathe. She risked a glance at Nicholas.

"Breakfast was nice," she said. "I really enjoyed the pancakes."

"I'm glad."

She could feel he was perplexed and fighting not to ask the question flashing behind his eyes.

And what could she do? Avoid being alone with either of them by hiding in the powder room until Laurie arrived?

He slipped the cleaning rag she'd forgotten she still held from her hand. "Don't worry. I'll clean it all up."

The double meaning was clear, and no doubt intentional.

The doorbell rang again.

"That's probably Laurie." She hoped it was. "We'll be in the library."

***

Lorenzo kept looking at her the same way he had in the hotel suite back in Vegas. As if he couldn't take his eyes off her and didn't want to try. Long, studying looks as if he were committing her features to memory.

The attention stirred her, but not the same way it had last week.

"I'll be right back," she told Lorenzo and Laurie. "I remembered some volumes in the nightstand upstairs."

Without intending to, the naïve romantic inside her fantasized about Lorenzo following her. Saying he'd thought of nothing but her since last Friday. Reaching for her with abandon because he'd felt the same instant, visceral connection she had thought she felt and could wait no longer to finish what they'd started.

Yet the image didn't shine. Rather, the edges were as tarnished and blackened as cheap jewelry. What had she been thinking in Vegas?

She located the books and noticed the fully-made bed. She hurried from the room. If she lingered and Nick found her there, he'd surely pressure her to sleep there tonight with him.

Something inside urged her to silently approach the library. Without knowing why she thought to do so, she went through the parlor to the side library entrance and listened at the doorway.

"You have an untouched, unforced beauty," Lorenzo said to Laurie.

"That's kind of you to say."

"I regret when Angelina introduced us, I didn't use the occasion to kiss your hand."

"Since I'm not sure how I'd respond to that, maybe it's better you didn't."

"Ah. You Americans. Always keeping your—how do you say?—personal space."

"I wasn't thinking of personal space. I was thinking of my husband."

"He would object to another man kissing your hand when he

meets you?"

"I think he might."

"But it is only a hand." Lorenzo lowered his voice. He murmured to Laurie.

"Excuse me a moment." Laurie hurried out, nearly walking right into Angelina.

Their eyes met with understanding. Laurie motioned her to the other end of the parlor.

"We're a pair," Laurie said. "You don't want to be alone with your husband, and I think I'd rather not be alone with Lorenzo." Her eyes widened. "Oh, my goodness, did you hear him? He really lays it on thick, if you know what I mean."

"I found the books," Angie said, grateful Laurie had no clue how terribly gullible and stupid Angelina had been in Vegas.

"I think I'll use your powder room. You okay going in there by yourself?"

"Yeah. I'm fine."

Angelina steeled her expression as she'd learned to do in dozens of beauty competitions and entered the library.

"These complete the set." She motioned to a stack near the window.

"You ladies have done well organizing the sets apart from the solo first editions. You have a larger collection than I'd envisioned. No matter, I'm certain we can sell them all for a very good price. I know a couple of collectors and dealers. Although we will have to photograph and catalog them. I brought a digital camera for that purpose. It is in my rental vehicle."

"I'll walk you out to get it," Angie said.

She needed to know. Although her instincts told her to be very careful, she wanted to be one hundred percent certain now she'd been one hundred percent mistaken then. Not only about his intentions last week, but also about him.

She purposely walked a little too close. Purposely let her arm brush against his as he held open the front door. They walked to his van—the type of vehicle he'd chosen surprised her—and he used the key fob to unlock the double doors. He opened them, and she stepped with him into the private alcove they provided, should someone look out from the house.

"You would like to pick up where we left off, no?" He moved to nuzzle her hair.

She backed away. "We're not alone. My husband's here."

"Ah. You'd rather indulge your indiscretions away from here, in secret."

"That's not what I meant," she said.

"Then you have forgiven him for not going with you to Rita's wedding? No more punishment is needed for Nick?"

"I wasn't punishing him."

"So you did want some fun while you were alone and in Vegas," he said.

"But you knew I was married."

"If you did not have an open marriage, why invite me to your room unless you planned to cheat?"

She wasn't about to admit to him how lonely she had been, or any other steeped-in-fairy-tales thought she'd had about him.

"We could have had a great time that night. I promise you." He motioned with his head. "I always rent a van when I travel to clients, in case I need to move items to ship. But a nice, flat surface can serve other purposes, no? Trust me, the risk of being caught raises the excitement."

She wanted to be disgusted but couldn't fault the man for correctly reading her signals in Vegas and thinking she'd be happy to see him here. Angelina knew Rita well enough to know if she had suspected

Lorenzo would take advantage of Angie, she wouldn't have asked him to watch for her in Vegas nor sent him here now. No, Angelina alone had put herself at risk in Vegas. If Nicholas hadn't called when he did …

A chill ran through her, giving her clarity of mind as if she'd been doused with ice water. This man was neither in love with her nor was he a piranha. He was simply shallow and open to sharing his bed with any willing woman. All she needed to do was keep their interactions light and on the surface. He'd consider her rejection to be simple non-interest and focus on the next possible partner.

"Laurie is a pastor's wife."

"No." His dark eyes flashed with mischief, then if possible, chagrin. "I have never had an American pastor's wife."

Well, that was good to know.

"She's my pastor's wife."

"Ah. I see. You returned from Vegas at your husband's arrest, and now find comfort in American religion and rules."

"I …" Angelina winced at the shame rising within. "I shouldn't have tried to find comfort in you. I'm sorry."

"Why?" He shrugged. "I would have enjoyed it."

***

"I'm so glad he's gone to check into his hotel." Laurie slumped into a leather club chair and covered her eyes with a hand. "I'm honestly embarrassed for him. I don't think I could have taken an entire afternoon of 'You have hurt your beautiful finger. Would you prefer I kiss it or find a bandage?'"

Angelina let out a laugh, as they'd both wanted to do all morning.

"You were playing chicken with me," Angie said. "Looking at me behind Lorenzo's back to see if I'd laugh first. That was not fair. That wasn't very pastor's-wife-like."

Laurie laughed, too, long and hard. She caught her breath.

"Oh, wait. I'm laughing so hard I hurt." Laurie's voice was high, and she wiped tears from her eyes. "Bless his heart, he has no clue how he sounds. Or maybe he does and thinks every woman he meets wants what he's offering. I feel bad for him. Or I will. After I stop laughing."

"I wouldn't have thought we could be friends. But you're fun to have around. And I mean that as a compliment."

"I'll take it as one."

"Can I confess something?" Angie asked. "For some mysterious reason, I believe I can talk to you, and I actually want to, if you're game."

"I'm game. Just please don't try to kiss my hand."

They broke into renewed laughter.

"I'm being serious!" Angelina said. "I'm having a moment, here. Maybe even a spiritual one, and you're being disruptive."

"I'm sorry. I'm sorry." Laurie straightened her face. A giggle escaped, and she bit her lip. "Go ahead. I'm here for you."

"I met him at Rita's wedding."

"I gathered that."

"Nicholas wasn't there."

"I knew that, too, from the fact he was arrested here while you were there."

"With the condition my marriage is in, I couldn't sit through the ceremony. Lorenzo followed me out and up to my room. To be honest, I more or less invited him in. No, I did invite him in."

As Angelina had hoped, sympathy filled Laurie's eyes. Imagine that. Laurie might actually understand.

"You must have been desperate," Laurie said. "I'm not laughing.

I'm not. I can imagine how his standard lines would have sounded to you right then."

"I thought—this is terribly embarrassing to admit—I thought we had an instant connection, you know? I felt so disconnected from Nicholas, so abandoned. Lorenzo was there, and I tell you in a manner of minutes I'd conjured a fantasy in my head like a scene from the best romance novel. Even his winks were evidence we were destined to be together."

"Oh, dear. You were in a bad place, weren't you?"

"You know what I see now? I was convinced I knew the truth about that man. I was absolutely certain I knew his heart inside and out. I knew he was the one I'd been waiting for all my life. I couldn't have been more wrong about him. And I'm starting to wonder if I'm wrong about Nicholas."

She shared everything he'd done that morning.

"I take it that's unusual."

"You bet. By now, after any disagreement between us he's normally asking me to commit to his new plan, making promises and extracting promises from me. I've never seen him take responsibility for damage to our marriage for more than a day or two. And he's never followed an apology with a change in behavior."

Angelina shifted in her seat and leaned closer to Laurie. Then she shared about Nick walking her to the carriage house.

"Isn't that a good thing?"

"It's freaking me out. He gave me a gift. I have a thing about gifts; I generally don't like them. He caught me so off-guard, I couldn't look at him. Then he asked that I let him walk me there each night and accept other gifts."

"Did you agree?"

"No. He told me I didn't have to answer him yet. He asked me to consider it. It's like an alien has invaded my husband. That's just not Nicholas."

"Maybe it is Nicholas without the forgetfulness and manipulation," Laurie said. "Maybe it's him when he's putting you first like you always wanted."

"How do I know which Nicholas is real? Which one is the true Nicholas? I was abysmally wrong about Lorenzo. This Nicholas almost seems as much a stranger. How do I know what's true and what's not?"

"At the risk of sounding lame," Laurie said, "I'm proud of you. Because you, my friend, are asking the right question. What is true? When I faced a near-catastrophe in my marriage a couple of years back, God continually directed me to Philippians 4:8, where believers are instructed to think first about what's true."

"I'm not sure I'm a believer. I'm definitely not a strong one."

"Have you ever opened your heart and life to God?"

"Yes. When we stayed with Daniel and Kay right after we first married. But ..."

"But what?"

She looked at Laurie. "This is when you'll probably stop being my friend."

"There's a challenge. Try me."

"God isn't fair. He asked too much of me. Nicholas is supposed to be the spiritual leader of our home. He should have grown and changed with me. But he never did, not for any length of time. Yet God always wanted me to forgive. To love him even after he hurt me, and forgot me, and neglected me."

Just thinking of it all, saying it all together like this, made her angry.

She rose. "Why should I have had to give first? Give all? Love first every time when he kept doing things wrong? I should have been getting more back."

"I take it you chose not to do what God asked."

"What He asked wasn't fair."

"You're right. God isn't fair when He asks us to love like He does. Constantly reaching, pursuing, and risking rejection is not fun. It's work, and it's tough, and very often, it hurts. I know it hurt me to do that with Pierce. But in those days when I had to give without receiving and love without getting what I wanted and needed, God taught me things about His love and presence I wouldn't have learned otherwise."

Angelina turned away, crossing her arms, drawing herself in. *Don't break. Don't crumble. She'll walk away at any moment.*

Laurie's hand rested on her shoulder. "Do you know God loves you that way? Enough to reach first? Give all first? Constantly risk your rejection?"

"I don't know how to believe that," she whispered. "Nicholas is the only person I gave a chance to love me long-term. When he didn't stay, I couldn't imagine anyone staying, especially a God who makes unfair demands. A God I can't see and touch."

"I think, now, you've gotten to the truth. Yes, your marriage has been a painful one. But it's your spirit that aches most. You've been longing for God. You're hungry for what only He can give. Here's something to ponder: Even if your husband had loved you well and grown toward God, if you'd refused God's leading and hadn't grown, wouldn't you have the same distance between you and God, between you and Nicholas as you do now? God's Word is true. We reap what we sow. You sowed distance, so you reaped distance."

Angelina closed her eyes and saw. Every time God had told her to reach for Nicholas. Every time she'd been encouraged to do what Scripture taught, to forgive. She'd said *no*, and had chosen distance.

"How can God love me now?" After all she'd done. After all she'd refused to do.

"He loves you even more than you hoped Nicholas would all these years."

"I find that hard to believe."

"I imagine you do."

But she wanted it to be true. Oh, how she wanted it to be true.

She took a chance. A huge, frightening step for her, and reached up to grasp Laurie's hand still resting on her shoulder.

It wasn't enough. *More!* her spirit screamed. *I need more love. More acceptance.*

She turned to Laurie and let herself be held. Let herself touch unconditional love from God, from a friend. Let herself receive comfort and support without judgment.

Warmth and light seemed to pour into her soul.

After long moments, she pulled away.

"My happy tears are soaking your beautiful hair," Laurie said.

"Believing God loves me this way isn't easy for me. But I really want to."

Chapter Twenty

Nicholas found the watch in a Ziploc bag in a rarely used side pocket of his briefcase. Bracelet style with jade stones in gold settings. The clasp, broken. He'd promised Angelina he'd have it repaired at the jewelry store where he'd purchased it in Birmingham. Probably three or four years ago.

Now he held it in his hand. Still broken.

He'd heard Lorenzo leave and had felt instant relief.

He'd heard the women laughing hysterically and had felt longing and even happiness for Angelina. Making friends was hard for her. Laurie seemed to be a great, if unlikely, match.

He put the plastic bag containing the watch in his inside jacket pocket and walked to the library.

"Ladies, Julius will be here any moment to pick me up. He's driving me to the impound lot to get my car. I don't know how long that'll take, but I should be back to cook supper."

The women looked at each other. Angelina gave a slight nod.

"I might leave before then," Laurie said. "Not that I don't enjoy your cooking, but I've got a baby girl at home who's getting cranky about not seeing her mama for two days."

"Will you be back tomorrow?" he asked.

"For a bit. Probably mid-morning like today."

"Good." Nicholas didn't want Angelina alone with Lorenzo for any length of time. He'd felt a vibe from the man he didn't like.

He looked at his wife. "Hearing you laugh made my day."

He left. He would have loved to have seen her reaction to that statement but wanted to keep his word about giving her space.

His phone chimed as he walked out the front door. *Abide in my love.* He stood looking back at the house, looking at the land with its white cross-fencing and winding driveway.

He stepped down and realized he couldn't go to Birmingham to have the watch repaired. It was in another county.

Julius pulled up. Nick slid into the front seat.

"I need you to look at a photo." Julius handed Nick his phone.

"Is this off social media?"

"Gavin Hawk's Facebook page. Cameron, our PI, says it can be a great resource when trying to find someone. Do you recognize anything in that picture?"

Gavin's lying, cheating, smiling face smiled at a woman. A long-haired blonde. He had his arm around her and held a wine glass in his hand. The background was dark and blurry and indiscernible.

"That's definitely him. I don't know the woman."

"He never mentioned a girlfriend? No pictures on his desk?"

"Not that I remember." He set the phone aside. "I wish I could remember something which would help find him."

"You will," Julius said. "When you least expect it, *pop.* You'll call me, I'll call Darrin Simon, and Gavin Hawk will be apprehended."

"You're more confident than I am."

"You took a hard hit last week. Still taking one, I imagine. How's Angelina?"

"I guess you knew she wasn't living in the house."

"I figured as much, after seeing her Monday. Pierce called and asked how he might best pray for you. He's big on praying for others. He credits his and Laurie making it through their big crisis to the whole church praying for them for months. He almost walked away from the ministry back then."

"I didn't realize that." Nick thought for a moment. "So Pierce would say, if you know someone going through a difficult time, someone who has a big decision to make, you should pray for them."

"Are you thinking of your wife?"

"Yeah. I know what I want, but I also know I've hurt her badly. Praying for her might be the best way I can love her while she decides whether or not she'll give our marriage another chance."

"I'm sure Pierce would agree with that. I know I do. And I'd add, do what you know you can to show her you care."

Nicholas remembered the watch in his pocket. "Do you know a good jeweler in this county who does repairs?"

***

Nicholas took the last bite of his supper—baked chicken and asparagus—and set aside his silverware. As he had for breakfast that morning, he'd taken his meal into his office, giving Angelina the option of eating in their beautiful kitchen, or any other room in the house she chose, without him crowding her or making her uncomfortable.

He closed the door. He wanted privacy for the next few minutes.

He knelt, another new habit.

"Dear God," he said. "I don't know if she will forgive me enough for us to start over again. She might not. I am finding comfort in talking to You. In listening to You and reading Your Word. I don't know if Angie's doing any of that. But I ask You to comfort her anyway. Help her heal from the wounds I inflicted. Amen."

Nick rose. The repaired watch was burning a hole in his denim shirt pocket.

He went to the kitchen, placed the leftovers in plastic containers, and wiped the countertops, repeating in his heart the prayer he'd just prayed. Amazingly, praying for her made him feel close to her in yet another new way.

A steady rain blew against the windows. As Nicholas turned off the kitchen lights, he heard Angelina making her way to the front closet. He beat her there, slipped his arms into his jacket.

His phoned chimed his reminder alarm—8 P.M.

"That's been going off all day again. Updates from Julius?" Angelina looked around him. "Would you hand me my jacket?"

He turned with her jacket in hand. "May I help you?" He held it out for her to slide in her arms.

She turned. "Thank you."

She adjusted the collar, and he couldn't help staring at her neck, her face, and into her eyes. He found the hint of fear, as a doe might have of a nearby hunter and something else that might have been hope. But he couldn't tell what she hoped for.

Love for her rose like a geyser from his core to his throat. *I love you. Forever and always and more every day.*

"You didn't answer me," she said.

"What? Right. The alarm on my phone. It's a reminder. For me."

Her brow quirked up. "Hmm."

"Okay for me to walk you back to the carriage house?"

She nodded.

"It's raining. Windy, too, I think. I should drive us."

She touched his arm. Even through his shirt and jacket, the contact with her was the most intimate he'd had in months. His chest tightened.

She'd reached for him. He couldn't help wondering if she'd done it out of reflex or because she'd actually wanted to.

"I like walking in the rain," she said.

He exhaled. "Okay."

Still determined not to push her as he had so many times before, he handed her an umbrella and took one for himself.

"Got your flashlight?" he asked. "Puddles."

"I've got it."

They exited the house. In the moonlight, the surrounding trees swayed amidst the gusts.

She shone the beam onto the ground. "I didn't realize the wind was so strong."

They walked as the wind howled and fought their umbrellas. In the distance, thunder rumbled, then growled. Lightning streaked across the dark sky.

"The rain seems to be worsening. Maybe we should hurry?" Angelina asked.

"Watch your step." The weather would shorten his precious seconds alone with her.

The rain quickened with a whoosh. Sheets of heavy drops caught their shoes and pants. Finally, they were close enough to the carriage house to activate the exterior light. Still, the heavy rain dulled its beam.

"This rainband might blow over in a minute," he said. "Head for the awning over the stable doors."

He cupped her elbow, and they jumped the water carving its way along the edge of the concrete. They lowered their umbrellas.

Angelina shook back her hair and raised her voice over the storm's volume. "If this doesn't let up, you'll have to walk back in it." She looked away. "Sorry, I didn't mean to hurt you by pointing out the proverbial elephant right here beside us."

"I promised you I wouldn't pressure you. I know you didn't say yes to me walking you back here, intending to invite me in. But you did say yes, so I hope you'll take the gift, too."

"Nicholas. I hope you didn't spend money we may not have."

"It's not new. It's a promise I made—I'm sorry to say I don't remember when." He pulled the jeweler's felt satchel from his pocket. "Let me hold the flashlight."

The bracelet spilled into her hand.

"I didn't remember having this. Where did you find it?"

"In my briefcase. No doubt I'd put it there, intending to take it back to the jeweler in Birmingham. The clasp works now. Julius knew a place that does delicate work of this type. I didn't have to pay a lot. I just had to wait."

"You did this today?"

"I did."

"I don't know what to say."

"You don't have to say anything, remember?" He grinned. "Believe it or not, this is fun for me. Giving you things and having you accept them. As I waited at the jeweler's today, I thought of all the times I'd seen you wearing multiple chains or bracelets. I found myself wondering if you couldn't pick one because you liked them all the same. And I remembered those round, hard metal ones. What are they called?"

"Bangles."

"Right. And the clink they made on your wrist when you raised or lowered your arm. I always liked that sound."

"I didn't think you paid that much attention."

"When I was near you, you usually had all of my attention."

"The rain's letting up," she said.

Now the drops pattered gently on the ground. The rain had brought a chill. She pulled her collar up around her neck.

"Angelina." He felt as if a stallion were galloping in his chest. "I'd like to do something I don't think I've ever done before."

"Don't ruin it. Don't ask me for anything after you promised you wouldn't."

"I'd like to pray. For us." He couldn't blame her for being skeptical and raising an eyebrow. "And for you. I'm sure that surprises you—"

"You're right about that."

"I know you must be tired. I won't take long. I promise."

"There's that word."

"You don't have to do anything except stay for another moment."

The debate raging behind her eyes proved he was both gaining ground and still had much ground to cover to win her trust.

"Do we have to join hands?" she asked.

"Only if you want to."

She kept hers at her sides as he bowed his head. His hands began to sweat.

"Dear God, thank You that I was released from prison, at least for now." He willed himself to breathe, his chest to relax. "Thank You for Julius, and Pierce, and Laurie. Thank You for being ready and willing to guide me through this uncertain journey, even though I'm to blame for the predicament me and my wife are in.

"Most of all, Lord, thank You for Angelina." He paused, grief and sorrow hit, then the words tumbled forth. "Thank You for whatever You gave her to cause her to stick with me this far. Thank You for her loyalty, for her artistic talent, and even for the parts of her that make her hesitant to trust me again. They're all her, and I know if she does open her heart to me again, it will be because she's completely committed to our marriage."

Suddenly his strength left as if he'd just run a gauntlet.

"Please show me what to do to help heal every wound I caused her," he whispered. "I was neglectful and far-sighted. I was selfish and careless. Worst of all, I didn't make sure she knew how much I loved her. For any parts I can't touch, I ask You to heal them. Please show us what to do about our future, and help us find Gavin Hawk, so I—we—can be cleared of suspicion. Amen."

"That was very unexpected."

"I surprised you?"

"Yes. This time in a good way."

"I prayed for you like that a couple of times today."

"Once you set your mind and focused, you always did jump in with both feet." She stowed the bracelet in her pocket and took back her flashlight. "That's all I can handle right now. Good night, Nicholas."

"Rain fell the day we married." Impatience to reach for her churned inside.

"I know."

"I miss you." *Wait*, he told himself. *Wait*. Not easy, but necessary.

"I know you do."

He watched her leave and recognized the pain of what he'd done to her time and again.

"Angelina, watch your step. Those stairs will be slippery."

Although the rain had now stopped, rather than immediately going back to the empty house, he stood alone under the awning, breathing in the freshly-washed air.

"Abide in my love, Angelina." He spoke to the night, knowing she wasn't yet ready to hear the words.

"Abide with me."

***

Angelina locked the door behind her. She placed the dripping umbrella on the kitchenette countertop and walked to the bank of windows over the horse stalls. With the break in the storm, the lane back to the house lay fully illuminated in moonlight.

She didn't see him. Not getting what he obviously wanted from her—a full conversation, more time, a touch—had he hurried away?

Was he already around the corner and out of sight?

Yet she felt him near. Because of the rain? Because her heart was thawing? Her love for him softening as the brittle ground had beneath the pounding rain?

Because the once naïve girl's heart inside her still clung to fairy-tales and stories?

As a child she'd often pictured herself as Juliet, Rapunzel, or Sleeping Beauty, watching and waiting for her prince. What she hadn't realized then, was those characters might have known their beloved on sight but could not have really known their men without living with them. Even if great love were involved, discovering who a person really was took time.

Otherwise, all you had was Juliet's musings. Rapunzel's rescue. And Sleeping Beauty's dreams.

The man who'd just prayed with her—she'd not known him before. She'd never lived with that man. Never been married to that man.

Was he real? What a twist that Nicholas' failure to be like her fantasies—unflawed and prince-like—had all but ruined their marriage, yet she had difficulty believing his newfound honesty and humility to be true. Even as she was drawn to him.

And it hit her: She'd taken a chance on him based on who she thought him to be. If she ended her marriage based on the same type of poor assumptions, she might make the biggest mistake of her life.

She needed to discover the truth about him.

He walked out from under the awning. Looked back over his shoulder and their eyes met.

He raised his chin, a clear signal to raise the window. She obliged.

"I once promised to cook breakfast for you on a regular basis, didn't I?" he called.

"Yes."

"May I make you an omelet in the morning?"

"If you'll stay and eat with me. I've eaten too many breakfasts alone."

He grinned, then turned and made his way down the path. If she were close enough, she knew exactly what his dimple would look like in the moonlight.

Nicholas. Her husband. The only person she'd let herself love. The only person she'd let close enough to love her. He seemed to be willing to do anything to be close to her again. The power to turn away was hers and hers alone.

If she chose the latter, wouldn't she be responsible for her own loneliness?

She didn't want to think about the implications. Didn't want to think about anything else today. But if she were being honest, she needed to go there.

On impulse, she scrolled through her cell contacts list and selected Kay's number. She hit dial, wished she'd merely sent a text, then was too embarrassed to hang up. Maybe Kay wouldn't answer.

"Hello?"

"It's Angelina. Long time, no see, right?"

"How are you? We just got back from a trip and heard from Pierce all you and Nick are going through. Can we do anything to help you?"

Her walls crumbled. She felt them fall and watched them turn to dust.

"Can I ask you something?" Her voice cracked. "How many times have I called you since we met?"

"I'm not sure. Maybe two or three."

"What about email? I didn't write you and hardly ever responded to yours. Right?"

"I suppose. Did you try to reach me, and I didn't know it?"

"No. Not at all. For ten sweet days in my life, you and Daniel were a loving constant."

"We've always cared about you and Nick."

"I know that." Yet she'd cast aside the friendship they'd offered. When her marriage and life hadn't looked the way she'd wanted them to, she'd rejected every available resource.

"Kay, if I come to The Barn Church Sunday morning, may I sit with you?"

"Of course. I'd be thrilled. Do you need to talk before then?"

"I'll let you know. Don't worry. Maybe, pray for me."

"I sure will. And you know, you can pray, too. God's right there waiting for you to speak to Him."

"Thanks." She hung up and sank to the floor to sit. She laid aside her phone and covered her face with her hands.

What if on one of his many trips, something had happened to Nicholas? If through accident or catastrophe he hadn't come home, she'd have had no one to blame but herself for her loneliness. She'd have had no one to blame for anything.

Including God.

The truth hurt. Deep.

"Dear God," she whispered. "I don't want to be lonely anymore."

A part of her stood to the side and cheered at the revelation, while another part wept. All these years. She'd missed out on friendships and support and encouragement and community, whether or not Nick was around, even after they'd moved back here to Rowe City.

"In my life. In my heart and spirit and every part that can be close to You. I want to be close to You."

She remembered walking to the altar at The Barn Church so long ago and feeling as if she were running into God's arms.

"I'm running to You, again," she cried. "Catch me. I want to feel your love for me and know it, see it in the kindness of others, like Laurie and Kay. I want to reach out and have real friends. I want," she gulped, "I want a life with Nicholas. Will You help us rebuild? Amen."

Her cell phone chimed, a text from Kay: *You are loved.*

She knew the message held only three words, but from deep inside a force added: *By God. By friends. By Nicholas.*

Laurie had suggested Angie seek truth in all things.

Maybe she'd discovered the truths she should start with. The most important truths of all.

She was loved. And she was not alone.

Chapter Twenty-one

"You have paint on your chin."

"And you just now tell me?" Angelina looked across the table at Nicholas and let herself revel in the tender omelet, the fluffy pancakes, and the flirtatious look in his eyes as he watched her wipe her chin. "I painted last night."

"At first, I thought it was butter or eggs," Nick said. "I didn't know."

"Because I've always been a sloppy eater?"

"No. But you are downing those pretty quickly. Do you need more pancakes?"

"Need? No. Want? Yes, but I shouldn't."

"Why not?"

"Because I don't want to gain five hundred pounds, that's why. Did I get it all off?"

"No. Come over by the sink."

She followed him. He wet a paper towel.

"No mirror here. You want me to do it?" His voice still held a playful tone.

"I ..."

She let herself look into his eyes. Let herself feel the jolt, the unexpected pull to touch.

She stepped closer to him and raised her chin in invitation. He steadied her jaw with his fingertips as he rubbed the spot.

"Must be oil-based," he said. "Doesn't want to come off with water. I don't want to hurt you."

Their eyes locked, and she knew he was giving her the option of backing away.

Don't turn away. Let him love you.

"I've nail polish remover upstairs in our bathroom if you still want to help me."

"I do. Want to help," he said.

She led the way. With the exception of coming up here to get the books the other day, she'd not been in this room in months. She'd moved out before Thanksgiving, not wanting to spend another holiday alone in this house. Thinking now, if she'd done differently, she could have spent the time with Pierce and Laurie and Daniel and Kay.

Angelina sighed and opened the medicine cabinet. She dabbed the liquid onto a clean cloth and handed it to him.

"That smells strong," he said. "You sure about this?"

"Yes. It's fine."

He worked at her jawline, then rinsed the rag and wiped the area clean.

"Done," he said.

"Nicholas."

Every ounce of love she'd ever had for him reignited. This man—who cooked for her, and touched her gently, and kept his word—was exactly who she wanted, who she thought she'd married so long ago.

"When you prayed with me last night, I was very uncomfortable," she said.

"That wasn't my intent."

"I know. I'm not saying that to make you feel bad. I don't remember you ever praying with me like that before."

"I'm sure you're right."

"As I said, at first I was uncomfortable. Then I went upstairs. Something pushed me—I don't mean physically, I mean inside—to ask questions and answer them. I've never had an experience like that before. I sensed, well, a presence with me."

"You mean God?"

Thinking this way was new to her, yet she knew what she'd experienced.

"Yes," she whispered. "Like when we first asked Him into our lives. When I woke this morning, I still felt Him in a good way."

"Then why do you look upset?"

"Because I'm uncomfortable again."

The need to tell him how close she'd come to breaking her marriage vows became a weight in her heart. She needed to tell him the truth. Not to hurt him, but so there would be no secrets, no lies between them.

Only truth.

Dread wrapped a large hand around her throat. The tension inside her threatened to tear her apart. Telling Nick would hurt him. But if she wasn't truthful about who she was, she couldn't expect him to be, either.

"If I ask you something, will you be honest with me?" she asked.

"To the best of my ability."

"All the weeks and months you traveled, were you always faithful to me?"

"Yes."

"No lonely nights? Attractive strangers across a crowded room?"

"I don't think I experience loneliness the same as you. Whenever I missed you, I told myself I was working toward our future. Like investing. One has to pay to get a return if that makes sense. I was always swamped with work. I worked, I ate, I slept. When I did get lonely, the feeling made me dream of you. There wasn't room for anyone else. There never has been."

"Thank you."

Angelina left the bathroom and stood by their bed. She wrapped her arms around her middle.

"When I went to Rita's wedding—my goodness, was that only a week ago? When I went to Vegas, I was in a really bad place. I couldn't believe you'd turned down a free weekend away with me. I felt like you were saying spending time with me wasn't valuable to you."

"I didn't mean it that way."

"I'm beginning to understand that, but at the time, I was really hurt. I didn't realize how hurt until I was sitting in the ceremony and suddenly I couldn't stand it. I mean, a wedding? When you think your own marriage is dead? I started crying. Couldn't stop. I ran out."

"I'm sorry, Angie."

"Don't misunderstand. I'm not telling you this to make you feel guilty." She sat on the edge of their bed and wrung her hands in her lap. "I was too needy. Too desperate."

She paused as he sat beside her. Then made herself look him in the eyes.

"Lorenzo was there. Rita had asked him to keep an eye out for me. No questionable motives on her part, just worried about me being alone there. I misinterpreted."

She told him what had happened. What she'd almost done.

"What's worse is, at the time, I thought I was mistaken about his interest. Now I know he was interested, but not particularly in me. He's interested in whoever's close by. I would've meant less to him than I thought I meant to you."

He took a deep breath, blew it out, and looked away. He was silent so long, she wondered if he might not respond. He might just leave.

"You didn't sleep with him." He tapped his thumbs against his thighs.

"No."

"But you wanted to."

"I wanted to feel connected to someone. I wanted to feel loved and focused on."

The way we used to get lost in each other, she thought.

"Telling you this is much harder than I thought it would be."

He wiped a hand across his brow, then pressed his knuckles there. "Did you kiss him?"

"No."

"Hold him? Did he hold you? Touch you?"

"No. Except for kissing my hand. At the time, I honestly thought you couldn't care less if he or anyone else did. You left me starving for companionship. Starving for my best friend and my lover."

He dropped his hand. "I knew there was something between you two."

"There was nothing between us except a lonely woman's conjured fantasy."

"You take one trip on your own, almost sleep with someone, and say there was and is nothing between the two of you?"

"Okay," she said. "Okay. I know you're mad. I understand why."

"If I hadn't been arrested and called you, would you have spent the weekend with him, then come home and filed for divorce?"

"I don't know! I know this doesn't make sense. I'm trying to be honest with you."

"Like your father was honest with your mother?" His voice rose. "He confessed after the fact, too, right? She knew if she received a gift he was 'sorry for his indiscretion.' Which is why until a couple of days ago you wouldn't accept my gifts. Or is your accepting them now your I'm sorry gift to me?"

"I can't win."

She stood. She rolled the chains at her neck between her fingers, then turned to face him.

"Would you send a starving person to jail for stealing bread to eat? Don't you answer that. You think about it. Because that's how you left me." Her voice cracked. "You left me hungry and in need. I married you to be a mate and to have a mate."

If Nicholas was going to be furious with her, she might as well completely unburden herself.

"Going to Las Vegas was not my first trip on my own."

"What? Where have you been? And when?"

"All over the world." She gestured wide. "Alone. To places I wanted to paint. I've been to Paris and a dozen or more other locations you didn't take me when you could have."

"A dozen or more?" Shock filled his voice. "And Paris? I might have liked to have known that. You know, in case something happened to you? There were terrorist attacks all over Europe last year and the year before. Several in Paris."

"Why would I have thought you cared? If you didn't want to stay with me, why would you care? You know what? *Yes*. Yes, I probably would have slept with Lorenzo. And regretted it. And felt horrible. And beaten myself up—just one more way I'm a failure because he wasn't the first man I considered giving myself to in the last couple of years."

Nick shook his head. "I can't believe what you're telling me."

He looked away, leaving her feeling dirty and tainted and rejected.

"I want to think I couldn't do it," she whispered. "I want to think if he'd actually touched me, I'd have recoiled. You're the only man I've ever been with, and I would never have pictured myself as someone who could break her marriage vows that way, especially after seeing what my mother went through. Maybe—given the right circumstances—anyone can fall."

"Was the first man a stranger, too?" he asked. "A random person you met while traveling?"

"No." Shame made forming words difficult. "I wasn't looking for anyone. He was just there."

"Did he reciprocate?"

"No. He didn't recognize or return my interest."

"So you didn't sleep with him, either. Well, that's something, at least."

He drew a deep breath, let it out. "I thought I'd figured out what to do to fix us. It's much harder when I'm not the only one in the wrong."

"I'm sorry. You don't have to say anything to me—my, the tables have turned, haven't they? I'm guilty. One hundred percent guilty of wanting someone to want me for more than a couple of days and at his convenience."

"That's not exactly fair."

"At least we agree on something."

He stood. She expected he'd leave. Or reach for her in an effort to talk her out of her feelings, but he didn't.

Instead, he went into the bathroom and splashed water on his face. He dried with a towel.

"Did I really make you feel unwanted?" he asked.

"Worse," she whispered. "You made me feel forgotten. I shouldn't have, but I admit I used that feeling to justify my actions. "

"You said to me once—maybe around our seventh anniversary, right before we moved here—that while I was away working time didn't stop for you. For you, time passed without me. That's what *forgotten* means, isn't it?"

"Yes."

The doorbell rang.

"Saved by the bell," Angelina said. "Or in this case, Laurie. I better let her in."

She descended the stairs.

***

Angelina opened the door for Laurie, who took one look at Angie's face and hugged her.

"What's wrong?" Laurie asked.

"You know, your sensitivity must come in handy in your marriage. I bet you always know when something's wrong with your husband."

"Not exactly. It's a catch twenty-two. Too often I pick up on too much. Or think everything bothering Pierce has to do with me. He sometimes says I'm an emotional minefield—no place is safe for him to step. It wouldn't take a mind-reader to see you're upset. Sorry I'm late. This morning I chased a two-year-old who decided to stuff her diaper with French toast. Syrup in poo, very sticky stuff. Don't worry; I washed my hands several times."

"You are so real. Not like any church person I ever imagined, even after meeting Daniel and Kay. I wish we'd been friends earlier."

"My fault, too. But let's deal with today."

"Come on in. Come back to the kitchen." She led the way, listening to be sure Nick was still upstairs, then lowered her voice. "Can I ask you about your and Pierce's troubles before Hope was born?"

"Yes."

She needed something to do with her hands, so she pushed up her sleeves, removed her bracelets, and cleaned up the kitchen. Laurie moved to help.

"No, you sit," Angie said. "I need to move to be able to think and talk. How long did it take to heal your relationship with Pierce?"

"We're still healing. We probably always will be. God doesn't work on everything in both of us at the same time. He works on a piece here, a piece there."

"So it's a back and forth thing. Two steps forward, one step back?"

"Hopefully, we don't take steps backward. Are you asking if it's a process full of uncertainty? In the beginning, it can be when you're not sure what the other person wants. Pierce and I resolved to work in the same direction, toward the same goal. We still do."

"I thought my love for Nicholas was dead. I thought I couldn't believe he would ever change. Blowing up the other night the way I did? Somehow saying it made me realize how much I've kept inside all these years. How much I've demonized him when he wasn't there, or how a memory can become slanted.

"Don't get me wrong, our marriage is a mess." Angelina opened the dishwasher to load. "But I'm beginning to think that's because each of us is a mess."

"I'd say you're right."

"I confessed to Nick this morning about Lorenzo and something else you probably don't know about."

"Are you okay?"

"His reaction isn't easy to accept, but I still think we took a step toward each other." She returned the butter to the fridge. "That probably doesn't make sense given what we're up against here."

"A miracle doesn't make sense. I think your spirit is stirring and waking up."

"I've never really felt this before, even when I first asked God into my life years ago. It's like there are parts of me I didn't know were dead, and they're coming alive."

"That's wonderful." Laurie wiped her eyes. "Sorry. Happy tears, I promise."

"Is it possible to live like this every day? To ask for God's work in your life and cooperate with it?"

"It sure is."

"Then that's what I want to do from now on," Angie said.

The doorbell rang again.

"Grand Central." Angelina headed for the front door. "Be right back."

She peered through the peephole to find Lorenzo waiting with camera in hand. She steeled herself and opened the door.

"Beautiful Angelina. You look unhappy." He leaned against the doorframe as if he owned the place and her. "Is the morning not pleasing to you?"

Back in Las Vegas, what had she thought she'd seen in this man?

"Hi. Laurie's in the kitchen. You can go ahead to the library. I'll be there in a moment."

"Ahh. Straight to business. The husband must still be home, no?—despite what I heard on the news this morning."

"Excuse me?"

"A witness has come forward in your little scandal," he said. "A woman who says she had many communications with your husband about money and other things."

"We haven't been watching the news," Angelina mumbled.

Yesterday, Julius had taken Nick to retrieve his impounded car. She'd thought that meant—well, she didn't know exactly. But combined with the fact neither of them had been contacted by the authorities since Nick's release, she'd assumed at least part of the legal crisis was over.

Lorenzo shrugged. "Maybe the woman is mistaken. If she is, the reporters will probably leave before lunch."

"What reporters?"

"The ones I steered through to pull into your driveway. They are lined up along the road." He entered, removed his coat, and moved toward the library.

"Laurie and I will be there in a moment." She peered outside then closed the door.

Angelina laid her brow against the doorframe. This woman coming forward. New evidence?

She was falling in love again with her husband. What would she do if he now had to leave her permanently, through no choice of his own?

***

Nicholas braced both hands on the bathroom sink as he relived the last minutes with his wife. What Angelina had just told him hurt. He hurt worse than he remembered hurting in his entire life.

He wanted to blame her. He wanted to believe no matter what he'd done, nothing could excuse what she'd almost done.

But if the situation were reversed …

"*We're all broken,*" Pierce had told him earlier that week.

No truer words.

His blasted phone chimed. *Abide in my love.*

Lorenzo's masculine voice rumbled up the stairs. Laurie was here, too, but still, Nick didn't want Lorenzo to be alone with Angelina even for a moment.

But what could Nick do? Behave like a clingy teenager, prop open the door to the kitchen and eavesdrop as they worked in the library?

Ah, yes. The kitchen, complete with dirty dishes from preparing breakfast, waited for him. At least he'd have an excuse to be downstairs, wouldn't he?

His heart skipped a beat. What might Angelina do if he were convicted and sent away to prison for years?

His phone vibrated in his hand. "Hey, Julius."

"I'm almost to your house. You're there, right?"

"Where else would I be? Sorry."

"Don't think twice about it. I know you're under a lot of stress."

He looked back at his and Angie's bed. Last night, he'd drifted to her side. When he'd pulled the comforter into place this morning, he'd considered simply sleeping on her side tonight to avoid disheveling the entire thing. Now, he wondered if he'd be able to sleep in their bed at all.

"Julius, are we any closer to clearing my name?"

"I'm afraid not. Do you know a woman named Trina Iles?"

"Not that I recall."

"She contacted the FBI when she didn't get expected dividend checks from PGI. She was interviewed by several news stations this morning."

"You told me not to watch the news."

"Better for you that you're following my instructions. She says she had an online video call with you before she invested."

"That's not true!"

"Don't panic. This might be a good thing. If we can prove she is mistaken, it'll be a big step toward convincing both the State Prosecutor and the FBI they need to broaden their investigation."

"Tell me what to do."

"Do you have a pink dress shirt?"

"Yeah."

"Put it on and come out fast," Julius said. "I'm dodging press to get in the driveway."

Nick headed for the closet. "Two minutes."

He changed quickly and hurried down the stairs. He found Laurie in the kitchen pouring a glass of juice.

"Hi, Laurie."

"Any news?" she asked. "Is everything okay?"

"I'm not sure. I've got to go with Julius. One of us will call when we know more."

"Are you coming back?"

"I don't know. I hope so. Did you clean up?"

"Angie did."

He hadn't seen her in the hall. Could he blame her if she were avoiding him?

"Nick, if you want me to I'll stay with her until we hear from you."

"Thanks. I need to go."

Outside, Nick climbed in Julius' car. They drove down the driveway and out onto the street. Photographers snapped pictures, journalists spoke into microphones, and video cameras recorded their exit.

"Wow, you weren't kidding about the press. Where are we going?"

"Back to the state prison. First, you'll participate in a police line-up. Don't worry; I'll tell you exactly what to do."

"And then?"

"I've scheduled a polygraph—a lie detector test. It won't be accepted as conclusive evidence, but it will add weight."

"If I pass. How quickly can they put me back in prison if I don't?"

"I don't want you to think about that right now."

Nicholas hung his head and took slow, deep breaths.

"Stay with me," Julius said. "They're going to make a recording of your voice to use for voice print analysis. Trina Iles also has a voicemail on her phone she says is you leaving a message about PGI. We want to prove the voice isn't yours."

"I can tell you they won't match."

"That's what we're counting on. Did you think of anywhere Gavin might go? Anywhere he might be?"

"No."

"We ID'd the blonde in the picture. Olivia Furtado. Does that name ring a bell?"

"I'm sorry. No."

"She's a model. Lives in New York. Travels a lot. Right now she's supposedly out of the country on assignment."

"Is Gavin with her?" Nick raised his head. He couldn't help thinking of what Angelina had just said. "Do you know for certain Gavin had a relationship with her, or was she just a random hook-up?"

"We don't know."

"Is the FBI reviewing her emails? Phone records?"

"That's trickier than it sounds," Julius said. "The woman resides in New York, which is neither Alabama nor Mississippi where Frances Sweeney lives. The feds would have to get search warrants in New York to focus on her, and they're not yet convinced Gavin's disappearance isn't coincidental to their investigation, so she's not a priority."

"He could be hiding at her place in New York."

"Cameron checked. Gavin's not there. We'll be another forty minutes to the prison. Sit back and try to relax." Julius paused. "How's Angelina?"

Nicholas looked out the passenger window at winter-withered fields. "That remains to be seen."

Chapter Twenty-two

Nicholas laid back against the headrest in the front seat of Julius' car and closed his eyes as they exited the parking lot.

He'd been in stressful situations before. He'd shaken hands with men who could easily run a small country. He'd given "here's the bad news" presentations to CEOs who looked as if they might like to throw him out the nearest high-rise window.

Yet nothing had prepared him for today.

"I let myself hope Trina Iles wouldn't recognize me."

"I'd hoped the same." Julius reached the highway and accelerated. "Who knows? She might remember another helpful detail tomorrow or the next day."

Although Nick had participated in three separate police line-ups, the spry eighty-one-year-old wasn't certain the man she'd spoken with online wasn't him. The man she'd seen had like coloring and facial features. Nick supposed he and Gavin could be mistaken for each other from the shoulders up given the right conditions—they both had dark hair, dark eyes, a similar shape to their faces. Add the pink dress shirt, and there you go.

Which meant Nicholas hadn't been absolved, but at least he hadn't been arrested again.

So they'd moved to the next phase. In a special room, he'd read from pre-printed cards while an FBI technician recorded his voice. Finally, he'd taken a lie detector test.

"The polygraph results are in your favor," Julius said. "Although the FBI will probably ask for its own."

"So I'll have to do that again."

"I'm sure it won't be scheduled until Monday. Take the weekend off."

At first, the technician had been robotic and monotone. *What is your name? What is today's date? Have you ever lived in Florida?* He documented each response.

As the questions were repeated, time had seemed to stop. Then, the mundane was set aside.

Is PGI your company? Have you ever stolen anything? Did you use PGI to steal millions from investors? What is today's date? Is PGI your company? Have you ever called Trina Iles or Frances Sweeney? Are you guilty of real estate fraud?

On and on the questions went. Nick had endured by using every bit of self-control at his disposal until *Did your wife conspire with you to commit real estate fraud?*

"I'm sorry I lost my temper during the polygraph. I'm so frustrated they're not looking for Gavin. He did this. Not me. Not Angie."

"I believe you. But you're going to have to manage your emotions better next time, and whenever they question you again. Seems you've got a slow boil, but you can't blow up. You understand?"

"I understand."

They rode on in silence. Two of the gifts he'd kept in the safe deposit box had been returned and were in a bag in Julius' trunk right now. Dare he offer Angelina one of those tonight? Neither he nor Julius knew why, but the multilayered necklace from the gold box was still being held as evidence.

With every moment that passed, every mile they drove, he grew more anxious at seeing his wife and possibly picking up where they'd left off in their earlier conversation. Even after hours apart, he still didn't know what to say to her.

Julius slowed at Nick's driveway.

"News vans are gone," Julius said. "That's a good sign. Must be something more spectacular to report."

Nick hoped Lorenzo was gone, too.

The sun sank lower behind them, the last rays almost making the white cross-fencing glow amber. They reached the dense stand of pine trees. Nick rolled down his window. He simply wanted to breathe air that didn't reek of accusation, despair, and stale human sweat or the bleach-based disinfectant that failed to cover their combined stench.

"You're not alone," Julius said. "I always feel like I need a shower and a spray of air freshener up my nose when I leave that place."

"I appreciate everything you've done for me."

"I know you're discouraged. Don't do something foolish and run. It'll make you look guilty."

"I'm not going to run. But I don't know how long I can afford to pay you, especially with the added expense of the private investigator. My priority might have to be providing for Angie and hoping the justice system actually does its job."

Julius stopped in front of the house.

Nick got out. "Thanks again."

"I'll pop the trunk."

"Right." Two of Angie's gifts waited there.

He closed the passenger door and retrieved the bag from the trunk, then watched his lawyer drive away.

***

Lorenzo's rental van was gone, as was Laurie's car. An unfamiliar sedan sat on the far side of the circle driveway.

Nicholas let himself in the front door. He sniffed. Fried chicken?

259

He quickly stowed the bag in his office, then followed the scent into the kitchen. Sure enough, an open bucket of chicken, side dishes, and biscuits covered one end of the counter.

Then he heard Daniel's belly laugh. He hadn't heard that sound in years. Despite his fatigue, he smiled.

"Oh, you're finally home. Poor thing. Let me hug your neck." Kay did so. "Rough day, I bet. Let's fix you a plate. Come back to the sunroom, prop your feet up, and eat. You can fill us in, or we'll talk about something else. Whatever you need."

"Is Angelina still here?"

"Yes." Kay handed him a plate. "We had Hope for the day, but by this afternoon that precious youngin' wanted her mama and nothing else would do. So we brought dinner and handed off my grandchild whom I adore but could not make happy. That's the beauty of being a grandparent. Your grandchildren visit, then you hand them right back to their parents and get a good night's rest.

"Anyway, Daniel and I stayed with Angelina in case you called with tough news."

He'd not even thought to call. Guess he hadn't fully learned that lesson, had he?

"Sorry, false alarm. Julius says we're good for the weekend, anyway."

"Wonderful. Then you and Angelina can get some rest."

"Angie's not sleeping here."

"I know." Kay's voice lowered, and she squeezed his hand in comfort. "She's been talking to me and Daniel for the last two hours. I've never seen her open up so much. It's a good sign."

"I guess that depends on what she's been telling you."

He'd had about all the accusations he could handle for one day.

"Now don't get defensive. Bring your dinner in here with us. You might be surprised at what she's shared."

She grabbed a pitcher of tea and carried it from the room. Nick prepared his plate and followed, passing through the library with its nearly empty shelves.

Consequences, he thought. Bad decisions usually had consequences. Angie was suffering—parting with her once-beloved possessions—because of his choice to invest with Gavin. Her bad decisions regarding men meant Nick now suffered.

He continued through the back parlor and out into the sunroom. He didn't recognize anything in the room. Not the white-washed wicker furniture with striped cushions nor the host of glass-topped tables scattered throughout. Small trees, their foliage shaped into perfect spheres—topiaries?—gave the illusion of perpetual spring brought indoors.

He did a double-take at the paint treatment on the walls, as Angelina had once mentioned this was her favorite room. Sky blue at the top, then lighter and lighter shades blended to white on the bottom third. Gradient color, she'd called it. The effect was calming, yet didn't match the overt elegance of the rest of the house. He couldn't shake the feeling if she spent time in here, it was so she could pretend she was elsewhere.

Nick took a chair opposite the loveseat occupied by Daniel and Kay. Angelina sat cross-legged on the nearby rug.

"Hello, Nick." Daniel nodded in his direction. "Glad they let you come home, son. Any news?"

"Oh, Daniel, let him eat," Kay said. "He'll tell us what he wants us to know soon enough."

"It's good to see you both." He updated them on the day's events. "I lost my temper today during the polygraph. Julius says it won't affect the results, but I'm not so sure."

"Anyone who's wrongfully accused is going to have some feelings about it, son." Daniel shifted in his seat. "If we'd been here when they arrested you, I'd have given that State Prosecutor a thing or two to think about."

Kay looked at Daniel with mild exasperation. "And gotten yourself arrested, too, no doubt. You can't just tell people what to do."

"Sure I can. I'm a preacher. I tell everyone what to do. Nicholas isn't guilty. I'd have told them that."

Kay chuckled. "The State Prosecutor would not have cared what you think."

Silence fell as he finished eating and set aside his plate.

"I'm really glad they didn't arrest you again," Angelina said. "Daniel and Kay have been here a while. I pretty much told them everything."

He hadn't expected that. "About?"

"About me not living here since before Thanksgiving, and why. About what I almost did in Las Vegas."

His chest tightened. "Did you tell them about the first guy? I don't even know where that happened."

He looked away from the hurt and embarrassment in her eyes.

"Yes," she said. "They know I've been terribly lonely for some time now, and how poorly I handled it."

He pressed his fingers to his forehead. "You call almost committing adultery twice handling loneliness poorly? Did you tell them you were probably a one-night stand away from leaving me?"

She jerked as if she'd been struck, then moved as if to stand. Kay placed a firm yet stilling hand on Angie's shoulder.

"I asked for their help," his wife whispered. "I want to keep what came in my heart last night. I'm tired of hurting alone. I'm tired of us hurting each other."

"How about you?" Daniel asked. "You ready to stop hurting each other? She's swallowed some tough truth about herself the last twenty-four hours. Don't think Kay and I went easy on her before you came home."

Kay placed a hand on her husband's knee. "Be easy now."

"If the truth hurts, it needs to," Daniel said. "I care about you two too much to let this go on any longer. I should've done something, Kay. I should've jerked a knot in his neck and sent you after her when they moved back."

"I don't think so," Kay said. "I think it took getting to this place before they'd listen. Now spit it out so they can move forward. These children have hurt long enough."

Daniel popped another piece of Juicy-Fruit into his mouth. Kay bit her lip.

"Don't laugh at me. This stuff serves many purposes. Not the least of which is stress relief." Daniel offered a stick to Nick. "Want some?"

Nicholas accepted. "Thanks." The same old Daniel. Ready to listen and help.

"Angie told us about the anniversaries and what not," Kay said. "About all the plans and starting over you two have done. How you'd make promises you didn't keep."

"I meant to keep them," Nick said. "But I didn't. I didn't listen to her, and I didn't listen to God. Since being arrested, I see where I went wrong."

"God often uses pressure to reveal where He wants to work in us," Kay said.

Nick raked a hand through his curls. "Until this morning, I thought I was mostly at fault for our problems. Now, I don't know what to do. I don't know how to get past what she told me."

"You're barking up the wrong tree." Daniel continued chomping his gum. "You've both got the same lousy habits. Ten years is long enough to prove your tactics failed. Son, you're an efficiency expert.

What's wrong with this picture?" He looked at Kay. "Help me out, here."

"Daniel's not angry at you two," Kay said. "Even though he might sound like it. What he's trying to say is you have to start with forgiving each other."

"Stop reacting to each other and blaming each other for your individual behavior." Daniel's eyes twinkled as he smacked his gum. "Refusing to forgive? You two are chasing your own tails. You work, and you're tired, but you've got nothing good to show for your efforts."

Kay pulled on Daniel's arm. "Come on. You've made your point. Let God get a word in. Goodnight, Nick and Angelina. You know where to find us."

"I'll walk you out," Nick said.

He followed them to the door. Hugged and thanked them both.

"How?" Nick asked. "How do I forgive her?"

"You can't without God's help and love," Kay said. "Look up I Peter 4:8. 'Love covers a multitude of sins.' If you two put your heads together, you'll figure out how to make your marriage a healthy one. Two becoming one is a mysterious teamwork only God can guide you through."

"Thanks, again, Kay."

***

Nick returned to the sunroom to find Angelina sitting on the love seat where Daniel and Kay had been. Her eyes were closed. She fiddled with the chains at her neck.

"Angelina." He stepped to her. "May I sit with you?"

She looked up at him and nodded. "Yes."

"What are you thinking?"

"I'm thinking *and here I thought you and I had nothing in common. No common ground whatsoever.*"

"You agree with what Daniel said?"

She nodded. "We made the same huge mistake over and over again."

"Yeah, we did."

She turned, and light from a nearby lamp reflected off one of her many necklaces. A silver chain with a cross.

He couldn't quote the scripture passage about the crucifixion. He probably couldn't even find it if pressed. But he remembered being at church last Easter Sunday morning. At the end of the service, a young girl of about sixteen stood and sang. The lyrics, something about watching Jesus die.

He'd sat in the back row beside Angelina and felt a stirring in his soul. Not merely from the girl's compelling voice, but from picturing Jesus hanging on the cross for him. The spikes through His hands and feet. The crown of thorns pressed into His scalp. The agony with which He took each breath, then spoke forgiveness to all who watched, all who wept, and all who gloated at His pain.

Love her like I love you. Forgive. Even when it's hard.

And it hit him: *Love covers a multitude of sins.* Love and forgiveness went hand-in-hand. Between him and God, and between him and others.

"Angie? I forgive you."

She hung her head. "For committing emotional adultery?"

His throat tightened. "For everything. I don't deserve it, but I hope you'll forgive me, too. In many ways, I did the same."

"I forgive you," she whispered.

Light dispelled the shadows in the corner of his heart. He felt it grow and spread, and he knew he and his wife had joined in a way they never had before.

Dear God, help me remember this moment above all others. Every time I don't know what to do to connect with her. Every time we argue. No matter what the future holds for me or my marriage, help me remember this.

His cell chimed.

"What is that reminder about?" Angelina asked.

"A scripture. And my feelings for you. Just a silly idea to help me remember."

She touched his hand with her fingertips. "It's not silly."

"It kind of is. A grown man. Married almost ten years. Needing help remembering basic relational practices."

She slid the phone from his grasp and read the screen. "'Abide in my love.' Where's it from?"

"Jesus said it to His disciples. It's what believers are supposed to do. I wanted to say it to you because it's what I want you to feel safe to do with me."

"The alarm idea, it's a good one." She returned his phone, her eyes downcast.

Love her. Pursue her. Nick's heart pounded at the quick, insistent prompts.

Yes, God, he thought. *I'll do it.*

So he looked at her as he had that day in the college cafe, letting his grin spread slow and easy. Letting himself remember how he'd felt that moment when he hadn't a clue what to say to the woman who, with a single look, had turned his heart inside out.

"Hey," he said.

She gave the same half-embarrassed smile as she had then. "Hey."

"That's not how it went the first time. You didn't say anything back. We know more now, though."

"Yeah, I think we do."

"May I walk you home?"

She smiled. "I'd like that."

"Great. But first, we have to go to the kitchen."

Chapter Twenty-three

Angelina followed Nick to the kitchen. Believing he truly forgave her was difficult.

Dear God, is it true? With Your help, can we really make this work?

"Close your eyes." He reached into the refrigerator.

She obliged. "Another gift? You know they make me uncomfortable."

"Nothing fancy." He placed a small package in her hands. "I saw it when I bought groceries. Open your eyes."

The red and gold wrapper did indeed resemble a present. "Chocolate?"

"Supposedly from Germany. I guess they're getting a jump on Valentine's Day."

Valentine's Day. Only a few weeks until their ten-year anniversary. Her whole body, her heart tensed at the thought.

He touched her arm. "Hey. You okay?"

"I'm scared." And she couldn't hide it. "Scared to believe tomorrow you won't change your mind about forgiving me. Scared we might start getting it right, then without warning, you'll be arrested again, but this time not come back."

"Julius is doing everything he can for us. I'm working with him in every way possible to be sure I'm with you on our anniversary. I do forgive you. Please believe me." He grinned, and his dimple flashed. "Try a bite. Doesn't chocolate make women feel like they're in love?"

She tore open the package and inhaled. "I'll let you know."

They donned their jackets and made their way to the carriage house. In contrast to last night's rain, the sky was clear. A blanket of stars against midnight blue.

"When Daniel and Kay were leaving, I realized something else we have in common," she said. "Neither of us had a good relationship with our father."

"I hadn't thought of that, but you're right."

"I wonder what other similarities we'd discover if we tried."

She wanted to find them. With a desperation that somehow linked the naïve, in-love girl of her youth to the woman she was today.

I didn't listen to God he'd told Daniel and Kay. The truth that neither had she weighed heavily in her mind.

Another area they matched.

All the times God had told her to reach for Nick. *Reach for him now.*

The times she'd chosen her own loneliness. *He's right here, and so am I.*

The times she'd comforted herself with things rather than letting God comfort and lead her. *I'll show you what to do, what to say. Reach for him.*

She grabbed his hand, felt him squeeze hers.

The texture was familiar. The grasp, an easy fit.

She heard the owl that lived on their property, the scurry of night creatures.

She stopped walking near her stairs. "I stockpiled my hurts. Boxed myself in like a hoarder stepping around every painful memory."

"I told myself providing financially was the most important thing."

Her burdened lessened. She stepped closer to him. "To distract myself, I bought things I didn't need and didn't want."

"I found security in making money, but no matter how much I made, it was never enough."

She felt her shoulders, her face, relax. She took his other hand and held tight. "I poured my heart into my art. I should have given it to God and you."

"When I was home, I couldn't fight your anger, so I took every excuse to leave."

"That's how we always messed up. I pull back as soon as I think I might end up alone, and you run from conflict. I want to do better than that."

She thought back to years ago and what Daniel had told them. *Everything you need to know about marriage you can learn from your relationship with God.*

What had she learned within the last twenty-four hours?

She'd reached for God and found Him right there. She'd clung to Him today while she'd made a difficult confession, this evening while talking with Daniel and Kay, and learning tough truths about herself.

Reach. Cling. Abide.

She wrapped her arms around him. "Abide with me."

His arms came around her, and they stood holding each other.

"I'm not good at remembering this," he said.

"Remembering what?"

"How good, how right, it feels to hold you. The whole world falls back into place when I hold you. I can't believe how easily I forget that."

She smiled against his chest. "Will you help me tomorrow? I'll be picking up the horses, then taking them and all of the tack to Matthews Stables."

He motioned to the horse trailer parked at the far end of the barn. "In that?"

She tilted her head. "Yes. I'll drive. I think I can sell it pretty easily next week. I haven't even put a thousand miles on it."

"You're sure that's what you want to do?"

"Yes. They're going to someone who will really love them." She paused. "How long before your phone chimes again?"

He checked the time. "Another twenty minutes. I love you, Angelina."

"I'm starting to believe you. The alarm's a good reminder for both of us. So, will you help me tomorrow?"

She felt him take a deep breath. "If I can. If Julius doesn't call. If I'm here."

"Right." For a few minutes, she'd forgotten. At any moment, Nick could be taken away from her for an indefinite length of time.

She snuggled in close and tightened her hold on him.

***

In the quiet, cool morning, Angelina loaded the tack—lead ropes, brushes and combs and hoof picks, blankets and saddles. She stacked large items in a wall of locked metal cabinets behind the seat. Small items went into a footlocker with heavy-duty casters, now secured beside the cabinets.

"You're up early."

She turned at Nick's voice and walked down the ramp to stand beside him.

"It happens occasionally. I didn't sleep much. I'll probably crash tonight. What's in the insulated bag?"

"Oatmeal loaded with nuts and dried fruit. I figured we'd need it. A cold front's moving in. Supposed to rain this evening and be in the thirties tonight."

"Then we better eat and get going."

"You loaded without me?" he asked.

"Can't move the feedbags by myself."

"I'll get them," he said. "I remembered you like extra brown sugar." He produced a container of warm oatmeal and a spoon.

"What about you?"

"I already ate."

She ate every bite while he loaded the feedbags. Within minutes, they both climbed into the cab.

"I'm glad you're driving." He sat the cooler at his feet. "This thing's bigger than it looks. Not knowing how long of a day we'd have, I packed sandwiches, too."

She caught his gaze. "You thought about me. About us."

"Yeah. I did. God helping me, I will from now on."

"Then let me say thank you for the oatmeal with extra brown sugar. Thank you for helping me today. And thank you in advance for lunch."

She cranked the engine and pulled forward.

"Just so you know," she said. "I'm happy to spend a Saturday with you instead of being alone."

She drove to Pete Bohannon's place, introduced the men to each other. Apollo and Zeus greeted her with nuzzles and nudges. Godiva, in a separate stall with her newborn, blinked with new mother pride.

"Watch your step," she said as Nick followed her and Pete into the stall.

"What are you going to name her?" Pete asked.

"I've decided not to keep them, Pete." Angelina brushed her fingers through the filly's blonde mane. "When we leave here, I'm giving them to Rachel Matthews. I'll let Rachel name her."

"She's a friendly little thing, not hesitant like her mother," Pete said. "Loves to interact with people. Loves attention."

"Then she'll be happy at Matthews Stables. Rachel will dote on her. Help us load them?"

"I'd be happy to. Can't hardly believe you're parting with them."

"I'm not giving them the time and attention they need," Angelina said. "I want better for them."

When the horses were loaded, she pulled onto the highway.

She glanced over at Nick. "What I said back there, it wasn't a slam against you."

"The comment about time and attention?"

"Yeah. They need more than I can give them."

"Don't worry about it."

She drove on. Tightening her grip on the wheel. Repeatedly glancing at her husband.

What had she been thinking when she'd asked him to accompany her this morning?

She hadn't been back to Matthews Stables since she'd removed her horses a week after the twins' birth. Removing them and herself had seemed her only option after making a fool of herself the way she had with Rick. So the morning after Godiva delivered the first time, Angelina had found a contractor and promised him top dollar to quickly spruce up the unused barn and stables on their property. Then she'd relocated the horses and hadn't looked back.

They passed dormant fields and cow pastures on the familiar route.

"You know, I could drop you at the house if you want." She knew she sounded lame. "Forget I said that. Unless, of course, you don't want to meet *the first man.*"

"Ah. I wondered why you were tensing up."

"What makes you say I was?"

"You've been switching hands on the steering wheel. Worrying your wedding rings with your thumb—you're wearing your wedding rings."

"I put them on this morning. It seemed right."

"Thank you," he said. "I think I can handle meeting the first man."

"It was a fantasy, Nicholas. Rick's not like Lorenzo."

The statement seemed to settle on the seat between them.

"What drew you? To him?" Nick asked.

"I was wrong to fantasize about him. To feed that fantasy."

"Nevertheless, some trait caught your eye. I need to know what it was. I'm not angry. I just need to know. Please."

She swallowed. In the past, moments like this were when he'd lose his temper, or bombast her with questions, or pressure her until she laid aside her feelings.

"I want to do better than we did before, too," he said.

"You were listening last night."

"Yes, I was. Trust me with the truth. There are things about you I need to re-learn, or even learn for the first time. What drew you to this man?"

"He's nurturing," she said. "He's as kind and gentle with people as he is with his horses."

"Thank you."

She slowed before the entrance to Matthews Stables.

"If it makes you feel any better, his wife knows," Angie said. "I'll be more uncomfortable doing this than you are."

***

Nick had expected stone pillars. An expansive, wrought iron gate. At the very least, a crossbeam arch and a big sign.

Instead, they turned in at a nondescript dirt driveway over an extra-wide metal culvert. The path was smooth and grassless from obvious repeated use and led past a ranch-style home on the right to a well-kept yet aged barn the size of a small warehouse.

Beyond the barn, the land opened to corrals and fenced pastures of countless acreage. Signs warned visitors to watch where they stepped

275

and to avoid touching electric wires atop the fences.

Angelina pulled around the side of the barn, and Nick realized the building was more than twice as deep as he'd thought. Through a typical farm gate, he saw the back of the barn was actually a two-story metal arena.

They stopped.

"Nick, I can do this by myself."

"Isn't that part of why we're where we are? No, I'm with you," he said. "I don't know how to handle the horses, but I can do the grunt work. Move the feed, move the tack."

Penance wasn't exactly the term he'd use to describe what he was about to do. A reboot, he thought. This time he'd stick through the tough moments.

A teenage girl ran out of the barn, her thick brown hair flying behind her. Angie opened her door and stepped down.

"Hey, Mrs. Rousseau! It's great to see you! Did you bring them already?" She squealed. "I can't believe you're parting with them. Can I see them?"

Nick got out and met them at the back of the trailer. He smelled hay and manure and heard a chorus of horse whinnies from the barn.

"Rachel, this is my husband, Nicholas."

"Hi, Mr. Rousseau. Nice to meet you."

"You, too." He thought he recognized her but couldn't quite place from where.

"Rachel is Julie and Rick's daughter," Angie said.

Of course. Julie and Rick Matthews, and their daughter Rachel. She sang in church last Easter Sunday morning.

"You have a terrific voice," Nick said.

"Thanks." She smiled and leaned toward Angelina, hiding her words behind her hand. "He's really hot."

Angelina laughed. "Yes, he is."

A rugged-looking man in denim, cowboy boots, and a black Stetson exited the barn and approached. "Rachel, are your chores done?"

Nick watched Angie's face and knew. Rick.

He wiped his hands on his jeans and tipped his hat. "Angelina. Good to see you."

"This is Nicholas. My husband."

Nicholas extended his hand and met hazel eyes in a tanned face. "My pleasure."

"Same." Rick nodded. "Rachel, don't touch a horse before you talk with Mrs. Rousseau about the deal we made."

"Yes, sir." She sighed as if tragedy had struck. "Daddy said I can only have them if I pay for them. But I don't have any money yet, so he and Mom came up with a payment plan. My first lesson in paying my own bills." She rolled her eyes.

"Rachel," Rick said.

"Okay. Okay," Rachel said. "Anyway, barring complications, and if she stays healthy, we'll breed Godiva once a year for the next six years until I'm through high school and college. We'll train and sell her offspring, and half the proceeds will go to you. If that's okay."

"That's a great plan," Angie said.

"We've got space clear," Rick said. "Rachel, go get a couple of lead ropes."

"Daddy."

"Go. Show me you can follow directions even when you don't want to."

"Yes, sir." She walked into the barn.

"I wanted a moment." Rick addressed them. "I've seen the news. Are you two going to regret this when your names are cleared?"

If Nicholas hadn't already liked Rick, the vote of confidence would have gotten his attention. "This was Angie's idea. It's her decision."

Her eyes said *thank you*.

"This is best." Angelina moved to stand by Nicholas, and as she had last night, took his hand. "For us all."

Rick nodded. "All right. I'll write up the agreement for Rachel's benefit, have her sign and mail you copies to sign, too, just for show. Rachel has a tendency to want to repeatedly renegotiate. A 'contract' will teach her about sticking to terms and to her word."

Rachel returned. She and Angelina unloaded the horses. Rick worked alongside Nicholas unloading the tack and feed bags. Then Rick grabbed two brooms, they returned to the trailer and swept it out.

"You've got a pretty place here," Nicholas said.

"Don't I know it," Rick said. "God's given me a lot. I'm better at remembering that than I used to be."

"Angelina told me what happened." Nicholas stopped and leaned on his broom. "I appreciate you not taking advantage when I wasn't around."

"There are more than two sides to every story. I've learned there's his, and hers, and somewhere between them is the truth. I figure you two are getting around to the truth. Am I right?"

"You could say that, yeah."

"Then I'll thank you for making my little girl very happy. God knows I couldn't buy those horses from you outright. This way they're Rachel's. It means more."

Rick offered his hand. Nick accepted.

"You'll see us at church," Nicholas said. "No need to be strangers."

"I appreciate that," Rick said. "Ya'll come see the horses any time."

"Thanks."

They finished sweeping, returned the brooms. Nicholas walked to the arena gate where Angelina stood watching Rachel walk Godiva.

"Are you still sure?" he asked.

"I'm sure," she said. "I just spoke with Julie in the tack room."

"I would have gone with you. You didn't have to do that alone."

"My mess. I should be the one to clean it up."

He waited, hoping she'd tell him what happened.

"I apologized for what I did, made sure she knew Rick did nothing wrong. Then I told her I haven't been this embarrassed in a long time. I expected an awkward silence and hard looks. Instead, she thanked me for thinking of Rachel. She said she forgives me. I almost didn't know what to say."

"What did you say?"

"What could I say, but thank you? I'm a little sad, though. I think she and I might have been friends." She paused. "Maybe one day. She and Laurie are friends, so, yeah, maybe one day."

He drew her closer. He kissed her hair and held his lips there.

"Can you imagine me having two female friends?" she asked.

"I think that'd be great. Add Kay, and you've got three."

"If things were different, I think you and Rick could have been friends. I'm sorry I might have ruined that."

"You didn't ruin it. And I'm not mad. We were both wrong. I'd rather hold on to you than a grudge. I love you."

She turned to him, chewing her bottom lip. For half a second, she gently touched her mouth to his, then laid her head on his shoulder. "I love you, too," she whispered.

The boulder sitting on his heart was lifted away. He actually felt his chest expand in relief, then tighten again. He wished he'd never bought that first property, never met Gavin Hawk.

He wished he'd valued his wife and marriage more than money.

"I couldn't help asking Julie why she was willing to forgive me," she said.

"What did she say?" He slid his arm around her waist.

Angelina fidgeted with the chains at her neck. "She said she figured I wouldn't apologize if I still wanted her husband. She laughed when she said it—kind of lightened the mood, you know? Then she said it's because God and Rick have forgiven her so much."

"I suppose we can relate to that."

"It's been a very humbling week for both of us."

"It has."

"We're starting over, aren't we?"

"Yes," he said. "I think we really are."

Chapter Twenty-four

She hadn't looked forward to going to church in a long time. Yet this morning, excitement simmered inside Angelina. Not simply because Nicholas was home and would be joining her. No, for the first time, she wanted to go. She wanted so badly to grow her relationship with God, if Nicholas backed out or were summoned by Julius at the last minute, she'd happily go to The Barn Church alone.

Sitting on the couch in the carriage house, she slipped on boots, her wedding rings, and the set of metal bracelets Nick had given her the night before. From a trip to India, he'd said, when he'd spent a couple of hours strolling an open market and watched a woman create jewelry from melted-down pennies. The artisan had worked with the same intensity Nick remembered seeing in Angelina when she painted.

Angelina gathered her purse, coat, and keys, and caught herself scanning her work area. She'd not worked on the desert painting, nor the two others waiting to be completed, in days. Glancing now at the bangles on her wrists, the urge to invite Nicholas into her workspace, to show him her work, swelled in her heart.

After church this morning, she might do just that.

She walked to the main house. They shared a meal of breakfast casserole, then Nick drove them to church in his car.

News vans sat at the edge of the full, grassy parking lot, no doubt waiting to pounce.

"Does Julius know about this?" she asked.

"I don't know," Nick said. "Do you see him? I'll pull up close to the doors so you can hurry inside without being accosted."

He stopped near the doors, and she stilled his hand.

"I'll stay with you if you want me to," she said. "So you don't have to face this alone."

"I always want you with me."

Julius knocked on Angie's window; she lowered it.

"Park around back. Pierce is waiting at the rear door."

"What about the media?"

He grinned. "Pierce has a plan."

They followed Julius' instructions and found Pierce waiting. He led them inside.

"Maybe we should leave," Nick told Pierce.

"Oh, no. Didn't you see the building is packed? Dad sees this as an opportunity. Says we should take advantage of it."

"I don't understand," Angelina said.

"That's right. You two wouldn't have watched the news this morning. The local affiliates dug up Julius' history and opened this morning with the headline *Local Ex-Thief and Drug Addict Defends Con Man From Same Local Church*. Dad suggested Julius offer a statement—from the pulpit. He's going to give his testimony first."

Angelina laughed. "No, he's not."

"Yes, he is."

"The press and nosey spectators won't stay to hear the truth," Nick said.

"They might not," Pierce said. "If they do, they'll hear the gospel, too."

Pierce turned to Angie. "You ready to be a spectacle?"

She certainly hadn't planned on it. Merely sitting with Kay in the front row was a huge step.

"We didn't string up a banner with your face plastered on it," Pierce said. "But texts between church members have been flying this morning. You're going to be welcomed, Angelina. Get ready for hugs."

"Look at my hands." She held them out so the men could see them shaking.

"Pierce. Give us a minute?" Nick asked.

"Sure. I'll be right back."

Pierce left them in the back hall.

Nick moved to stand in front of her. "We should get remarried here."

"Nicholas! That's too fast."

"I know. I'm jumping the gun. Sorry. Some habits die hard." He grinned. "Although I would love the chance to marry you again, do it right and include God this time."

"Can we just get through this morning?"

"You stopped shaking. Guess I distracted you enough, huh?"

"I suppose you did."

Pierce returned. "I just made an announcement to the congregation. Dad's cleared the front two rows and aisle on one side for the media. He's going to get them."

Angelina blinked. "You're kidding."

"You know my dad," Pierce said. "Do you think I'm kidding?"

They waited a few minutes. Then, Pierce ushered them into the sanctuary from the door behind the stage. Bulbs flashed. Reporters spoke into television cameras. Laurie and Kay flanked Angelina as Julius took Nick aside. The congregation stood, and Angelina caught the gaze of Clyde and Millie Newman. Deacon Floyd and his little wife. And finally, Daniel.

Her church, she thought. These people were her church family.

The choir started to sing "How Great Thou Art."

She joined arms with Laurie and Kay and walked down the steps to sit with her friends. How great, indeed.

The song ended. During other services she'd attended, Angelina remembered listening as the choir and congregation sang several songs. But this morning, they stopped after one. Daniel stepped to the pulpit and motioned for Julius to join him. He explained about the media's presence in the service, about Nick's predicament, and encouraged folks to pray for Nick and Angelina.

She felt eyes on her. Some of those gazes were probably full of speculation and judgment. But she let herself glance up and to each side. Mostly she saw compassion. Several mouthed *Praying for you.* Deacon Floyd's wife crossed her arms over her heart, an obvious gesture of love and care.

Kay patted Angie's knee, and Angelina felt her heart open to the people around her. No matter what the future held for Nick, she need never be alone or lonely again.

Julius stepped to the microphone. "Good morning, everyone. Some of you will remember me as the kid who, years ago, stole from the church, went into drug rehab, then became a lawyer. That's what happened, but it's not what I want you to take away from this morning.

"I grew up attending this church. I watched my parents live godly lives. I heard sound, scriptural teaching. I learned—I knew right from wrong, and I knew about Jesus and His death for us.

"What I didn't know was everything I needed for every moment of my life was already waiting for me at the foot of the cross. I didn't know the gifts—presents, if you will—which waited for me to simply open and receive."

Presents.

As Angelina listened to Julius, the word prompted an image to form in her spirit.

Gifts. For her. Strewn around the base of the cross. Waiting for her to open.

Waiting. For her to receive and use and enjoy.

She looked over at Nick.

She'd thought she understood God's love in providing for her salvation, then thought she'd lost it when she'd come so close to committing adultery.

She'd thought she understood Nick's love in marrying her, then thought she'd lost it when he'd repeatedly left her.

Love didn't work that way. Not God's love. Not real love.

Love continued offering.

Gift after gift. Present after present.

A smile spread across her face. Not the practiced, pageant smile she'd learned to depend on to keep others at bay. No, this smile came from deep inside—the smile of a child who'd discovered the joy of being loved and wanted and valued. The smile of a woman who knew she was loved and wanted and remembered.

She wanted every gift God had for her.

She wanted every present from Nick she'd refused to open before.

And it's only been a few days, she thought. Only a few days since she'd re-opened her life and heart to God, to Nick.

What wonderful things could happen if she continued on this path for the next week? Month? Year?

Angelina looked to heaven.

Dear God, I want it all—forgiveness, mercy, wisdom, strength—all of You and everything You have for me. And if You grant me time with Nick, I vow I'll receive and appreciate every moment, every gift he gives, too.

***

"That was some service." Nicholas walked with Angelina to the carriage house. "I'm still surprised a few of the media actually stayed."

"Did you know about Julius being injured while playing football, then getting addicted to painkillers and other drugs?" she asked.

"No. But I believe it. Believable, too, that he thought sports were his only path to a successful life, so being hurt would seem to threaten his whole future."

"I'm glad we've got him on our side."

"Me, too," he said. "He's good at calming me down, that's for sure. Sometimes I still can't believe all that's happening. I'll probably have to take another polygraph this week. Julius says it's another step toward my absolution."

Knowing at any moment, his time with her could be taken away was starting to wear on his nerves. *Dear God, please give me more time with her.*

They stopped.

"Thank you for lunch," she said.

Before they'd left for church that morning, he'd placed a roast, carrots, and potatoes in the oven, set the temperature and the timer.

"I must confess, I didn't know the timer on the stove worked that way," she said.

"Stick with me. You feel brave enough, one morning this week I'll teach you how to make the perfect omelet."

Angelina turned the bracelets at her wrist.

"Too fast again, huh?" he asked. "Sorry."

"No, I … would you like to see my paintings?"

His heart sputtered and settled into a heavy rhythm. "I'd love to."

He followed her up the stairs. She unlocked and opened the door. Sunlight streamed in the rows of windows on both sides of the long room. To his right sat a small kitchenette. To his left, shelves of art supplies, some untouched, some partially used. A thick stack of blank canvases rested against that wall. The remaining perimeter was lined with stacks of completed paintings, easels holding works in progress, and long tables of brushes, paints, rags, and solvents.

A sectional sofa dominated the center of the room. Two open suitcases rested on a large, matching hassock.

"Living this simply really doesn't bother you?" He walked to the middle of the space.

"No."

"That might be a good thing since we probably won't get our money back or be able to keep the house."

"I told you I didn't care about the house."

"I'm beginning to believe that."

He stepped closer to her work. He saw waterfalls. A beach that looked too crisp, too beautiful to be real. Monuments he recognized as being in Spain and Portugal.

"Are these for your show?"

"Yes."

"You painted all of these?"

"I had a lot of time on my hands."

"Your perspective, your talent—I feel as if I could reach out and touch stone or water or sand."

Joy bloomed on her face. "Thank you. I'm pretty nervous about the show. I've kept in touch with galleries back in Birmingham, but I didn't share about my art with anyone here. Until the radio spots about the exhibition aired, I don't even think anyone at church knew I painted. Somehow, it seems right you're the first to see it all."

"How will you move them?"

"By truck on Thursday. I've just begun preparing the packing lists. I'll have to oversee the process and stay in Mobile in a hotel until the show Saturday."

"I wish I could be there."

"Can Julius ask special permission for you to leave the county?"

"I don't know. I'll see. I'd give almost anything to be there for you."

He again surveyed the expansive work she'd done. "You must be proud of all this. Don't artists name their paintings or groups of paintings? These are amazing. How did you remember the details? How did you know what colors to choose? What techniques to use?"

She laughed. "Are you my first groupie? My first obsessed fan?"

"Yes. I always will be. I want to take you back to all of these places. I want to experience them with you and see them through your eyes."

His memory pricked, and his gaze sharpened. She'd visited Paris without him, too.

He scanned the stacks but found no French scenes or Paris landmarks. Then, he spied a dark cloth draped over a solitary stack of paintings at the far end of the room.

"Is that Paris?" he asked.

She turned away, hugging her elbows, and nodded.

"May I look at them?"

She nodded again.

"Are you crying?"

She didn't answer.

He lifted the drape.

The bank of the Seine. The Eiffel Tower. A quaint café. The unique, nearly transparent pyramid-shaped entrance to the Louvre—she'd created both a day and a night version, complete with a starry sky and what must have been hundreds of glowing lights.

In the left forefront of each, she stood, always wearing a red cape. Her long dark hair bordering her right shoulder. Her head turned so the viewer saw a swath of her cheek as if looking over her shoulder at the object of her perusal.

As he replaced the drape, a packing list fluttered to the ground beside his feet. *Eleven pieces. Series Title: The Lonely Woman.*

He rushed to her and turned her in his arms. She wept silently, her body quaking with long-buried hurt.

"I'm so sorry, Angelina."

Feeling helpless and awkward, he kissed her hair. Then her face, her tears.

Then he simply held on and rocked her while she cried.

Her chest shook against his. Her tears dampened his shirt.

"I'm sorry, my love." How he wanted to turn away from the pain he'd caused. "Don't hold the pain inside. Don't hold it between us. Forgive me. I was reckless and blind and focused on all the wrong things."

Finally, she drew back and looked up at him. "You've never let me cry before. Never held me or comforted me."

His eyes misted. "It was wrong of me. As long as I live, if I can get to you, you'll never cry alone again. Come sit down."

He led her to the couch. She snuggled up to his side.

He stroked her hair. After some time, he realized her breathing had gotten deep and even. He closed his eyes, and for the first time in months, slept beside his wife.

***

She was warm and safe and held.

Angelina breathed in, her husband's scent confirming he hadn't only held her while she cried but had continued to hold her while she napped.

She opened her eyes. Daylight was fading to dusk. The temperature dropping from yesterday's cold front, which was expected to stay a few days.

She burrowed against her husband and nuzzled his neck. How she'd missed him.

He woke with a start and moved to sit up. She tightened her hold on him.

"What time is it?" he asked.

"Almost six-thirty. Your alarm hasn't sounded."

"I turned it off for church. Guess I forgot to reset it."

She shifted, placing her head and a hand on his heart. "Tell me again you love me."

"I love you, Angelina. I hate it's taken me this long to learn how to show you."

She raised her head to look up at him. "I love you, too, Nicholas. Always and forever."

She wanted him to stay. She wanted to become one with him again and feel all the things she'd always wanted to feel.

But asking. Reaching. Being the first to touch was so risky.

He studied her.

The gift she wanted was within reach. If only she dared.

She touched his face. "Will you love me now? Be with me now?"

"Are you sure? I don't want you to do something because you feel pressured or because you're afraid I'll get mad and revert back to how I was."

"Not everything from before was bad."

He kissed her with tenderness and hunger. "I'm as nervous as I was our first time," he said.

"It is our first time."

"Tell me what you need."

"I want us to focus on each other," she said. "I want to feel every moment, every touch, and know we're thinking only of each other."

They took their time. Spent time. He whispered against her skin and made her tremble. She touched and stole his breath.

Wanting to be one with him, she reached for him. He loved her with a reverence that brought tears to her eyes, and she didn't try to hide them.

After, they lay in each other's arms.

"Will you stay tonight?" she asked.

"Does any part of this couch convert into a bed?"

"We are kind of squished together, aren't we? No, this isn't a sleeper sofa. We could toss all the cushions on the floor, sort of make a mattress."

"That might work."

She propped up on an elbow and drew images on his chest with her fingers.

"Let's hide here for the next few days," she said. "Just us. I'll call Laurie and Lorenzo and tell them we don't need them until Thursday. You call Julius and ask him not to schedule anything. Please?"

"Whatever will we do with all that time, Mrs. Rousseau?"

"Sleep in."

"Ugh."

"Take a walk."

"Better," he said.

"You can teach me to make an omelet."

He shook a finger and rolled on top of her. "Oh, no. No cooking for you tomorrow. If we're taking the day off, I won't risk you getting miffed at me telling you how to do something."

"Then you'll have to cook me breakfast again." She twirled the curls at his brow. "I'll need lots of pancakes."

He kissed the tip of her nose. "I'll be more than happy to make you lots of pancakes."

"Then I'll be more than happy to eat them."

Chapter Twenty-five

"I can't believe I let you talk me into teaching you how to cook a turkey." Nicholas spoke over his shoulder as Angelina entered the butler's pantry.

"I did okay with the omelet this morning. Let's keep going. The oven is preheating, and I'm ready."

He turned and saw she'd donned latex gloves that reached to her elbows. He laughed and leaned back against the counter where the turkey sat.

"What are those for?" he asked.

"I don't want to touch it."

He laughed again. "But you want to cook one?"

"I've always wanted to know how to cook a turkey."

"Is that why you had one in the freezer? Hoping one day, you'd be able to cook it? How old is this thing?"

"I don't know. Do frozen turkeys expire?"

He checked the label but found no "best by" date.

"I guess we'll find out. If it stinks up the house, we probably shouldn't eat it."

She came close and raised her gloved hands like a surgeon preparing to operate. "Where do I start?"

"Go grab the kitchen scissors."

She scurried away, and he pulled out his phone. When she returned, he snapped a picture of her with her gloves and the scissors. She gasped. He leaned over for a selfie with her and snapped another.

"You said we didn't have photos of the two of us," he said.

"So you took one now? Should we have included the turkey?"

"If you want."

She cringed. "Only if it turns out to be edible."

"Lower it into the sink. Trust me." He showed her how to remove the wrapping and the metal wire at the neck. "Now, reach in and remove the giblet bag."

"Excuse me?"

Her eyebrow winged up, as did the corner of her pretty mouth. He couldn't help but kiss her.

"Will you kiss me like that every time we cook together?" she asked.

"I just might."

He turned away, fighting guilt.

"We should have more memories like this," he said. "I shouldn't have let so much time pass apart from you."

After the entire weekend with no trip to the prison, no new news, he couldn't shake the feeling he was now living on borrowed time.

"And I should've been grateful when you were home," she said. "There. We were both dysfunctional idiots. Something else we have in common. Let's move on."

She stood there with the giblet bag in one gloved hand, the scissors in the other. He'd never loved her more.

He took her face in his hands and kissed her again. "My brave, fierce Angelina. Brave enough to tackle a turkey. Fierce enough to keep me on track."

Her eyes filled with surprise and innocent joy. "I've never been brave."

"You're the bravest person I know. I keep thinking about your art. How you traveled alone. How you put so much emotion into your paintings. Only the bravest of the brave can do that."

She smiled the killer smile that knocked him back and made him think of beaches and long nights in a private room.

"What?" she asked.

"Your smile always gets me."

"Really?" She smiled again.

"Really."

His cell chimed.

"Abide with me," Angelina said. "I enjoy abiding with you like this. I don't need this house. All I need is you."

"It's not the reminder. It's a text."

He read the screen. *Polygraph this Thursday morning. Pick you up at 11 A.M. Will update as I get more info. Relax.*

"What's wrong?" she asked. "Is it Julius? Bad news?"

"I have to take another polygraph this Thursday."

She tossed the giblet bag and scissors into the sink. Snapped off her gloves and wrapped her arms around him.

"I should go back through all the documents I have," he said. "The emails. Find something he can use to clear me."

"Julius is doing everything he can. I know the waiting and uncertainty are unbearable. They are for me, too. Don't close off from me. Don't leave me."

"Angie, I don't want to have to leave you. That's what's driving me crazy."

***

Angelina slipped the turkey into the oven, then set aside the oven mitts.

"Want to set the dining room table for us to eat in there?" Nick asked. "We've hardly ever done that."

"True." She thought of the crystal and china, the copper chargers she'd purchased years ago but never used.

She shook her head. "How long will this take to cook?"

"Hours."

"I need to show you something."

She led him to the dining room. From the china cabinet, she removed the copper chargers, napkin rings, ice bucket and tongs. She added the mugs, challises, the colander and cookie cutters, spreading all across the massive table.

"I bought all this the day you came home for our seventh anniversary."

"That's a lot. That's before we had this house."

"I didn't need them. Didn't even want them, really, although at the time I thought I did."

She lifted a mug. "All this time, I've told myself I never cared about money. Still, I used it to comfort myself even when I knew better. I have a lot of things like this—not what I purchased for the house while working with Rita—things I bought, no, indulged in. Will you help me sell them?"

"If that's really what you want to do. It kind of makes me feel bad."

She laid her head on his shoulder. "You shouldn't feel bad about these. I knew I spent too much money. We both lacked self-control, we simply manifested it in our own unique way."

They took pictures of the items. Then they worked in their master suite. Nick packed a few things to bring back to the carriage house. She set aside designer purses she knew could be sold quickly through a specialty website.

She opened and took pictures of the handmade quilt and pillow shams they'd purchased in Gatlinburg. "We never used this, either."

When the turkey was done, Nick carved it into thin slices for sandwiches they ate over paper towels. She didn't miss the chargers, the crystal, or the china. They returned to the carriage house, bringing leftovers and Nick's small bag of essentials. He placed ads on eBay while she put the finishing touches on her desert painting.

"The bedding is sold," Nick said from the couch.

"Told you. *Buy it now* always works."

Angelina laid aside her paint brush and checked her watch. "Too late to go to the post office now. I can ship it in the morning."

"I'll go with you. We can send the notification right away."

Dear God, she prayed. *Can we keep this closeness? This life?*

"Selling the bedroom furniture wouldn't be difficult," she said. "I bet we could do it locally on Craig's List."

"But that's one of the few things we chose together."

"True. Giving it up would sting, but not as much as the Bev Doolittle painting. We'd have trouble fitting the furniture in a smaller master bedroom. The painting, we can hang anywhere."

"Good idea. Whoa." Nick set aside his laptop and rose.

"What?" Fear rippled through her. She lunged for the computer. "What?"

"Angie. Don't. Why didn't I see this coming?" He wiped a hand over his face. "I'm sorry."

A local news clip video played in the top corner of the screen. The background a split screen of The Barn Church there in Rowe City, and Fairchild's gallery in Mobile. She turned up the volume.

"*… the couple attended church together yesterday morning. Speculation ranges from the local artist being an innocent bystander to an accomplice in a regional real estate scam. In either case, only time will tell if the related press over her husband's arrest and legal troubles will benefit or hinder Angelina Rousseau's premier exhibition, Fairchild's first event of the season.*"

The image changed to her headshot beside Nick's mug shot.

"*To date, this reporter has been unable to confirm Mrs. Rousseau has retained a criminal attorney, although confidential sources state she might be in the market for a divorce lawyer. It appears she moved out of the couple's mansion before Thanksgiving. Since Mrs. Rousseau never traveled abroad with her husband, many wonder if his intent was to hide criminal activities from her or to remove her from suspicion in the event he was caught."*

She went back to her painting, drank from a nearby bottle of water.

Their eyes met.

Why hadn't he taken her with him?

The question and the old hurt that accompanied it seemed to jump at her. Important? Or at this point, petty? Others obviously wondered, but for different reasons.

Dear God, to move forward, do we have to talk about every single mistake we made? And if we miss one, will that be the one that comes back to bite us?

She didn't want to always put Nicholas on the defensive. Still, if the wound was deep and stopped her from moving forward ...

Talk about the ones I bring to the surface. And don't leave Me out of the conversation.

Remember, for where two or three have gathered together in My name, I am there in their midst.

"Can we pray?" she asked. "Right now?"

He came to her. "Yes."

"Dear God, I think You just brought up in me a hurt I have to address. So I must ask my husband about it. Help me ask without accusation. Listen without judgment. Bring healing to me, and if at all possible, make us closer to each other and to You."

She opened her eyes to find Nick watching her.

She swallowed. "Why didn't you ever take me with you?"

"Too many reasons and none of them are good enough. At first, it was the money, and you were in school."

"But summers. I was off in the summer."

"Then, I worried I wouldn't be able to spend enough time with you. I didn't want you to feel angry and cheated while I worked, and I didn't want to break another promise."

"So you didn't try."

He nodded. "Later, I worried about your safety as terror attacks became more frequent, especially in Europe. In the end, I admit we fought so much when I was home, being away was a relief. Work was something I was good at. If we'd traveled together and fought while I was trying to work, I don't know if I would have been able to do my job."

He sighed. "And of course, I always wanted to make more money for us. That's all of it. Every stupid reason I had."

"Sounds like you had the list ready."

"You asked when they let you see me in prison. The look on your face, the emptiness in your eyes—I knew you were gone, and I knew it was my fault. At night when I laid there alone in the dark, I asked myself the same question and came up with the answer in case you ever asked again. Please forgive me. I didn't know the harm I was causing."

"But you knew you were telling me *no*. Every time you said *yes* to someone or something else, you said *no* to me."

He placed his hands on her shoulders. "I have many reasons, but no real excuse. Forgive me. I'm asking for mercy, Angie. I was young and stupid, and if I could go back and do it over again, I'd tell you *yes* every single time. From now on, I won't leave because I'm distracted. I won't leave when I'm angry or when there's strife between us."

Forgive. Don't sow distance this time. Forgive. Like I do.

How? How do I forgive him?

He's already changing and keeping his word. He's staying, right now, even when there's strife between you. Don't close your heart to him or Me.

The power is yours. Don't say no.

Her heart trembled. For a moment, her breath stuck in her lungs.

Not all mercy is for you to keep.

Pressure built in her chest.

Some mercy is to be given to others.

"I forgive you." She pressed her cheek to his. "I forgive you."

He wrapped her in his arms. "Thank you."

Peace swept through her. Peace that didn't make sense, yet settled quickly in her heart.

She breathed it in deep. Clean and clear and fresh.

Their tears mingled, and they held each other as they cried.

Chapter Twenty-six

For the fourth morning in a row, Nicholas walked to the main house to prepare breakfast. Silly, maybe. He could've stocked Angie's small fridge with a few things, but somehow starting the day this way was more fun. Soon, Laurie and Lorenzo would arrive to continue their work. Later, Angelina would leave for Mobile. Tonight, he'd be the one alone in the big house.

Still, the future lay before them, full of love and possibilities. He was so full of gratitude, he couldn't help smiling, despite the polygraph looming before him later that morning.

He rounded the corner of the house to the sound of approaching sirens. He stopped, hoping they would drive past his property.

The sound grew. Joined now by flashing lights. All coming toward him up the lane.

He almost turned around and ran back to the carriage house. But if the next few moments were going to be really bad, he didn't want Angelina to remember him as a coward.

Four cars stopped in his driveway—two marked, two unmarked—positioned to bar his exit. The sirens stopped, but the red and blue lights still flashed.

A policeman exited the first car. "Nicholas Rousseau. Stop where you are. Put your hands up. You are under arrest."

He complied.

"Nick? Nick!" His wife's cries nearly broke his heart.

She ran straight to him and stopped as the officer lowered his hands to cuff them behind his back.

"Step back, ma'am." Another officer blocked her path.

"What's happened?" Angelina asked. "Why are you taking him again? Nicholas?"

"You're under arrest on suspicion of the murder of Gavin Hawk. You have the right to remain silent." The officer binding his hands recited the Miranda warning.

"Murder?" his wife cried.

"Angie, call Julius," Nick called over his shoulder.

"Where are you taking him?" she asked.

"Straight to the state prison, ma'am. Please stay back."

"I love you, Angelina!"

Nick ducked into the back of the police cruiser. The car lurched forward. He looked out the rear window, keeping Angelina in sight as long as possible.

Murder?

If Gavin was dead, Nick's life might be over, too.

***

Angelina could only stare as the police cruiser carrying Nicholas drove away.

Dear God, help. Help us.

Another officer approached. She remembered him from the day she'd returned from Vegas.

"Detective Niles. What's going on?"

"Ma'am, we need to search your property again. Will you let us in?"

She withdrew her keys from her pocket. "Will you need to search the carriage house, too? Go through my paintings again?"

"Possibly. We also need to ask you some questions."

"Ask me now."

"You don't want an attorney present?"

"I don't need one. And neither should my husband. He's innocent."

"You know that for a fact? Have you spent every moment with him since his release last Tuesday?"

"No."

The officer looked at her with mildly restrained doubt.

"So, he can't use you as an alibi?" Niles asked.

"He doesn't need an alibi. I know he's innocent. I know him."

She unlocked the door and opened it wide. "Search away. Anywhere you want. We've nothing to hide. If you need to check my art again, you have to do it in my presence. But you better hurry. My paintings and I will be leaving soon."

Laurie pulled in and hurried to Angelina. "What in the world?"

Angie started to shake. She relayed what happened. "I don't know the details."

Laurie took her hand and pulled her aside. "What can I do?"

"I should care about the art show, but right now all I can think about is Nick. We reconciled. We've spent days together, and they were the best ever."

Tears shimmered in Laurie's eyes. "You know me, they're happy tears."

"I'm happy, too. For the first time in a long, long time. I love him. I want this to be over. I want my life with him."

"Of course you do."

And what if she had to wait? Days or weeks for Nick to be released. Or years, if—heaven forbid—he was convicted of crimes she knew he didn't commit.

"If the worst happens, I'll have you and Pierce, Kay, and Daniel, and my church family for support, won't I?"

"Absolutely. We're here for the long haul."

The truck arrived. Angie and Laurie worked together loading the paintings—a tedious task as the officers re-examined each piece. Finally, all was secured, and the truck drove away. After sending Laurie home, Angelina packed her bag. She locked the carriage house and descended the stairs behind Detective Niles.

"I have to leave," she said. "Would you mind making sure the house is secure when you're done there?"

"Where's the art show?"

"Mobile." She rattled off the address.

"Not sure how the state prosecutor is going to feel about you being in another county."

"I'm not missing my first exhibition. I'll be back Saturday evening. Probably by way of the prison to see my husband."

He looked at her long and hard. "You better give me the name of your hotel."

She complied. Placed her suitcase in her car and got in. She wove through cops and law enforcement vehicles, passed her house and the line of pines. Reporters and a television crew all but blocked her driveway.

She slowed. *Please, just let me through*, she thought.

Bulbs flashed bright, the LED glare blinding her. A reporter yelled into his microphone even as he pounded on her window and trotted beside her car.

"Do you believe your husband is guilty of real estate fraud? Did you know of his schemes? Were you already planning to divorce?"

The television cameraman was at her front bumper, leaning over the hood yet walking backward. Why wouldn't they leave her alone?

Finally, she reached the road. She hit the horn, jerked the wheel around the tip of the news van, and floored it.

***

"What happened, Nick? Did you finally snap? Where's the body? Will we ever find Gavin Hawk?"

Once again, Nick found himself in an interview room, wearing prison-orange scrubs and sandals, his hands bound with handcuffs and secured around the metal bar at the end of the table. Facing him sat State Prosecutor Darrin Simon, looking morning fresh with his tailored suit and gleaming white teeth.

Stay calm, he told himself.

"My client knows nothing of Gavin Hawk's current condition or location," Julius said.

"When's the last time you saw Gavin Hawk?" Simon asked.

Nick waited for Julius' nod. "I told you before. I met with him in his Mobile office before I left on my last trip to Spain. About four months ago."

"What did you two talk about?"

Again Julius nodded.

"He showed me concept drawings for suites in the resort. He even had a drawing of the view from above."

"Tell me about the drawings."

"The building was shaped like a pyramid. That shape, combined with the way the strip of land jutted out, meant rooms on two sides faced the beach. The third side was for offices, maintenance, laundry, and such."

"A pyramid," Simon said. "Like on PGI's logo?"

"Yes. What does it matter?"

"Ever see a pyramid like this?" Simon slid photos to Julius, who handed them to Nick.

The pyramid of black onyx was stamped with the golden PGI logo.

"This was supposed to be the hotel trademark," Nick said. "About eight inches high. One in every room or something. Gavin was psyched about it. He had me hold it to feel how heavy it was. Made of real stone, I think."

"So you held one in his office." Simon took back the photos.

"My client already disclosed he did indeed hold one, at Gavin Hawk's request."

"Which would explain your fingerprints, of course."

Nicholas looked at Julius, who stayed him with a hand.

"I think you should tell us the significance of this item," Julius said.

"Your voice print was not a match with Trina Iles' voicemail recording. She turned over email correspondence—between her and you, or someone using your name—to us. We traced them back. They didn't come from your computer."

"I told you I never met the woman. Never talked with her. I didn't do this."

"Yes, you did tell me that. And I didn't exactly listen, did I?" Simon tapped the photos on the table between them. "Did you get impatient? Thinking your name would never be cleared, did you figure if you're going to jail for the rest of your life, you might as well kill Gavin for doing this to you?"

Nick jerked back. "No!"

"I'd believe it, after seeing you during the polygraph last Friday."

"I was frustrated. I've never been in a situation like this before."

"There's blood on the pyramid from Hawk's office. His blood and hair. Your fingerprints. Nothing else."

"That's enough," Julius said. "I'd like to confer with my client."

Simon stood. "You've got ten minutes." He left.

"Julius?"

"It's bad, Nick. This is bad. They can hold you for a while. No bail because you would have had to leave the county to go to Gavin's office. Tell me everything you did since your release."

Nick filled him in, then sighed. "So, they finally believed I might not be guilty of fraud, and what? Searched Gavin's offices and apartment over the weekend?"

"They're not sure you're innocent, but they did searches yesterday. I was told after I arrived here this morning."

"That's what Simon meant about being impatient and losing my temper. He thinks I finally found Gavin and killed him. Gavin could be anywhere. Can they prosecute me for murder without finding a body?"

"It's been done before," Julius said. "We're going to dig in here. We'll go over every detail again from the beginning. I had the photo of Gavin enlarged." He removed it from his briefcase. "Is there anything that jogs your memory? The woman, Gavin's clothes, the background?"

Nick concentrated. The hard copy showed a wider view of the scene, but the background was still blurry and dark as if the picture were taken in a small, poorly lit space.

Like a cell. The kind he might spend the rest of his life in.

"Angelina and I—we just started over. I can't lose my life with her. I don't care about the money or the house. But they can't take my life with my wife."

"When Prosecutor Simon comes back, don't answer any questions. We need to buy time for me to look at their evidence, review it with you, and plan a strategy."

"I won't go back home this time, will I?"

"I'm afraid not. They think you left the county and killed someone." He paused. "And Nick, I've got more bad news from our PI. Cameron discovered Gavin owes tens of millions in gambling debts."

"That would explain why he formed the dummy corporation and

framed me, wouldn't it?"

"It could. But gambling debts of that kind mean he's into some dangerous stuff. If someone's trying to collect and Gavin's lying low, we may never find him. Or worse, if someone's already gotten to him and couldn't collect, he could already be dead. We may never be able to prove you're innocent."

Nick looked at his hands, bound and bare. They'd taken his wedding ring when they booked him.

"Call Angelina for me. Tell her I love her. Tell her I'm so proud of her. Tell her I'll be thinking of her and only her. But don't tell her the rest, okay? Let her get through the art show without knowing I might never come home."

***

On Saturday morning, Angelina looked out the second-story office window at Fairchild's Gallery, which dominated a prominent corner near Mobile's Garden District. With fifteen-foot high ceilings and strategically placed lighting, Fairchild's would give her work the best possible debut.

Except Nicholas wouldn't be there. As of last night, there'd been no progress in his case, and Gavin Hawk was still nowhere to be found.

The morning was clear. The temperature, January crisp.

The gallery air was scented with spice and pine—a nod to winter. An elegant brunch would be served buffet style throughout the show and auction from ten to two, courtesy of Antoni's Restaurant across the street. She gazed there now, at the brass-paned windows flanking deep wine double-doors, and the private patio on the side with its mythical Greek statues.

From the corner of her eye, camera lights flashed. She recoiled from the window. Although the latest charges against Nick had not yet been made public, Thursday night, reporters had ambushed her at the hotel. They'd also followed her on each trip to the gallery.

Thankfully, this time, the camera wasn't aimed at her, but rather at a photo shoot taking place outside Antoni's. A woman draped herself against a stone god and lifted her face to the sun.

Angelina turned from the window, checked her makeup in the full-length mirror by the door. The cobalt sheath dress seemed to shimmer around her. She should feel confident. Elated.

Instead, her heart ached. Long hours of preparation for the art show meant she hadn't seen Nicholas since Thursday morning. She hoped if she left early enough, she'd make it to the prison before visiting hours ended today.

Angelina texted Julius. *Any news?*

He responded. *Not yet. You'll be the first to know.*

She checked her watch. The next four hours would be tricky. But she could do it—maintain her composure, interact with the public. She placed her phone in her purse and stowed it in a cabinet. She squared her shoulders, rode down in the elevator, and pasted on her beauty pageant smile.

Zane Fairchild, wearing his signature silver-gray tux, met her as the doors opened. He took her hand and guided her through a series of doors to the reception area in the building's center.

"My dear, you look lovely." His bald head shone under the high lights. "Not to sound insensitive, but the publicity surrounding your husband's situation has afforded us a sold-out event. It's standing-room only in the gallery. Antoni's is scrambling to feed all the guests."

"So, attendance is high?"

"Indeed. Angelina, what can I do to help? Nick's predicament is impossible, I know. The timing, despicable. Can you persevere?"

She still couldn't believe Nick had been charged with murder and couldn't bring herself to discuss that with Mr. Fairchild or anyone else. The world would know soon enough, but hopefully not until after her show.

"I'll be fine. I appreciate this opportunity and all you've done for me. However, I will leave when the final auction ends."

"I understand. I'll sneak you out the back if I have to."

"Thank you."

He kissed her cheek. "I'm terribly proud of you, my dear. You'll do well today. I can feel it."

"Thank you, again."

Mr. Fairchild assigned an intern, Darla, to escort her throughout the reception area and gallery. She steered Angelina around and through the displays to insure all attendees saw her, greeted her, and had just enough time before the auction to glimpse each piece of her work.

She led Angelina to a private viewing booth on the right of the auditorium. On screens and through a series of well-placed microphones she could see and hear each bid, be it live or from an online buyer.

The sale began.

"That guy in the back is either a jerk, or he has money," Darla mumbled. "Sorry. I noticed the same bidder bumping up the opening bids of the first two pieces, then bowing out."

"Do people do that? Bump up the prices?"

"Sometimes. Sometimes it's a jerk, sometimes it's someone who can't make up his mind. Either way, it's more money for you and the gallery. I'll be curious to see if he actually buys anything."

Mr. Fairchild sold the waterfall series. The Seychelles Islands set. Other single works, including the monuments of Spain and Portugal. He'd warned her he would hold *The Lonely Woman* series until the end.

"The crowd will stay," he'd assured her. "And we'll sell it all."

Now, Angelina sat forward on the edge of her seat as the first three pieces of *The Lonely Woman* were placed on easels on the stage.

And she remembered. Nicholas, viewing them slowly as if using them to see into her soul. Reaching for her with sorrow in his voice. For the first time, holding her while she cried.

The way they'd loved each other.

Dear God, please bring my husband back to me.

Bidding resumed. The prices quickly rose.

As Mr. Fairchild had predicted, each piece sold. Angelina's mind spun at the purchase prices. Still, sadness spread at parting with such personal work.

I'll paint more, she thought. I'll paint and sell, paint and sell for as long as it takes to free Nicholas.

The side door to the viewing room opened.

Mr. Fairchild approached with open arms. "Angelina. Did I not tell you we would fare well today?" He kissed her cheek. "Already I am being asked if you will take commissions. Don't worry. I'll hold them off until your legal troubles are resolved."

"Thank you. I really must go."

She hurried upstairs to his office, retrieved her purse. Her phone buzzed. Julius.

"Hello?"

"Angelina. Are you on your way?"

"No. I'm about to leave."

"Glad I caught you. Don't come tonight. You won't be able to see him."

"But I can be there in time."

"They're about to do the polygraph they didn't do on Thursday. Stay by your phone."

"I'm going straight home. Call me with updates, no matter the time."

Chapter Twenty-seven

In the same small room as before, Nicholas sat in the designated chair. Julius leaned over his shoulder. "No matter what they throw at you, stay in control, or they will bury you."

His attorney left, the technician entered. A different man than had performed the first polygraph. Nick tried to steady his breathing. He knew how intense and precarious the process would be.

The technician wired him up. "I was told you've been through this type of test before. Would you like me to explain the procedure?"

"That's not necessary."

"Then let's begin. What is your name?"

Same first question as last time. "Nicholas Rousseau."

"What is your *full* name?"

"Sorry." He should have remembered.

"What is your full name?"

"Nicholas Francois Rousseau."

"What day is today?"

"Saturday."

He stared ahead, blocking out the bleak surroundings. Focusing on the routine, the technician's tone. Last time, they'd continued this type of mundane questions for many minutes.

"Did you kill Gavin Hawk?"

Nick jolted. "No."

"Have you ever done bodily harm to anyone?"

Sure. He'd gotten into fights like any other boy in elementary school. "Yes."

"Have you ever done bodily harm to Gavin Hawk?"

"No."

Sweat soaked his armpits and ran down his spine.

"Did the gold box from your safe deposit box contain a necklace for your wife?"

"Yes."

"Did you know the necklace was stolen?"

Stolen? "No."

His heart raced. Stay calm. Breathe.

"Did you steal the necklace kept in the gold box in your safe deposit box?"

"No."

"Are the investment documents in your safe deposit box real?"

"Yes."

The seconds became minutes. The minutes, surely an hour.

"Since your arrest, have you spoken with Gavin Hawk?"

"No."

"Do you know where Gavin Hawk is?"

"No."

The questions struck like punches. Stealing his breath, threatening to double him over.

Dear God, help me. Julius was right. They're going to lock me away.

Abide with Me. Wherever you are, abide with Me.

"Did you kill Gavin Hawk?"

Despair crept over him and worked its way inside.

All his efforts to provide for Angie had been in vain. Without knowing, he'd sabotaged them.

Never again would he get the opportunity to take care of her. He'd be here, or in some other prison. And she'd be out there, alone.

"Repeating the question. Did you kill Gavin Hawk?"

"No."

Dear God, only a miracle will get me out of here. If that never happens, please take care of my wife. Provide for her and stay with her always.

***

"The State Prosecutor says Nicholas could have forged his documents as easily as we claim Gavin did," Julius said.

Phone in hand, Angelina ran up the carriage house stairs. "We have to do something."

"He has an answer for every suspicion we raise concerning Gavin and balks at Gavin faking his death to further frame Nick. We have to prepare the defense of the century before Monday's hearing."

She went inside, locking the door behind her. "How can I help?"

"I don't know. Maybe we should start at the beginning. What's throwing me off is the real estate fraud investigative team is now working with local FBI agents on another angle. Remember the necklace in the gold box?"

"The one they kept."

"It's stolen."

"That can't be."

"I'm telling you what I just learned after they finished the polygraph."

She sank onto the couch. "How's Nick?"

"He's in bad shape, Angie. I've never seen him this discouraged. Simon's mad. He's right in the middle of a power struggle between two groups of federal agents. He's putting a lot of pressure on Nick, trying to break him. He's offering a deal for a confession."

"But Nick didn't do any of the things he's accused of."

"I've seen lesser men break. Ten years, versus life in prison, or the possibility of capital punishment. A deal would guarantee he'd come home at some point, as opposed to a trial where the worst could happen."

She couldn't think about that.

"We have to find Gavin," she said. "I made enough at the sale. If I budget wisely, I can keep us afloat. Hire another private investigator. Do whatever you have to."

"Cameron's been in Mobile for days. He's got no leads."

She rubbed her forehead. "I should have stayed and helped him search. I was right there. Can you and I meet tomorrow? Just so I know all we're up against?"

"If it'll help you feel better, I'll make time. After I see Nick in the morning, I'll come to you."

She ended the call, watched through the windows as evening approached.

Another sunset alone. How many had she spent by herself? Too many to count.

Dear God, I didn't want to feel this way ever again. Wrestling the loneliness I always battled when Nick had been gone for a couple of days and the sadness settled in. My heart was ripped away from his and torn open so many times. It can't be right for me to hurt this way anymore.

She needed to paint. To get the pain out.

She grabbed a blank canvas and set it on an empty easel. She loaded a palette with blots of color, chose a brush.

No image came. No texture. No shape.

Her fingers itched. She turned the easel. Flipped the canvas to vertical. Flipped it back.

Still, she had no idea where to begin. No vision for where she would end.

The pain blossomed.

I'm right here.

But I can't see You, she thought. *I can't touch You. How would I know if You leave?*

I don't leave. I never leave.

She slashed black across the white cotton. She could feel the darkness pressing in. Feel herself huddling up to hide in solitude.

Self-preservation became the goal. Like every time before, her heart wanted to shut down and close itself off to avoid being hurt.

She made another full stroke of black.

Keep your heart open to Me, to Nick. Abide with Me.

She flung down the brush, stepped away from the canvas. Curled up on the couch with her blanket.

You don't have to be alone. Abide with Me. Abide …

Sunlight speared across her face. She opened her eyes to morning.

Sunday morning.

She stayed still. She didn't want to be alone. She wanted God's presence.

"I open my heart to You, Lord," she whispered.

She didn't want a heart full of loneliness. She wanted a heart full of love.

"I open my heart to Nick, too."

Abide with Me.

"Yes, Lord. I will abide with You."

She wanted companionship and friendship, learning and laughter.

Angelina rose and dressed for church. This morning she'd go by herself, but not alone.

***

Angelina helped Kay clear the table. "Laurie, lunch was great, but I could have met with Julius at my place."

"Nonsense." Laurie rinsed lunch dishes in the kitchen sink. "One or two more here on a Sunday afternoon isn't a problem. Besides, the men are already napping in the rocking chairs on the porch."

"Hope's already napping on Daniel," Kay said.

"Knock, knock." Julius stuck his head around the porch door.

"Come on in," Laurie said. "Take over the table. Kay and I'll be in the living room if you need us." They left the kitchen.

"Julius, I'll be right back." She followed the women. "Laurie, Kay."

They turned, and Angelina extended her arms, a request to them both. The group hug made her feel warm and safe and welcomed.

"You both mean so much to me." She dabbed at her eyes, then looked at Laurie. "Look, we match. Happy tears."

Kay squeezed her hand. "We're right here if you need us."

She returned to the table. "How's Nick? Should I go see him this afternoon?"

"Honestly?" Julius unloaded documents from his briefcase. "He was pretty quiet this morning. I think we'd help him most by strategizing for tomorrow's hearing."

"Right." *Dear God, I love Nick so much. Please show us what to do.* "Tell me everything, from the beginning."

He laid out the sequence of events from the first arrest, through yesterday's polygraph.

Angelina sat beside Julius. "If Gavin is alive, and he hasn't been seen since he left his office the night before Nick's first arrest, he's covered his tracks well."

Julius spread pictures before her. "You remember his office?"

"Yes. I went there a couple of times years ago after Nick first met him."

"See anything out of place?"

"I don't know if I remember enough to tell."

"What about this woman?"

The selfie of Gavin and the long-haired blonde looked as if it had been taken in a bar or dimly-lit restaurant.

"Who's the woman?" Angie tapped the photo.

"We believe his girlfriend, but can't confirm. She's a model, supposedly out of the country on assignment."

A model?

Her memory pricked. "I saw her yesterday outside a restaurant in Mobile."

"When?"

"Before my art show."

Julius' smile spread. "You're sure?"

"Absolutely."

He whipped out his phone. "Cameron. You still in Mobile? I need you to talk to Angelina. She thinks she saw Olivia Furtado there yesterday."

She gave Cameron every detail.

"I'm on it," Cameron said. "Tell Julius I'll call back after I get to Antoni's."

She ended the call and handed Julius back his phone.

"I think we should drive to the prison." Julius gathered his documents. "If we get a break, I want to be able to tell Nick in person."

"Will they let me see him?"

"I'll call ahead and ask. Since you couldn't see him last night, they might make an exception."

"Go. I'm right behind you. Just let me fill Laurie and the others in. I want them praying for us."

Chapter Twenty-eight

Nicholas looked up when Julius entered the interview room. He knew what he had to do. Ten years was ten years, was ten years.

This time, he'd use that time as wisely as possible and hope Angelina would forgive him for all his actions had and would cost her.

"I want to take the deal. I'll start my sentence now, or as soon as they'll let me."

Julius glanced at the officer who'd been waiting with Nick. "Can you leave us alone, please?"

The officer complied.

His attorney made sure the door had fully latched. "I know what you're thinking. I want you to listen to me."

"Julius, I want you to call Simon right now and take the deal. I'll sign it in blood if I have to, right now."

Julius raised his hands. "Hold on."

"Do you work for me, or not?" He couldn't hold his composure much longer. "Don't you have to do what I want?"

"Yes. First, just listen."

Nick shook his head.

"Five minutes?" His attorney's eyes darted to the one-way mirror. "You know you can trust me."

Nick's gaze locked on Julius. Someone was watching? Someone was listening.

His attorney's face relaxed. "Let me fill you in. You knew when I left here earlier I was going to meet Angelina. We reviewed all that's happened, including various photos. Yesterday, Angie saw Gavin's girlfriend—the one we believed to be working abroad—in Mobile outside a restaurant called Antoni's. Cameron has spoken with the owner there. Olivia Furtado, the model to be featured in Antoni's new promotional flyers, is really Olivia Furtado-Knight, daughter of Jarrod Knight, casino boat line owner."

Nicholas got a glimmer of insight. "Does Knight own the casino boat Gavin took me and others on?"

"Yes, he does. And until recently, when his little girl got her heart broken by a boyfriend who disappeared and stopped returning her calls, he'd extended a very large credit line to Gavin Hawk, a frequent boat visitor and gambler."

The glimmer flashed bright. "Gavin framed me and ditched the girlfriend."

"We believe he was using her as a buffer with Knight, to buy time to pay his debts."

"Which brings us back to all the money he stole."

Julius nodded. "That's what we believe. We also believe the jewelry was a side job for Hawk. You said he accompanied you to the jewelry gallery, right? Did he influence your choice?"

"Actually, he did. We narrowed it down to two or three. I chose."

"The Feds say you're not the only client Gavin steered toward jewelry when on the boat. Possibilities are high they'll be arresting the gallery owners for selling stolen goods. They believe Gavin took a cut each time one of his clients made a purchase. But being a terrible gambler …"

"He lost more than he acquired and couldn't repay his debts," Nicholas reasoned.

"Some people always want more."

"God knows I was like that." He took a deep breath. "What now?"

"Cameron just texted me. He spoke with Furtado by phone. She had no idea about the real estate scheme Gavin was into, so she's doubly mad now at being deceived by a crook. She said the authorities should check one of her father's casino boats, which is currently docked for re-provisioning. It seems she and Gavin had used a suite there more than once as a private getaway. Knight's just given his permission for the search. The Feds and local authorities are moving in now."

Nicholas wiped a hand over his face. "How long? Hours?"

"Maybe. How about I get you some water? Something to eat?"

"Just water, thanks."

Julius left. Nicholas turned toward the glass. Were detectives watching? Was State Prosecutor Simon? Other federal agents?

Julius didn't return. Nick tried to count the minutes. Knew he'd sat alone at least ten, twenty.

He put his head down on the table.

Dear God, could this nightmare be over soon? In days or hours, can I be home again with Angelina for good?

Abide with Me. Wherever you are, abide with Me.

The door opened.

Julius' smile said it all. "We got him. There'll be some paperwork. Procedure might take a day or so, but even though we can't get your money back, I thought you'd like to see someone. For the record, Simon cleared it." He motioned toward the mirror. "And of course, he's watching."

Angelina rushed into the room and into his arms. She kissed him, and he held on to the woman he loved more than anything else.

"You're going to be free," she said. "It's almost over."

"Thank God." Nick pressed his face to hers. "Thank You, God. Angie, I'm so sorry my greed and insecurity nearly ruined our lives. I'll never make another big decision or big purchase without talking with you first."

"You mean no more gifts?"

"Only inexpensive ones, and only once in a while."

"Fine with me. Although I'm glad now you bought that necklace."

Epilogue

Epilogue

Valentine's Day, tenth anniversary

Angelina stopped before the sanctuary's double doors. She slipped her arm through Daniel's and gave in to the urge to bend and kiss his cheek.

"You're a beautiful bride," Daniel said. "Can't believe you won't let me chew gum."

"You smack too loudly."

"I can be discreet."

"But you never are."

"Shh, you two." Kay straightened the train of Angelina's thrift store gown. "You'll miss your cue."

"Daniel," Angelina whispered. "I was never given away before. Thank you for doing this for us today."

"You're gonna make this old man cry," he said. "Now I really need my gum."

The wedding march began. Angelina heard the rustle of fabric as her friends and church family stood. Deacon Floyd and Clyde Newman opened the doors.

She scanned The Barn Church sanctuary from the rafters, to the pews, to the stage.

Laurie stood at the front on the left, holding Hope's hand. A pile of red rose petals lay at the child's feet. Pierce stood in the center, holding his Bible. On the right, Nicholas waited, wearing a dark suit.

As Daniel escorted Angelina down the aisle, her eyes met her husband's. *Hey*, Nick mouthed, and she couldn't help smiling.

They reached the front. This time, Daniel kissed her cheek, then turned her to face Nicholas and went to his seat.

"I've never loved you more," Nick said.

"Nor I you."

"Abide with me?"

"Forever and always."

Pierce cleared his throat. "You're not exactly supposed to start without me."

The crowd chuckled. Deacon Floyd's *ha-ha* echoed in the vaulted space.

Someone giggled. Someone popped gum.

"Daniel," Kay whispered. "Where did you get that?"

"I have friends."

The laughter rumbled, then grew.

"Hurry up and kiss her!" Clyde yelled from the back.

"Shush, you," Millie said. "They're not done yet. Haven't even started, really."

Angelina's shoulders shook. "This is very different from the courthouse and McNuggets and French Fries."

"Ree-ries! Ree-ries!" Hope took off and ran straight to Daniel. "Papa, ree-ries!"

"Soon, baby girl. Soon." He scooped her up. "Now, let's watch these two get married again."

"Dearly beloved," Pierce said. "We are gathered here today, to witness the reunion of this man and woman. Nicholas, Angelina, please join hands."

They complied. Nicholas stepped closer.

"You're so beautiful," Nick said. "I can hardly believe you'd marry me again."

"I'm just glad you asked me again."

"Okay," Pierce lowered his Bible. "Are we doing this by the book, or are we flying by the seat of our pants?"

"By the book," they said in unison.

Again, the crowd laughed.

Nicholas kissed her forehead. "Never again will we leave God or His Word behind."

"Never," Angelina said.

She turned to Pierce. "We're ready."

Discussion Questions

1. At the opening of the story, we see Angelina in Las Vegas at a wedding. The beauty and romance of the ceremony is in direct contrast to her unhappiness in her marriage. When have you looked at your marriage and seen it lacking? To what or whom did you attribute that lack? Discuss that Angelina's real hurts led to fantasizing about a different life and another man. Do you see a link between Angelina's spiritual condition and the condition of her marriage? Why, or why not?

2. From the start of the marriage, we see Angie's naivety. As a newlywed, about what aspects of marriage were you naïve? Did that naivety cause any problems? What problems did it cause, and how?

3. From the start of the marriage, we see Nick's focus on providing for Angelina. While that goal can be a manifestation of love and is a good trait for a husband, Nick's desire is rooted in negative childhood experiences. What goals do you have, which on the surface might appear normal or good, yet they originate in a negative experience? How can you work with God to sort healthy goals from unhealthy goals? Is it possible for a goal to be "good" yet not of God?

4. At six months married, Angie and Nick have already discovered profound personality differences between them. Nick is an

extrovert, while Angie is an introvert. Nick is a morning person, while Angie prefers to sleep in whenever possible. What personality differences are present in your marriage? What problems have these personality differences caused? Discuss how a personality trait (such as Nick's compulsiveness and Angie's self-inflicted solitude) can lead to bigger problems and challenges in a marriage.

5. Obviously, God orchestrated the meeting between Nick and Angie, and Daniel and Kay. Who has God placed in your life to help you on your walk with Him? To help you in your marriage? Do you need to seek out counsel for an immediate need? For long-term support? Daniel and Kay constantly direct Nick and Angie to explore a personal relationship with God. Discuss why that starting point is best for any marriage.

6. Angelina and Nick are drawn to God in different ways. What aspect of God draws Nick? What aspect of God draws Angie? Discuss how husbands and wives relate to God differently, because of gender, background, hurts, or life experience. What traits of God draw you most? What traits of God most draw your mate to Him? How can sharing those needs and insights bring a deeper spiritual connection to your marriage?

7. When Angelina and Nick drive back to St. Augustine for their belongings, they believe God is leading them back to Rowe City and a job for Nick at Benson's Hardware. Then, the new job presents itself, which means leaving their new friends and support system. Discuss how receiving an unexpected provision can mean giving up something else. What might Angie and Nick have done to keep their newfound support from Daniel and Kay?

When has God met one need for your family, yet simultaneously created another? How did you react? Did that reaction help or hinder your marriage?

8. Nick doesn't come home as planned for their first anniversary. What do you think of Angie's reactions—her panic, anger, and detachment? What do you think of Nick's actions—his neglect, avoidance, and attempt at reconciliation? Does it matter who did wrong first? Discuss what Nick and Angie could have done at each point to diffuse the conflict.

9. On the night of their third anniversary, we see a reunited and refocused marriage. Discuss how the previous two anniversaries affected Angie's expectations. Angie has spent three years having conflicts with Nick regarding his gifts, but doesn't tell him why she dislikes them until their third anniversary. When have you reacted negatively to your mate because of someone else's actions, or because of a previous experience? Is it difficult for you and your mate to create your own meaning for items or experiences you've seen in other, possibly failed, relationships? Why, or why not?

10. Also at the third year mark, we see Nick and Angie active in church and growing spiritually. Did you think Nick would purchase the duplexes without Angie's knowledge and agreement? Why, or why not? What did you think of Angie's reaction? When Angie returns home, she refuses to reconcile with Nick or listen to God about their problems, and instead funnels her emotions into her paintings. What coping mechanisms do you use when conflict is present in your marriage? What should you do instead? How can you learn to have a healthy response rather than an unhealthy one?

11. At year seven, do you believe Angelina and Nick are as active in church as they were at year three? Why, or why not? Do you believe they are growing spiritually? What actions do you think support your opinion? Both Angie and Nick voice being scared about the condition of their marriage. Discuss what they could have done to address that fear.

12. With regard to the early years of Nick and Angie's marriage, which character do you relate to most? Why? What do you see as their most problematic habits? Why? In your marriage, is it difficult to address fear without placing blame? Why, or why not? Discuss the difference between placing blame and assigning personal responsibility.

13. At this point, what marital problems are Angelina's responsibility? Which ones are Nick's? Discuss how marital conflict can be cyclical and complicated. What conflict in your marriage is most challenging? Can you trace it to the early years of your marriage?

14. If the usher (Lorenzo) hadn't pursued Angelina at the wedding, would Angelina have found another coping mechanism for her loneliness? At this point, do you think Nick is as lonely as Angelina is? Why, or why not?

15. When Angelina learns of Nick's arrest, she's more concerned with the condition of her paintings than she is her husband. What things (children, job, possessions, status, pride, hobbies) are more important to you than your mate and marriage? What caused this discrepancy? Discuss how disappointment, hurt, conflict, and dysfunction can create a scenario where husbands and wives no longer focus on each other. Is there any area where

you put other things such as those listed above, ahead of your mate? What problem is that causing in your marriage now? What bigger problems can that behavior lead to? What can you do now to stop that behavior? What do you need from God to stop that behavior?

16. By the first time Angelina is questioned by the state prosecutor, she is already contemplating divorce. Discuss how most of her musings involve avoiding future pain, rather than considering the origin of her current pain. How might Angelina's marriage have been different if she'd obeyed God in the first ten years of her marriage? Even though Nicholas is clueless to the condition of his marriage, he does vividly remember times when he refused to do as God instructed. How might Nick's life and marriage have been different, if he had obeyed God? Do you think he still would he have been arrested? Why, or why not? In what area have you refused to obey God in your marriage? What consequences are you living with now, because of that decision?

17. Nick's arrest pushes him to repentance, yet after years of disappointment, Angelina can't believe he is truly changing. Discuss how years of negative experience in a relationship can make trusting difficult. What do you think Angelina fears most with regard to trusting Nick again? What negative behaviors have injured trust in your marriage? What might God want you to do to rebuild that trust and closeness?

18. When Angie confides in Laurie regarding her marriage, Laurie responds "We reap what we sow. You sowed distance, so you reaped distance." How did Angie and Nick sow distance into their marriage? How do you sow distance or conflict into your

marriage? The law of sowing and reaping is reciprocal: by examining what we reap, we can determine what we have sown. What unwanted harvests are you reaping in your marriage? What did you sow to reap that undesired outcome? From now on, what can you sow instead, in effort to reap a better harvest? What is keeping you from sowing those good things?

19. Neither Nick nor Angie had a healthy relationship with their earthly father. Discuss how finding shared pain or lack with our mate can create common ground. What wounds or lacks do you and your mate have in common? How can both of you approach God about those areas? How can intimacy and closeness be enhanced by sharing God's provision and healing with each other?

20. In the end, Nick and Angelina see their own contributions to the dysfunction in their marriage. And God instructs them to do now all He'd told them to do from the beginning. What lessons from God are you still learning regarding your faith? Regarding your behavior in your marriage? Discuss God's willingness to continually teach us even when we've failed. How does God use Nick and Angie's obedience to satisfy their spiritual hunger? To grow the love in their marriage? In what area of your marriage might love grow stronger if you are obedient to God? What is God asking of you regarding that area?

*If you or someone you love wants information or instruction about handling conflict in marriage, please visit my web site www.shelliearnold.com. There, check out YOUR MARRIAGE resources.

www.ingramcontent.com/pod-product-compliance
Lightning Source LLC
Chambersburg PA
CBHW070608300726
48975CB00006B/1755